THE GILDED HOOP

Netta Muskett

HOUSE OF STRATUS

This edition published in 2014 by House of Stratus, an imprint of Stratus Books Ltd, Lisandra House, Fore St., Looe, Cornwall, PL13 1AD, UK.

www.houseofstratus.com

Typeset by House of Stratus.

A catalogue record for this book is available from the British Library and the Library of Congress.

ISBN 0755142837
EAN 978 0755142835

Chapter One

Gail gave a cursory glance at herself in the long mirror and did not agree that she looked 'marvellous'. She felt silly in the pseudo-Elizabethan costume hired for the occasion and wondered how on earth she had let herself be trapped into this. She was playing the part of Katharina in the village production of *The Taming of the Shrew*, but she knew she was no actress.

It was Mr. Chives who had persuaded her into it. Mr. Chives whose secretary and general factotum she had been for the past three years, ever since Jeffrey Templar had found her the job and had managed to persuade Mr. Chives that she was not too young and inexperienced at eighteen, though she had really known nothing.

She was deeply indebted to old Mr. Chives for those years, for she had come to him homeless, penniless, broken by the suicide of her father as his only escape from a long term of imprisonment for embezzlement and fraud, and knowing herself to be completely unfitted by her expensive schools for the kind of life she had never expected to live. Mr. Chives must have put up with a lot from her at the beginning, and this ridiculous business of Katharina was almost the first thing he had asked her to do that she really hated doing. He was a patron of the village dramatic society, taking an active interest in it, and when their Katharina had been taken ill he had suggested her and asked her to do it as a favour to him.

'But I can't act. I shall be hopeless,' she told him.

'Never mind. You'll look beautiful and you can be a shrew, you know!'

But she was not even sure she looked beautiful in the red velvet gown which did not suit her marmalade-coloured hair (her own word for it, though it was browner than that).

1

The audience had gathered noisily in the village hall, and amongst them the Miller family, who had brought with them a visitor who had turned up at the last moment and been ecstatically welcomed.

Kipling Delaney did not have much free time, but yesterday had been the last night of a long and successful run, and he was tired and had escaped, as he liked to do, to the people he called 'his family', though they were unrelated, and to the place he thought of as 'home'.

'Oh Kippy, we're going out,' said Cora Miller regretfully when he walked in. 'I'm afraid we've got to go.'

'He can come with us,' cried Ethne, hanging on his arm.

'Course you can! What a lark!' chipped in Rex, who was twelve.

'You'd be bored stiff, old man. It's a village presentation of *The Taming of the Shrew*. What are you going to drink, by the way?' said Mr. Miller. 'There's some whisky left over from Christmas.'

'That'll be fine, but why do you think I should be bored by any sort of presentation of *The Taming of the Shrew*? It's years since I've played it but I bet I could remember all Petruchio's lines. Somehow one always does remember Shakespeare. What's their Katharina like?'

'Not particularly good but a smasher to look at,' said Rex. 'Old Petruchio's Bob Jay at the grocer's and you should see his wig! Makes his face look like a boiled suet pudding!'

'Now, Rex, that isn't kind,' admonished his mother. 'Actually it's very brave of him to keep on with the part because he's not at all well.'

In fact, at that very moment Mr. Wilkie, the fussy little stage manager, was assuring poor Bob that there was nothing the matter with him but nerves and that he would be alright once he was on.

From a hole in the curtain, the girl playing Bianca saw the Millers arrive.

'They've brought a man with them,' she reported, 'and isn't he an eyeful! Tall, dark and handsome? I'll say he is. Wonder who he is?'

'Ladies, ladies, off the stage *please*!' said the harassed Mr. Wilkie and the curtain wobbled up uncertainly and the play began.

Kipling Delaney watched it with interest and with no feeling of superiority or contempt, though he realised that none of them could act, certainly not the Katharina. He imagined Gay Manners in the part.

She would have played it to perfection, being by nature a shrew. He was getting very tired of Gay, who had been his leading lady too long. It was refreshing to be watching someone who couldn't act for toffee but was as lovely as this girl to look at. He found himself interested by her. She offered contradictions. Her eyes were cold, but her mouth was warmly feminine. She moved as if under careful control, but he could picture her pulsing with restless life. How old was she? he wondered. She might be any age. She gave the impression of having passed through deep waters, but her voice and the way she used it were virginal, so he decided that they had not been love troubles.

And then he realised that something was the matter with the Petruchio, who had been a poor thing at best but was now falling to bits physically as well as mentally, for his wig was over one eye and his rapier, which Kip had thought a curious addition to the costume, was trailing by its silken cord and finally clattered to the floor altogether.

This was the last straw for poor Bob Jay, and, gripping his middle in both hands, he hurried from the stage, leaving both players and audience nonplussed.

Mr. Wilkie, after a hurried altercation back stage, had the curtains drawn, and himself offered a soothing assurance to the audience that the play would go on in a few minutes.

'It'll be a shame if they make him go on,' said Mrs. Miller. 'He must have been feeling very bad this morning, because he served me with a pound of sausages when I'd distinctly asked for cheese.'

'They can't go on with the play without the hero,' said Ethne.

'No understudies?' asked Kip.

'There aren't enough in the dramatic society for that,' she said.

'I'm so sorry,' said Cora. 'It does seem a shame. People have looked forward to it so much, and the players will be so disappointed, but I don't see what else they can do but ask us all to go away without seeing any more.'

Kip whispered to her, and no one but the Millers saw him slip away and round behind the curtain, where he walked straight into the distracted little stage manager, who was about to ask the audience to leave.

'I wonder if I can help you?' asked Kip. 'I know Petruchio's part fairly well, if I could have a prompter ready in case I find I have forgotten. The clothes won't fit me very well, but I noticed they were on the big side for your Petruchio.'

Mr. Wilkie eyed him doubtfully. Some London nob, he decided, who fancied himself at amateur theatricals and would probably make a mess of the part, but perhaps even that would be better than calling the thing off half-way through.

'You say you've acted in the part?' he asked.

'Yes,' said Kip with a little smile, relieved to find that he was not recognised.

'And you think you could manage it? Mind you, we pride ourselves in Heatherley on our dramatic shows, but of course everybody will know you aren't one of our members.'

'That's so,' said Kip gravely, 'so if I let the show down a bit, I shall probably be forgiven and my delinquencies not laid at the feet of the Society.'

'That's about it, Mr.—I didn't catch your name.'

'Geer,' said Kip, giving his second Christian name.

'Right. I'll go and tell the audience, though perhaps I won't mention the name as it's not known down this way. You don't mind?'

'I'd prefer it that way,' said Kip. 'Where do I find the clothes?'

Mr. Wilkie called someone and dispatched him with Kip to the room where poor Bob had been helped out of the doublet and hose before being taken home.

The clothes were a tight fit, but they looked infinitely better on him than they had on Bob Jay, especially as he kept his own dark hair uncovered by the wig, and refused the rapier.

When he was ready, Mr. Wilkie came in again, eyed him with a faint disapproval, but was glad to see him actually in the costume.

'I do hope everything will be alright,' he said nervously. 'I've spoken to Miss Marlin about it (she's Katharina, you know) and she says she knows your part as well as her own now and will be able to help you. She can give you the tip about the bits of business we do, side-play and so on. Remember, you're acting. Don't be yourself too much.'

'Alright. I'll remember,' said Kipling Delaney gravely, but his eyes twinkled and when, a few minutes later, he was being introduced to Gail Marlin, the twinkle remained in them, slightly disconcerting her.

'It's very good of you to come to our rescue,' she said with stiff formality.

'I shall enjoy it,' he said with a smile, thinking that it was amusing to find her a little prim madam, after all, though she should not have been, not with that mouth.

He found himself looking at it, the sensitive lips curved but not too full for beauty, the upper one short, its line classically beautiful. Gail, realising his look, found herself flushing crimson and felt insanely angry.

Mr. Wilkie, fussing along, told them that the audience had cheered his statement that a member of the audience, who preferred not to give his name, had nobly offered to take over Petruchio's part.

'Don't you worry,' he said, patting Kip's arm, a procedure which looked very odd, since Mr. Wilkie's little round bald head barely reached to the younger man's shoulder. Don't you worry. They won't be critical, will they, Miss Marlin? If you make mistakes, don't get flurried. I'm going to prompt you myself, and we'll get you through alright. Now I think we're ready!'

He bustled off with another encouraging smile and pat, and again Gail read amusement in Kip's eyes and resented it. She thought he was feeling superior, and secretly hoped he would get taken down a peg or two by finding he had forgotten his part.

Directly he was on the stage, however, she realised her hopes were doomed to frustration, for he was completely master of his part, of the stage, of all of them, even though with the consummate skill of an experienced actor he contrived to subordinate his part to those of others when the script so required it.

His appearance in the play changed the whole performance, infused it with new life. Everybody reacted to it, even Katharina herself, or perhaps more than any of them Katharina. It was impossible not to feel that they were those very people, and the treatment which this new Petruchio so vigorously meted out to his unwilling and disagreeable bride stung her to a shrewishness which she would never have achieved under Bob Jay's almost apologetic harassing of her.

And so to the last scene, with Katharina finally subdued, with her meek surrender to this all-conquering lord:

Thy husband is thy lord, thy life, thy keeper,
Thy head, thy sovereign …
… place your hands below your husband's foot
In token of which duty, if he please,
My hand is ready, may it do him ease.

The tone was perfect. Meek, subdued, a little anxious, but, as she finished the speech, Gail's eyes looked up into his and he read no such humility there, no such anxiety for his goodwill towards her, and he laughed aloud, answering that look in her eyes as he swept her into his arms, lifted her from the floor, held her there with his laughing, good-looking face tilted back to look at her.

'Why, there's a wench! Come on, and kiss me, Kate,' and the kiss he gave her, his mouth on hers, was no stage affair but a kiss that left her furious, but utterly helpless.

Lucentio spoke his line, and Vincentio, but she did not hear them, and then Kip swung her to her feet again and, an arm about her, prepared to take her off the stage with a loving 'Come, Kate, we'll to bed!' and the next minute they were in the wings.

He held her, a hand on her arm.

'Don't run away, Katharina,' he said, laughing, knowing how angry she was, enjoying the fact that he had roused her and found just the fire he had felt sure lay beneath the cool, prim exterior. 'We shall have to take a curtain, you know.'

'You go by yourself then,' she said, trying to get free, but realising she might as well give in at once, for she could not shake off his hand. 'It's you they want, not me.'

The stage manager came beamingly towards them.

'Well, how did I do?' asked Kip with a smile.

'Oh, very well, very well indeed, considering,' admitted Mr. Wilkie, who had felt a little aggrieved that not once had he had to prompt the stranger. 'I think you ought to join a dramatic society, you know. With a little help, just to rub off the corners, you know, you'd be quite a useful addition to a little society. I'd like to have had you with us. I should quite have enjoyed, in fact, having the chance to polish you up a bit.'

'Sorry I can't have that privilege,' said Kip with the easy grace which was natural to him. 'Still, you'll have Bob Jay back, you know, and I don't want to steal his thunder. They're clapping still. Shall we go on, Kate?'

'There's no need for you to put your arm round me,' said Gail with spirit, feeling that he had been getting at little Mr. Wilkie, who did not appear to have realised that this man, whoever he was, was right out of their class as an actor.

'Oh, but don't you think there is?' asked Kip mischievously, keeping his arm about her shoulders. 'After all, we don't want to destroy the illusion that you've lost your shrewish nature in the interests of true love,' and he marched her on to the stage, and she had to bow and smile, to the audience and to him, with that wild, unreasonable anger in her heart.

Again and again they returned, Kip refusing to go on alone, though they shouted for him, and when they came off for the last time they found their way barred by two excited young men with notebooks and pencils.

'I say, sir, would you mind telling me who you are?' asked one.

'Sorry. Really I'd rather remain incog.,' said Kip, trying to elude them.

It was in vain, however, for the other spoke up quickly.

'No good kidding,' he said. 'You're Kipling Delaney, aren't you?'

Kip heard the little gasp Gail gave, and did not attempt to hold her back any longer.

'Alright. I give in,' he told the reporters with a smile. 'Any chance of your keeping this out of the paper?'

'Not a ghost of one, Mr. Delaney, No, sir! This one's ours. Care to tell us what brought you down here? Looking for new talent or anything? Have you found any?'

'I came here for a couple of days' rest and no publicity. If you must mention my name, give that young man Bray—or Jay?—a boost, will you? After all, he did a hero's job in turning up at all when he must have been feeling very seedy.'

'Alright, Mr. Delaney. We'll attend to it,' they assured him, and Kip went off to the dressing-room which the other men of the company had vacated, awed by the discovery of his identity.

When he had changed, he joined them in the passage outside and stood chatting in easy fashion with them, entirely at home, as one would imagine him being in any circumstances.

Gail came at last, stopping short at sight of him.

'Miss Marlin—'

'Please, Mr. Delaney. I have to go,' she said in a clear, very prim voice to hide her discomfort.

'Keep him waiting,' said Kip teasingly. 'It won't hurt him, you know.'

'There's no one—' began Gail hotly, and then stopped.

Idiot that she was! That was just what he had been wanting to know, of course, and she'd stepped right into the trap and told him, like any schoolgirl.

'Why are you so angry with me? What have I done, Katharina?'

'Done? Do you think I don't realise how you have been enjoying this? Laughing at us and making fun of us, all of us—and poor Mr. Wilkie. Letting him go on about giving you a few lessons, and he's the nicest little man, much too nice for you to be making fun of—'

He held her arm.

'Look here, Katharina, you've got hold of the wrong idea. I haven't been laughing at you, any of you, or making fun of anyone. I wanted to help you out of a difficulty, and thought I'd done so. I confess I was a bit tickled at Mr. Wilkie, but believe me, it wasn't a rotten sort of amusement.'

'Then why didn't you tell him? Why did you let him ramble on like that?' demanded Gail furiously.

'I didn't want him to know. I didn't think anyone would recognise me in that get-up, and down here in a village hall. Anyway, why are we sparring like this, Katharina? I don't want to.'

He could not say any more, for Ethne Miller came in from the street by the door near them, looking for him.

'Kippy, aren't you coming?' she asked, and then saw Gail.

'I expect you two know each other,' said Kip. 'Ethne's an old friend of mine, Miss Marlin. In fact, I used to bath her.'

'Kippy!' remonstrated the girl with a blush.

'Well, truth will out, sweetheart,' said Kip, 'and a more delectable young person in the bath I never have seen.'

'Now, Kippy!' begged the girl, and he stopped his teasing to speak to Gail again.

'Do you go our way, or can we go yours?' he asked. 'I'm putting up at the 'Lamb', but I'm in no hurry and I know this young baggage would stay out all night if I let her. Have the others gone, Ethne?'

'Yes,' she said, 'Mom said I could wait for you. We can go round by The Coombe, Miss Marlin.'

But Gail refused.

'What about snow-balling with us tomorrow afternoon?' he asked, sensing her loneliness, hating the thought of a girl going off like that, alone into the night.

'I work for my living!' she told him, and left them.

'Nice girl,' he said to Ethne, tucking her hand into his arm. 'A bit queer in her manner, though. Sort of—frightened. Is she always like that?'

'Well, we don't know her very well. She doesn't mix with us. She's a bit ikey, I think,' said Ethne, who was hail-fellow-well-met with everyone. 'Not that she's any reason to be. Far from it.'

Kip gave her arm a little pinch.

'You know, you're getting distinctly catty, my pet,' he told her. 'What's poor Gail Marlin done to you?'

'Oh, nothing, but seeing who she is, she's no right to give herself airs. Her father was a rotter. Do you remember the case? Jeremy K. Marlin, the financier, who embezzled thousands and thousands and then shot himself to escape imprisonment. He was her father.'

'Was he? Yes, I do remember that,' said Kip, casting his mind back. It was hazy because at that time he was so much preoccupied over

Gilda, but the case had made a stir. 'So she's that Marlin, is she? Poor kid.'

'Poor people her father robbed,' retorted Ethne. 'Fancy you asking her to come snow-balling with us! She wouldn't come. I could have told you that. She won't go anywhere,' and there was a touch of scorn in the young voice.

'Look here, young woman, you and I are going to have a row if you grow claws and stick them into people. She seemed to me a very nice girl, and it's my belief that she's shy and self-conscious rather than stuck-up. What she wants is a little friendliness. She works at The Coombe, does she?'

'Yes. For old Mr. Chives,' said Ethne, inclined to be a little sulky.

Kip took no notice of her sulks, knowing she was naturally sunny and sweet and would recover.

'Chives? Is that by any chance the man who's interested in old national costumes? I've got a book he wrote, and I've been in touch with him once over a period play on which we wanted expert advice.'

'Yes, I believe he does something like that,' said Ethne. 'He wanted to design the costumes for our play, but we couldn't afford to have them made. Miss Marlin's a sort of secretary-companion to him.'

'I see. Interesting,' said Kip, and changed the subject.

Chapter Two

'A car,' said Gail. 'Do you want visitors?'

John Chives peered out of the window with his short-sighted eyes.

'See who it is, my dear. If it's the man from Solomon's, I'll have a word with him, but I'm feeling very tired today.'

It was not the man from Solomon's.

It was Kipling Delaney.

Gail saw him getting out of his car and drew a quick little breath. She had not realised until this moment how much he had been in her thoughts all the morning, nor how exciting in retrospect last night had been.

'It's Mr. Delaney,' she said. 'Do you want to see him?'

Mr. Chives had already learned all about last night, having insisted on Gail describing the play to him in detail, and having been greatly tickled by the thought of the trick the great actor had played on them all, especially his quiet, prim secretary.

'Yes. Yes, I certainly do,' he said with vigour, and a few moments later Kip was coming into the room, bringing with him a breath of the glorious, frosty afternoon, the cold so keen that the winter sunshine vied with it but could not conquer it.

Snow lay thick on fields and hedges and roofs, and in the gutters were little rivers of ice.

'Mr. Chives, I had to come and see you as I was so near. It was too good a chance to miss,' he said, taking the old man's thin, delicate hand in his and bowing over it with a grace which Gail told herself scornfully was theatrical but which was actually the homage which he paid naturally to age and distinction.

'I am more than happy that you did not miss it,' said Chives. 'You'll have something? Whisky? Port? Or have you acquired the pernicious sherry habit yet?'

Kip laughed.

'I'm afraid I have,' he said.

'Gail, get the No. 49, will you? And two glasses.'

'You know you ought not to have it,' she warned him.

'I know, you tyrant. It isn't for me but for you. We can't let so honoured a guest drink alone,' with a little contented chuckle.

When she had gone, Kip spoke of her.

'Nice girl,' he said. 'She did very well last night, though she's nervous.'

'Yes. She ought to get about more. Never goes outside the door without me unless I send her, and she doubles back like a hare rather than meet anyone. It isn't natural, and I dare say I've got the reputation in the village of being a nigger-driver. Today, now, she ought to be out. I can't go because of my infernal rheumatism, but she ought to be revelling in all this. They tell me there will be skating tonight on the old millpond.'

'Yes. I'm going with the Miller's. Know them?'

'Slightly. Mrs. Miller's a fine woman and that's a nice girl she has. A bit young for my Gail, but I think they'd have been friendly if she'd let them. Pity. She ought to have friends, do the things other young people do here. What about getting her to go with you to the skating tonight?'

'Well, if she would come and you can spare her, I am sure the Millers would be delighted,' he said, and when Gail returned with the sherry and the two glasses, Mr. Chives put the suggestion to her at once.

'Gail, can you skate?' he asked her.

'I could once,' she said. 'Why?'

'There's to be skating at the old mill-pond tonight, and I think it would be a good idea for you to go along. Kipling Delaney tells me his friends the Millers are going, and you could join them.'

'I don't think skating is very attractive to me now,' said Gail quietly and distantly. 'Your sherry, Mr. Delaney.'

'You're having some, Gail? That's right. Put a bit of colour and warmth into you. Now no nonsense about tonight. I've told Kipling that you'll go.'

'I'll call for you, Miss Marlin,' said Kip. 'What time? About seven? There's to be supper on the ice, which I believe is a time-honoured custom difficult to revive in our mild winters.'

They talked of winters John Chives had known, and before he went, Kip contrived to justify his visit by poring over soma sketches of old costumes and woven materials which had been reproduced from prints.

"These are very interesting—and extraordinarily well done,' he said at last. 'Who did them?'

'Why, Gail here,' said Mr. Chives, well pleased to have her work approved. 'She's got quite a flair for this sort of thing.'

'I compliment you, Miss Marlin,' said Kip, and was delighted with her blushes, a rarity in the days of female emancipation. 'I shan't lose sight of you. It isn't easy to get this sort of thing well done nowadays. Modernism and the school of futuristic art seems to creep into everything. Thank you, Mr. Chives. I shall look forward to seeing your book in due course. Perhaps Miss Marlin will let me know when it is published.'

John Chives sighed.

'I'm an old man, Kipling,' he said. 'I sometimes feel I am just dawdling on the edge of eternity, waiting for it almost with impatience, and I wonder if the book will ever get finished, and if the world will be much the worse off if it never sees Chives on Period Costumes,' with a smile, shaking the younger man's hand in farewell.

'Don't say that, or even think it,' said Kip, and to Gail, as she went with him to the door: 'I shall see you tonight, then?'

She made a last half-hearted protest.

'I haven't any skates, now.'

He looked down at her small, narrow feet in their workmanlike shoes.

'You leave it to me. I'll call at seven. You'll be ready? Wrap up warmly. It'll be freezing hard, or so we hope,' and he was gone, with that warm, friendly smile which had so strange a power to penetrate the fastnesses within which she had learned to hide her wounded, frightened self.

'Well, so that's Kipling Delaney, is it?' said Chives when she rejoined him. 'I like him. No side about him. Just a simple, decent chap, keen on his job. Put down the address and telephone number he gave us, Gail. I'd like to keep in touch with him,' and she wrote it down in the little book of addresses in her small, firm handwriting.

'His wife was killed in a railway accident some years ago, wasn't she?' asked Gail, reluctant to go back into the Middle Ages so soon.

'Was she? Yes, I believe she was. I remember something about it. Shocking business. Yes. Shocking. By the way, I think tomorrow you had better go up to the British Museum again and have a look at those prints. You remember we were not quite sure about them.'

So there they were, back in the past again, though for the rest of their working hours, which were until teatime, Gail's mind kept harking back to the present and to the immediate future. Now that she was being obliged to go out, to meet people, to take part in their fun, her youth responded to it and she knew she was looking forward to the evening.

In the old days she had loved skating and had been several times with her father to the winter sports in Switzerland, and Austria, and amongst the galaxy of skating stars there, she had twinkled gaily.

Somewhere or other she had one of her old skating dresses, though she could not imagine why she had kept it all these years. Perhaps some kindly Fate had been watching over her after all, and had not let her throw it away when she had made a scrap-heap of everything else that might remind her of past days.

When she was free, she ran up to her room and hunted out the dress, found it badly creased but not moth-eaten as she had feared. An iron was all that was needed, for her figure had altered very little. It had the same slender lines, and if they were not quite so boyish, the little curves and hollows added to rather than detracted from the appearance of the dress.

It was scarlet and white, a short, circular skirt of scarlet bound with white braid, a tight-fitting white jersey with a red collar and cuffs, jaunty little red cap with long, swinging tassels of white. She even found the scarlet gloves with the little white bears knitted into their backs.

Boots? Yes, even those were tucked away into the bottom of the box, long white kid boots which she cleaned with loving care and remembered, grief mingling with every memory, the occasions on which she had worn them before.

She looked at herself in the mirror as she had not done for years, and her heart gave a little throb of pleased surprise at what she saw. Her skin was smooth, her eyes clear, the brown hair curling in little fronds beneath her cap was both strong and silky.

She took a few dancing steps about her room and gave a little breathless laugh of joy at her lissome energy, feeling the springs of the old vitality still buoyant within her.

'I'm going to enjoy it!' she told herself exultantly, and when she ran down to greet Kipling Delaney in the hall, that light was still in her eyes and her cheeks were softly flushed, and she looked younger and more vitally alive than so far he had thought possible.

'I've got the skates,' he told her, but did not say that he had spent the afternoon tearing about from place to place to buy some for her. 'Had we better see if they fit? I managed to get two different sizes for safety,' and he produced four gleaming skates from his big pockets, and Gail sat down on the chair in the hall.

Her appearance had surprised him until he remembered what Ethne had told him, that she was Jeremy K. Marlin's daughter and must have been accustomed to all the trappings of the rich. Carefully pressed, the scarlet and white outfit looked like new, and he wondered for a moment what effect she would produce on Heatherley in such a kit.

The first skate he tried on fitted perfectly, and soon they were speeding along the hard road in his car, Gail with the half-sweet, half-bitter feeling of having been caught back into the past, except that in place of her grey-haired father was this very presentable young man.

'Grumpy would have liked him,' she thought, with that pang inseparable from such a memory. 'And he would have liked Grumpy.'

Strange that in all these years this was the first time she had been able consciously to think of her father by the old nickname of love.

'Now mind. You belong to me tonight,' Kip told her as they rounded the last bend and came in sight of the sheet of ice where couples were skimming or struggling, according to experience. 'No racing off with other men for hours at a stretch.'

She smiled. Life could be good in patches, even now.

'Don't worry about that,' she said, 'I'm not really known very well, and they all have their own friends. But don't forget Ethne Miller will expect some of your time.'

'I won't forget. I'll do my duty there, though I don't fancy she'll be short of partners of her own age. After all, I'm middle-aged to her,' with a glance at Gail which assured her that he did not feel she so regarded him.

'How old are you?' she asked him, and blushed as soon as the unpremeditated words were out.

'Thirty-five,' he said. 'And you're what?'

'Twenty-one,' said Gail. 'Fancy calling yourself middle-aged!'

'So I am, to sixteen,' he said. 'Anyway, there's Ethne now, skating with one of her boyfriends, so shall we park here and put on our skates? The car will be sheltered a bit by that hedge.'

She was grateful to him for a suggestion which relieved her of the need to join the crowd at the other side of the ice. Her first glimpse of the skaters had been a shock, for she realised that her appearance in the skating-dress would cause a stir. None of them wore special clothes for the sport but were in their everyday garments, coats and skirts, big coats, furs. She had never skated in England before, except at a fashionable rink, and it had not occurred to her that she would be unique in clothes which had seemed the only possible rig for such an event.

When Kip had put her skates on, getting her to sit on the running board of the car, she expressed her fears to him.

'I ought not to have come,' she said shrinkingly, 'not like this, anyway,' indicating her long white boots and scarlet skirt.

'Why not? You're just right,' he told her, not understanding.

'I shan't be to Heatherley,' she retorted grimly. 'Look at the others.'

He glanced at them indifferently, but saw her point.

'You'll feel alright once we're started,' he consoled her.

'After all, it's you who are in correct kit, not they.'

'That's the whole point,' she said. 'I've never been really accepted in Heatherley. They think I'm proud and feel superior to them, and they'll consider my appearing got up like this as just further evidence of my feeling of superiority, whereas actually—do you know about me, Mr. Delaney? Who I am? Who my father was?'

The tone of her voice hurt him inexpressibly. It was hard, with the defiant hardness which covered a wound still raw, still so tender to the touch that she feared even the gentlest of fingers, that shell of hardness her only protection.

'Yes,' he said gently, fixing his own skates. 'Yes, I do know.'

'Who told you?'

'Ethne Miller.'

'What did I tell you?' she asked. 'That's how they think of me. That's how they've always thought of me – as Jeremy K. Marlin's daughter, never as myself, Gail Marlin. And tonight they'll all realise that I am still his daughter because a kit like this is outside the scope of Mr. Chive's hired help!'

He stood up beside her, getting the feel of the skates, his hand beside hers on the bonnet of the car.

'Don't be so bitter about it, Gail,' he said. 'Aren't you stressing the point in your own mind too much? Have you ever given them the chance to know Gail Marlin? They're nice people, kindly, good-natured people, but they're like everybody else in the world, ready to take you at your own valuation since you give them no chance to value you themselves – and the view you give them is that of your father's daughter. But come along. We came here to skate and enjoy ourselves, and that's what we're going to do. Ready?' putting a hand beneath her elbow.

They walked gingerly across the foot or two of frozen grass, and then Kip took her two hands strongly in his and swung her out over the roughened edges of the ice into its smooth centre, and almost immediately Gail forgot everything in the rapture of that most thrilling movement on earth, skimming over smooth ice with a partner as perfect as she was herself.

All eyes were quickly upon them, and some of the comments were just what Gail had anticipated, but they were friendly, good-natured people for the most part, and they were soon lost to everything but admiration of that swift perfection of movement.

Someone had brought a gramophone, and Kip and Gail were left alone in the centre of the ice as they danced.

'Enjoying it?' asked Kip superfluously, for her cheeks were rosy and her eyes like stars and her lips softly parted. She was entranced with happiness and he knew it, and felt within his own being something to which he had long been a stranger, a sense of excitement, of anticipation, of adventure. He had believed his capacity for excitement dead, and adventure for him a thing to be forgotten.

'I'm loving every second of it,' she told him, and her voice was filled with that warmth and light which made her eyes like stars.

'I shall have to take Ethne for a turn,' he said at last, regretfully, and at once her radiance dimmed a little. 'Don't look like that. Why are you so frightened? You're like a nervous little bird that's been kept in a cage.'

'Perhaps that's what I am,' said Gail, her voice not quite steady.

'Well, come out of your cage. Nobody's going to hurt you except yourself, and it's just silly to do that, isn't it? There's a man who's had his eyes on you all the time and is longing to skate with you. See the one I mean? Blue and white muffler – speaking to Mrs. Miller now.'

Gail glanced in the direction he indicated.

'Yes. Joe Tenner, the chemist,' she said.

'You know him?'

'Yes,' said Gail, to whom Joe had always contrived to address a few remarks when she went into the shop for medicine for Mr. Chives.

He had once asked her to go to the pictures with him, but she had refused so swiftly and decidedly that he had never dared to ask her again.

'Alright. Well, you skate with him whilst I do my duty by Ethne, and Cora if she wants to skate, and then I'll come back for you and take you to supper. You won't let Tenner persuade you into going with him?'

'No,' promised Gail faintly, her hands instinctively tightening on Kip's as he skated with her towards the chairs and rugs, which had been arranged for the non-skaters near the tables on which the buffet supper was being spread.

Kip smiled at the chemist.

'I've seen you eyeing my partner and probably wondering what noxious poison you could fix up for me,' he said in his friendly fashion. 'Do you want me to hand her over to you?'

'If she will—will you, Miss Marlin?' he asked, flushing with delight, and Gail found herself gliding away with him, missing the smooth perfection of Kip's movements, missing his comforting presence, his easy speech, missing everything about him, but knowing that she was far more at ease with Joe Tenner now than she would have been an hour or two ago. Kip had given her confidence in herself.

Kip skated with Ethne, who was a beginner, but a courageous one.

'Enjoying yourself with Gail Marlin, weren't you?' she asked.

'Not having such a bad time yourself, young woman, are you?' he returned, squeezing her hands. 'You're doing well, poppet. Don't forget to bend your knees and swing—swing—that's fine.'

'How long does it take to skate like Gail?' she asked, breathless but delighted.

'You'd get the hang of it in two or three weeks of this,' he told her.

'But we never get two or three weeks of it in England,' said Ethne. 'I suppose she learned abroad? She must have had a good time when she was young.'

He laughed.

'Young? She isn't exactly a Methuselah now,' he told her. 'Will you go out of your way to be nice to her, Ethne? She wants to be friendly with you all, but she feels you're all remembering about her father and it makes her self-conscious and reserved.'

Ethne gave him a quick look, a look which assured him she was growing up.

'What are you taking so much interest in her for?' she asked.

'I'll spank you, youngster, if you talk to me like that,' said Kip, laughing, but as they skated in silence for a bit, he was thinking of her words.

Was he taking a special interest in Gail Marlin? Perhaps he was, but after all, why not? Where was the harm? It was unlikely they would meet again after tonight, for he was going back to London tomorrow, to get down to work on a new play.

Mrs. Miller would not skate.

'I'm so bad at it for one thing, Kip, and for another there's the supper to see to, and those who don't skate can give a hand there. You go back to Miss Marlin,' with a little mischievous smile.

And back to Gail he went, finding that by this time Tenner had lost her to another partner and he in turn to yet another, so that she had been passed from hand to hand by the time Kip got her to himself again.

'One quick round and then supper?' he suggested, and she nodded happily and gave herself up again to the rapture of this night.

He brought her a stool and a rug, and plied her with sandwiches, cakes and hot coffee, kept her more or less to himself and yet encouraged the somewhat shy overtures of people who wanted to be near the great Kipling Delaney, and insisted on Gail's participation in the conversation.

But he could see that she was tired, in spite of, or perhaps because of, the extent of her enjoyment, and when they had skated again for a little time, he suggested taking her home.

'I don't want to leave off, really,' she said, a wistful note creeping into her voice. 'I don't think I'm tired.'

'I know you are,' he said. 'All that excitement last night, and working all day and now skating for four, nearly five hours. Listen! That's midnight striking, and it's starting to snow again.'

'Alright. Let's go then,' she said regretfully, and when she was in the car again, and he beside her, he laid a hand for a moment on hers. It was a friendly gesture, not one which could either frighten or embarrass her.

'Thank you for this evening,' he said. 'It's one of those to remember, isn't it?'

She nodded. Her eyes were soft. She was like someone come to life out of unconscious sleep.

'I shall remember it all my life,' she told him.

'You're very sweet, Gail,' he said, and because it was dangerous to sit there like that, in the intimacy of the dark, silent car, he switched on the engine and busied himself with lights and various gadgets until the pregnant moment had passed.

They spoke very little on the way to The Coombe, but at the last he told her of tomorrow.

'I'd like to feel we are going to meet again,' he said, 'but this is the end of my brief holiday. I've got to get back to work tomorrow.'

'Are you acting tomorrow? I've got to go up to London for Mr. Chives, and if I get done in time, I might manage to get to a matinee,' said Gail, feeling that she must see him again, even if only from a seat in the gallery.

'No, we're going into production with a new play,' he said, 'but if you're going up in the morning, why not let me run you up? It'll be warmer and more comfortable than the trains this weather even if I can't bring you back.'

He regretted the words directly he had spoken them. He was a fool to keep this contact open. He should recognise the symptoms and be warned in time, for both their sakes.

But he could not take back the invitation, and Gail caught at it eagerly.

'I should love that,' she said happily. 'I could be ready any time you like, the earlier the better.'

They fixed a time, and her eyes were bright when they said good night, bright with the memory of tonight and the promise of tomorrow. Looking into them, Kip cursed himself, but had neither the will nor the power to dim their brightness.

'Good night, Mr. Delaney,' she said with that look.

'My friends all call me Kip,' he said.

'It would be a cheek for me to call you that,' she said.

'Why, when a kid like Ethne does it?'

'Then—good night, Kip,' she said very softly, and again he cursed himself. What had come over him to be so weak about a girl? Heaven knew he had had to suppress enough of them in the last few years to have the technique off pat, and yet he had not only let Gail look at him and speak to him like that, but at the last moment he had pulled her to him, had been madly ready to kiss her but for her instant withdrawal, so that he had had to let her go with just: 'Good night, Gail. See you in the morning.'

'Well,' he told himself very decidedly when he was driving back to the 'Lamb', 'this drive up to town tomorrow must be the end. She's too dangerous and I, it seems, too vulnerable! Fancy being bowled over by a chit like that, who hadn't even any intention of doing it or hasn't an earthly idea she's done it!'

But the next day he was even a little bit madder, for on an impulse, when he set her down outside the British Museum, he made a lunch appointment with her.

Gay Manners, the leading lady of whom he was sick and tired, but who seemed to have fastened herself on his productions like a limpet, made a fuss when he declined to take her to lunch.

'But, Kip, we always lunch together during rehearsals,' she said pettishly.

She was small and blonde and exquisite, and she was over thirty, but no one but her maid knew it, though Kip guessed it. She spent half her life keeping at bay the lines and wrinkles which threatened the peace of the other half. It had always irked her that she had never been able to attach Kip Delaney to her chariot, and she was no nearer success now than she had been six years ago, when he had been attracted by her and made a little light love to her.

'Sorry, Gay, but this isn't exactly a rehearsal. It's more an informal discussion. We're not really cast yet.'

She shrugged her thin shoulders.

'I'm not sure that I like your play, Kip. It isn't a patch on *Fly by Night* and the heroine really isn't the right style.'

'She's right for the play,' retorted Kip,

'Well, she isn't right for me,' said Gay. 'I'm not at all sure that I should be doing a wise thing in taking on the part.'

If she thought she was going to reduce him to despair and pleading by that, she was mistaken, for, to her horror, he accepted the suggestion quite calmly.

'I'm not sure either, Gay,' he said.

'Must nip along now or I shall be late. Can I drop you anywhere?'

'Thanks. You've done so,' said Gay angrily, and walked away, whilst Kip got into his car and hurried to the appointment with Gail.

He found her a little shy again, and decided that it was easier to get her to talk of his affairs than of hers.

'I've been through a nasty little spot this morning,' he told her. 'I've sacked my leading lady.'

'Not Gay Manners?' asked Gail, for the two names had become linked almost to an indissoluble point in the public mind.

'Gay Manners,' said Kip. 'I'm producing my own play and the girl in it doesn't fit that type. I wish I felt there were any chance of making you an actress, Gail. You've got a lot of what it takes – you look nice, you move well, your voice is good, you can articulate without mouthing your words – you're young.' She laughed. It was so good to be with him again, even if she could not recapture last night's enchantment.

'You needn't go on with the list,' she said. 'I'm not an actress and never shall be. I only made a fairly good show of Katharina the other night because there's something of the shrew in me!' He laughed.

'I won't have that,' he said, 'though a woman who is all sugar soon becomes insipid. I've always preferred a savoury to a sweet –which reminds me, what are you having to follow? I suggest Crêpe Suzette, sort of pancakes with brandy and cointreau. They cook them here whilst you watch. Exciting, indigestible, very nice. Try them?'

Gail had reached a stage when she would have tried almost anything he suggested, whilst at the same time, deep in her heart, she knew by some infallible instinct that he would not suggest anything she would regret trying.

It was strange, when she thought about it, how deeply she felt she could trust him. He was more like Jeffrey Templar, though younger and of a quite different way of life.

It was that memory which took her into the City when, the lunch over, Kip had to get back to a discussion which would be considerably complicated by his announcement that Gay would not be the leading lady.

They had made no arrangements for meeting again. Gail had felt disappointed, but after all, what had she expected? What right had she to assume that he had any real interest in her?

So it had just been: 'Well—goodbye, Gail. Thank you for coming.'

'Goodbye, Kip, and it was a lovely lunch. Thank you.' Miss White received her at the offices of Templar, Thwaites and Company with a wintry smile.

'Yes, Mr. Templar is in, Miss Marlin. Is he expecting you?'

'No, I just came on the off-chance,' said Gail, and presently she was shaking Jeffrey Templar's firm hand and smiling into his twinkling blue eyes.

'Well, stranger?' he said. 'More trouble?'

At first she had been a fairly regular visitor to his office, but when she had settled down with Mr. Chives, she felt hesitant about bothering so busy a man as Jeffrey Templar with her small affairs, and none could, she felt, be much smaller than what had been left for her when the complexities of Jeremy Marlin's business had been cleared up.

'No. No trouble,' she said. 'I was in town and thought I'd come and see you. Am I in the way?'

'Of course you're not,' said Jeffrey, and thought how very different she was now from what she had been. Thank heaven she was past that corner of the road. 'What have you been doing with yourself?'

She told him of her work, to which recital he listened with the patient indulgence of the man to whom period costumes could be of no possible interest, and at length she came to last night, and the skating party, via the night of the theatricals.

He chuckled over the thought of Kipling Delaney's escapade.

'Do you know him?' asked Gail.

'No. I've seen him on the stage, though I don't go in for theatres much. Clever man, I imagine, in his own line.'

'Very,' said Gail, and went back to the skating, and he watched her reflectively, listened to the new warmth of her voice, realised, as Kip had done, that she had come to life.

'Well, he seems to have made an impression on you,' he said. 'Seeing him again?'

She coloured.

'You have a knack of digging out the very things one has intended to keep buried,' she said. 'I've just had lunch with him.'

'Hm. Well, my dear, I hope you know what you're doing, but stage folk are notoriously unreliable, you know,' watching her with that small, slightly mischievous smile of his.

'I think that's libel,' she said.

'Not between ourselves. Be careful what you're doing with that young man, though, I wouldn't get mixed up in any affairs if I were you.'

'I don't think Kipling Delaney could possibly be called an affair, where anyone like me is concerned,' said Gail.

He had only a few minutes to give her in between clients, and soon she was on her way again, but those few minutes had served to prove to her that she had been right in connecting these two men in her own mind, Jeffrey Templar and Kipling Delaney.

Though the lawyer had nothing physically in common with the actor, not even age, the former having at least ten years start of the latter, there was that intangible link between them which put them into the same class in Gail's mind, almost in her affections. Both had that quality of reliability which one felt at once and without need of proof. There was the same kindliness, the little glints of somewhat pawky humour, the same wide tolerance. Gail felt that Kip did the little hidden kindnesses which she knew Jeffrey Templar did. How marvellous to be the woman Jeffrey Templar loved! And how marvellous for the one whom someday Kip would love!

And so thinking, her mind came with a shock to Gilda Delaney, whom beyond doubt Kip had loved. She wondered if he loved her still, if that exquisite memory would forever lock his heart against all other comers.

What sort of a fool was she to dream that he admired her, Gail, with her hair that was just brown and her very ordinary grey eyes and her big mouth and her shy, awkward ways?

She went back to Heatherley and her work, resolute in her intention to put Kip out of her mind. That had been a lovely, exciting memory, and whenever she went to the theatre and saw him on the stage, she would hug to herself the thought of those few days and get a thrill out of them because to all the people about her he would be Kipling Delaney, as unattainable and remote as the planets, whilst to her, Gail Marlin, he had once been just 'Kip'.

She found it easier to dismiss him from her mind than she had feared because, a few days later, Mr. Chives had a stroke and was confined to his bed, powerless to move, even to speak for some weeks.

A nurse came to relieve Gail, and Cora Miller, for whom everybody sent in time of trouble, came in and out until there was no question about the bond of sympathy and friendship between her and the grateful girl on whose shoulders most of the responsibility seemed to rest, for Mr. Chives had no relations and only a few business friends.

When he died, mercifully in the end, Gail felt utterly bereft.

There was not much money, for his work had been more for pleasure than profit, and had not earned him much. What there was had been left to charities, and Gail found herself again looking for a job, though considerably better qualified to obtain one than when she had come to Heatherley.

In the final clearing up of the old man's affairs she had had to write a number of letters, and went through the address book, toying with the temptation, to write to Kip.

He had asked her to keep him in touch with Mr. Chives' book, now never to be completed. Was that not sufficient reason? She refused to use to herself the word 'excuse' and sat down to write to Kip in the dismantled study from which, in a few days, the rest of the furniture and books would go to the sale.

> *Dear Mr. Delaney (she wrote, after tearing up the sheet which had begun Dear Kip), I think you may not have heard of the death of Mr. Chives, so I am writing to tell you of it. I am sorry to say he had not finished the book, but the manuscript and the illustrations have been left in his Will to the British Museum if they wish to accept the bequest, which I think they will do. If, therefore, you wish to make any notes about them for future reference, you will know where they may be seen.*
>
>

Yours very sincerely,
Gail Marlin.
>

Two days later, his reply came, and she felt her heart race as she opened the envelope which bore the seal of the Irving Theatre, which was Kip's own playhouse.

My Dear Gail,

I'm so sorry. No. I had not heard. I have been very busy lately. What are you going to do now? Will you come up and tell me? I could lunch almost any day if you will ring up my secretary, Paul Bray, at Irving 2190 and tell him which day suits you best. We can talk then.

Kip.

Chapter Three

'I feel you're doing this because you're sorry for me,' said Gail.

Kipling Delaney faced her across the luncheon table where they had gone for what he warned her was a quick lunch, as he was drivingly busy.

'Don't talk rot,' he said. 'I don't do those things. If I did, I should be surrounded by such a crowd that I shouldn't be able to move. I'm offering you the job because I want someone for it, and you fit it better than anyone I know. If you don't want it, say so, but if you do, let's come to the point without a lot of haggling. Do you want it?'

'Oh, Kip, you know I do,' she said.

He gave her one of his sudden, attractive smiles.

'That's alright, then. Bray will settle things like salary with you. I don't want you to live in, of course, but there is a block of flats near mine where you could probably get a decent little crib. I can't have you miles away, so if they cost more than you think you can afford, tell Bray and he'll put it on to your salary.'

She felt bewildered at this high-handed, open-handed treatment.

'I may not be worth it,' she said, distressed.

'You'll be worth it alright,' he said. 'I wanted your help directly I saw those sketches you did for Chives, but I couldn't in decency suggest your leaving him to come to me. I can use that talent of yours, but you'll be asked to do a lot of other things, and when I'm in a bad temper, I shall curse you and expect you to turn up, smiling again, when I feel better. Going to mind that?'

Again he smiled at her, and she felt, as did everybody else who came into contact with Kip Delaney, that she could forgive him anything but casting her adrift from him.

'I don't know – but if I do, I shan't let you know,' she said, and he nodded approvingly.

'Well, then, that's settled,' he said. 'I've got to go now. I'll tell Bray. Let me see, today's Thursday. Start on Monday. If you can't get a flat by then, Bray will get you fixed up for the time being.'

How used she was to get to the phrase 'Ask Bray.'

She rose to leave the restaurant.

'I don't know how to thank you, Kip,' she said uncomfortably. 'I suppose I ought not to call you Kip now?'

'Why not? Everybody else does,' he told her casually, and brushed aside her thanks, which were unpalatable, for he knew his act was not entirely altruistic. She had a talent he could use, but apart from that, he was going to like having her about, and his capability for doing good work depended largely on the happiness and contentment of his personal environment. If he liked anyone in his employ, he was willing to overlook much; if he disliked that person, he or she must go, no matter what the quality of the work done.

Gail went back to Heatherley walking on air, but first, and with a feeling of utter unreality, she went to find the block of flats where Kip lived and the pair of old-fashioned, tall houses in the rear which had been converted into what was described outside as 'self-contained chambers'.

Kip had given her his card to use there, and the porter nodded and at once became more expansive.

'I'm going to work for Mr. Delaney,' she explained.

'We've had one or two of his people here,' he said. 'A very nice gentleman. The only flat we've got empty just now is on the top,' and he took her by an old-fashioned lift to a tiny suite of rooms with sloping roofs and dormer windows, two rooms opening one from the other, a miniature bathroom and a passage which connected it with the front door and also did duty as kitchen, being fitted with small gas cooker and cupboards.

Her heart was lifted up. Kip meant what he said. He wanted her, needed her, and she would make it her business to see that his need of her remained active.

'I'll have to see Mr. Delaney again first,' she said. I—I haven't really fixed up anything about salary with him yet, but I suppose he would expect me to be able to pay this rent as he told me to come here?'

'That'll be alright, Miss Marlin. We used to have the young lady who was with Kipling Delaney before Mr. Bray. She had this very flat, as it happens. If you see Mr. Bray and then come back here, you can have a word about what colours you would like the place done up in. The telephone's included, except for trunk calls, and light and gas are on slot meters. I empty the dust every day.'

Everyone seemed to know Mr. Bray, she thought, but she could not bring herself to call and see him in case Kip had not yet told him of her advent.

But the next morning came a telephone call to her as she went on with her work of clearing and listing at The Coombe.

'Miss Gail Marlin? My name is Bray. Mr. Kipling Delaney told me to get in touch with you.'

She told him about No. 7 Albery House and its rent.

'That will be alright, Miss Marlin. Mr. Delaney would expect you to pay as much as that. If the flat is not ready, I will arrange accommodation for you. I understand you are to be here on Monday. Ten o'clock please. Your salary will be four hundred pounds a year plus the rent of your flat, if that is acceptable to you.'

'Quite,' said Gail, whose head at that moment was quite incapable of assimilating figures and did not know whether she were being offered a pittance or a munificence, and did not greatly care. What mattered was that she was going to work for Kip, be with Kip, see him every day, be associated with his life, a part of it, however small.

She spared a few minutes to ring up Jeffrey Templar and tell him of her stupendous good luck.

Typically, he was more concerned with her personal wellbeing and safety than the brilliance of her job.

'What do you know of the man, Gail? Is he respectable?' he asked in his blunt fashion.

She laughed. He could hear the lilt in her voice, and smiled a little.

'I should say eminently so,' she told him gaily. 'And he's going to pay me eight pounds a week and the rent of my flat!'

'You ought to have seen me first, you know, Gail,' he said, the smile turned to a frown. 'A man ought not to be making himself responsible for the rent of a flat for you.'

'Don't be idiotic,' retorted this recrudescence of the old Gail. 'It's merely a business deal, part of my salary, as he wants me to be conveniently near where he lives. And it's going to be decorated to suit me, and I'm going to have a home again – a home of my own, my very own!'

He could not resist the appeal of those last words.

'Well, keep in touch with me in case you get yourself in a mess,' he said tolerantly.

'Alright,' said Gail happily.

He hoped she had not fallen for this actor fellow, but to his mind most girls were incapable of managing their own lives with any success, which was why they ought to be guarded and cherished until delivered safely into the hands of an impeccable husband. A husband was also one of the things which he felt indispensable to a woman, and though he sincerely hoped Gail would not get herself mixed up in any funny business with Kipling Delaney, the best thing she could do, if he were a decent sort, was to marry him.

Gail had not got as far as that. All that mattered was that she was going to Kip, and the few days that intervened passed like a happy dream.

Promptly at ten on the following Monday, a raw February morning of wind and rain, she was presenting herself at the elegant double doors of No. 1 The Close, a large flat on the ground floor, situated at the back of the block so that its windows could look out on a surprising garden, high-walled and surrounded by trees, which gave it the appearance of being in a distant suburb rather than within sound of Big Ben.

As she was admitted by a trim, soft-voiced maid and led along thickly carpeted corridors, she was caught back again into the past, and had a tumultuous feeling of home-coming.

She followed the maid into a little lobby, shut off by thick double doors from the rest of the flat and offering a choice of three doors.

The maid opened the one on the right.

'This will be your own office, Miss Marlin,' she said. 'There is a cloakroom through that door, and the room connects with the workroom by this one. If you will leave your hat and coat here, you will find Mr. Bray in the room opposite this. Have you everything you need?'

'Yes, thank you,' said Gail, with a smile.

'I look after these rooms, so if you need anything, will you ask for me on the house telephone? My name is Ethel.'

'Thank you,' said Gail again, and felt already the efficiency of Kip's home, the smooth running of the wheels which only wealth can accomplish. 'I hope I have come to stay.'

The girl smiled and Gail, left alone, took stock of her new quarters.

It was a small, square room, with a window overlooking the side of the garden. A little cloakroom was equipped with all she might need, even down to a bowl of powder. The third door was tempting, but Gail did not open it, going instead across the lobby and knocking at the door opposite her own.

The secretary's room was similar to hers, except that it looked out on the street, was larger, and possessed a finer galaxy of files, safes and bookshelves.

Paul Bray was a quiet, grey little man, quite unlike what Gail had anticipated. He was to become a part of her life, and yet she never discovered anything of his private affairs, knew nothing of his family, his friends, his pursuits – nothing that went beyond the bounds of Kipling Delaney's offices and the theatre. His second name was Efficiency. He stood between Kip and the world, a small, utterly reliable buffer, immovable, inconspicuous, undefeatable.

He greeted Gail with a quiet, friendly smile over the top of his horn-rimmed glasses.

'Good morning, Miss Marlin. Ethel told me you were here. Mr. Delaney wishes you to become acquainted with the routine, and especially to know where everything is kept and to help to keep it in its place. That, you will find, is a not inconsiderable part of your job.'

'Is it a new job, or am I taking someone's place?' asked Gail.

'Actually I have not had an assistant for some months, the last having left to—er—to be married, I believe. Mr. Delaney likes to wait until he finds the right person,' and he took her into the room which everyone called the workroom, a large, almost circular room, one wall of which consisted of French windows, half a dozen of them, leading out to a paved terrace and by a broad step down to the garden, with its perfectly kept lawn, and its flower-beds filled with the promise of the earliest spring flowers.

It was a restful room, a room in which one felt at once glad to be in and loth to leave.

The floor was entirely covered by a plain grey carpet. A huge couch and three or four deep chairs were covered in dull blue leather, and at the windows hung heavy curtains of the same shade. A grand piano in plain dark wood was given the place of importance in the room, next in importance being Kip's desk, a huge, workmanlike affair on which stood miniature stage sets, piles of manuscript and a massive, silver-framed blotter.

Bray saw her eyes rest on this for a moment.

'That's the only piece of silver he will use,' he said. 'People give him hundreds of presents in the year, but eventually they find their way to various charities. He won't keep any of them for himself.'

'Was this a very special one?' asked Gail, indicating the blotter.

'His wife gave it to him before they were married, and he's used it ever since,' said Bray, but his tone did not invite further inquiries, and Gail was quick to adapt herself to his wishes.

Kip did not appear during the morning and in the afternoon, as there was nothing for her to do, she went off to inspect her new flat, in the hands of the decorators.

John Chives had added a codicil to his Will in which he left 'to my dear young friend, Miss Gail Marlin, any or all of my furniture which she may care to possess.' She had had nothing on which to spend her salary at The Coombe, so she could buy herself whatever else she needed, chiefly kitchenware and curtains.

Bray had said there would be no need for her to go back to The Close that day, so, though she regretted not having been able to see Kip, she decided she would seize the opportunity of going to the hairdressers.

It was not to be, for on the landing outside the new flat she ran full tilt into Kip.

'Oh—it's you!' she said, in a little breathless whisper.

'I guessed you would be round here,' he said. 'May I look in? Like it?' and he threaded his way between the ladders, bending his tall head until he stood in the room which was to be her bedroom.

'I love it,' she had answered him softly, and he looked down at her curly brown head and smiled.

'Odd little thing, aren't you?' he asked, and she did not mind his thinking of her as 'little', though she was well above medium height, because he was so much taller. 'Going to be utterly pleased with yourself in this eagle's nest, aren't you?'

'Utterly,' said Gail, smiling back at him in a way which made him look as far from her eyes as he could.

Damn it, the child was so devilishly appealing.

'Bray tells me you seem to have absorbed quite a lot today, so what about seeing materialised the sort of work you'll be doing for me very soon? Like to come back with me to the rehearsal?'

'Oh, Kip, yes!' she said eagerly. 'Are you sure it's alright to call you that? Mr. Bray always says Mr. Delaney.'

He smiled.

'He's the only one who ever gives me that dignity,' he said. 'Bray's the sort who has to go his own way and take his own time, and he's nothing if not conventional, though how on earth he contrives to make himself fit into my crazy coach is always a mystery. He would as soon think of calling his employer by a nickname as of coming to work in his pyjamas, though I frequently work in mine. Will that shock you?' with a quizzical smile at her.

'I don't expect so,' said Gail soberly, and then they both laughed, for no apparent reason.

It is on those pointless laughs that many friendships are made.

Gail went with him to the theatre, a strange, shrouded, echoing place, where hammers and voices and jarring instruments in process of tuning vied with one another to make the most noise. Men touched their caps to Kip as he and Gail threaded their way between bits of fantastic-looking scenery and articles in crazy juxtaposition with one another, a gilt bed looking obscene when placed beside a painted stream in a meadow.

'Aren't you acting in the play?' asked Gail.

'Yes, but my understudy is going on tonight so that I can get the view of the audience of the thing. It's to be hoped that distance lends enchantment to the view. Heaven knows something will have to!'

He paused to speak to one or two people and introduced Gail.

'Miss Marlin, Bray's assistant,' he said as a rule, but to Priscilla Grant, who was waiting quietly in the wings, he added a little more.

'I want you two to know each other. Priscilla is my new leading lady and Gail my new assistant secretary, both of you feeling a bit uncertain of yourselves, but with no justification in the world. Gail's going to have a flat in Albery House. Go and see her some time, Priscilla.'

Priscilla had no beauty, but she had that which makes it superfluous. She had charm, personality, a deep and lovely voice, and her presence was full of restfulness.

She smiled at Gail.

'Are you nervous?' she asked.

'Horribly,' said Gail, 'though I haven't got your ordeal to go through. If I had, I should pass right out.'

They laughed, and a wild little thrill of jealousy shot through Gail. If Kip were surrounded daily by such women as this, what chance would she ever have?

'I sincerely hope I don't let Kip down like that,' said Priscilla. 'Be merciless to me tonight, Kip. It's better than having to be merciful to me on Thursday. I'd better go now. Where will you be?'

'Everywhere. Got a notebook, Gail? Well, pop down to the room marked Business Manager and ask them for a pad and come back to me in the dress circle.'

The play had started when she rejoined him, wondering how she was going to make notes in the dark, but he produced a torch and held it for her whilst she jotted down his comments.

Gail was absorbed in it, gripped by it, and when the first act came to an end, her eyes were frankly wet. Kip laughed at her, but there was no unkindness in the laughter. There was even a little throb of satisfaction. The play was different from anything he had done before, deeper, less spectacular, making a different appeal. Would they like it, these people who were coming to him so confident that he would not fail them? There had been a great urge in his soul when he had written it. He felt that the whole world was riding on the gay roundabout of a circus, whilst beneath them, the sounds deadened by the jingling music of the hurdy-gurdy, a madman fashioned sticks of dynamite, infernal machines, terrific fireworks on which were written 'Light at this end and retire immediately'.

'Well?' he asked her when it was over.

'I think it's marvellous,' said Gail, and meant it.

He sighed.

'I wonder. Perhaps they'll prefer the mixture as before – pretty heroine, dashing hero, chorus with lines and legs, music they can whistle in the bath.'

'This will make them think,' said Gail.

'Do you think they want to? It's a gruesome business nowadays, thinking. Far better to make so much noise that no one can think. Bang the drums. Shriek out the saxophones. Life's gay. Life's wonderful. It must be to make all this noise! On with the dance, let joy be unrefined.'

There was an unusual note of bitterness in his voice and Gail could find nothing to say, and a moment later he patted her hand.

'Come along. Let's go down. Never mind my burblings. I always get a fit of the blues before a new production.'

'What about these notes?'

'Oh—type them out and give them to me tomorrow. I shan't bother any of them tonight. They're tired and so am I. I'll have a go at them tomorrow. Goodnight, Gail.'

'Goodnight, Kip,' she returned, but he was gone without waiting to hear her reply.

She walked to the boarding-house where Paul Bray had obtained a room for her, her head in the clouds though her feet trod London's streets.

She was working for Kip. She had actually started working for him. Tomorrow she would see him, and the day after, and the next day. What more could human heart desire?

But in the days that followed, those tumultuous, nerve-racked, hideous days before the fatal 'First Night', what little she saw of Kip showed her a restless, driven, anxious man with too many of the strings in his own hands, too many details to examine, too many little difficulties to solve. She was sent here and there, diving into files, spending hours looking for something which, when she had found it, had lost its value and was no longer needed. She sat for hours at the telephone until her ears buzzed and her throat ached and her head felt it would burst. She received a dozen different orders all at once, everybody wanting something done once it was known that there was an assistant to Paul Bray.

Bray himself sat in his room like a small grey spider, spinning his webs, immovable, imperturbable, getting through incredible tasks, sorting out muddles, solving seemingly insoluble problems, taking out of Kip's hands whatever he would let fall, or was obliged to let fall.

'Why does he try to do so much himself?' asked Gail, sharing a picnic lunch with Bray on the day of the opening at the theatre.

She had wondered how she was going to find time to go out for it, when Ethel had appeared with a loaded tray of sandwiches, delicately cut and served, fruit and a huge Thermos jug of coffee.

'That's the way he's made,' said Bray. 'Better eat whilst you can,' but before he started, he went across to the door of the workroom.

Kip was surrounded by a crowd of people. Someone was playing softly on the piano.

'For God's sake, stop that row,' said Kip, and the pianist was silent. 'What's the matter, Bray?'

'Better come and eat something,' he said.

'Alright. In five minutes,' said Kip.

When the five minutes had gone, Bray went to the door again.

'Mr. Delaney.'

'Well, what's up now?' asked Kip irritably.

'Better come and eat something,' said Bray.

'Oh—five minutes. Alright, curse you. I'll come now,' and this time he came through to the secretary's room, shirt-sleeved, untidy, looking worn out.

They did not speak to him, though Gail crossed the room and turned the keys in both doors, at which Bray nodded approval. Then they waited on him, anticipating his needs, Bray at the end producing a bottle of liqueur brandy and measuring out a thimbleful into his chief's coffee before giving it to him.

'Thanks,' said Kip, the first word he had spoken to them, but they knew that their silent service, their unspoken sympathy, had done as much work as the sandwiches and the coffee and the brandy.

Gail took the empty cup from him, and he smiled at her and stretched his legs and lay back in the easy chair before the fire. Two minutes later he was asleep, and Bray went back to his desk and turned over his papers quietly whilst Gail tiptoed out of the room and got on with her work.

Kip had sent tickets for the Millers and arranged for Gail to go with them to the theatre that night.

Somehow or other she had managed to move into her new flat, and she was thankful of its bright peace after the turmoil of Kip's workrooms.

Their seats were in the stalls, and she wore a dress of hyacinth blue with a big blue scarab pinned to it 'for luck'. It was a survival of other days. Her father had bought it for her in a Moorish market they had visited. It had not brought him much luck, poor darling.

The play was undoubtedly a success. It might not have produced the laughter that so often had made Kip's plays memorable, but it gave the audience something else, a sweetness, a width of outlook, a glimpse of an ideal, to which they were not unresponsive.

Kip made his customary very short, graceful speech, saw to it that everyone shared the honours with him, even the stage hands, and at last people could go home.

Chapter Four

As Bray had said, once Kip's play was in being, and playing to his usual crowded houses, life for those about him grew easier and more regular.

Promptly at ten each morning Gail presented herself at the side door of No. 1 The Close, of which only she and Bray, besides Kip himself, had a key. A stack of letters awaited her attention, and she found that it took her most of the morning to deal with them. Kip was conscientious towards his enormous crowd of admirers, and there was no question of his 'fan mail' being thrust unread into the waste-paper basket.

Autographs, photographs, subscriptions small and large, jobs of work, recommendations, requests for his services or his company at stone-layings, bazaar-openings, hospital fetes – these came in by every post, and Gail quickly learned what to do with them, though the cost of being famous appalled her, and she felt it must be impossible for anyone to go through the year, and through year after year, with such an enormous extraneous call on his income.

All letters marked 'Personal' went in to Bray unopened, though often he brought them back to her, the designation on the envelope being mere camouflage for another begging letter.

She was disappointed that she did not see more of Kip himself. Sometimes a whole day passed without her seeing him at all, whilst on other days he would come in for tea, spend an hour or so closeted with Bray, and merely look in on Gail before he left the offices.

One of her jobs was the collection and filing of press cuttings, and Kip was amused at her reactions to them.

'Don't take them so seriously,' he told her when, a few days after the first night of *The Roundabout*, the critics were still chewing over his ingress into serious plays. 'No one else does, and the box office is the best weather-vane.'

'But this man seems to think you have no business to write a play with a purpose,' she said. 'He suggests in quite a superior tone that your business is merely to amuse.'

He laughed and re-read the notice.

'Poor old Chute,' he said. 'Got chronic dyspepsia. Was probably never amused in his life, and feels that a mere mountebank has no right to try to steal the thunder of the gods. Well, perhaps he's right. After all, in this world what better can you do for your fellows than make them laugh? Make them forget that they're sitting on a volcano?'

'In other words, keep the roundabout turning to the tune of the hurdy-gurdy,' said Gail, with a curl of her lip.

Kip laughed again, and threw the cutting down on the pile and prepared to leave her.

'Don't take life, or me, too seriously, my dear,' he said.

'You haven't had your tea, Kip,' she reminded him as he reached the door.

Anything to keep him there a little longer, to add to the number of those jealously held minutes.

'I've promised to have it in the house today,' he said. 'You know that if you want to see the show again at any time, Bray can give you a seat, don't you?'

'Yes, thank you, Kip,' said Gail, and he was gone.

She sat wondering what he had meant by warning her not to take him too seriously. Did he know just how seriously she was taking him? Had he guessed that he was the sun, moon and stars of her life? His presence heaven itself? Every moment spent working for him a moment of worship? This house her temple and this room its altar?

'I hope he does. I want him to,' she told herself. 'Even if I'm never anything to him (and why should I expect to be?) I think I'd want him to know how I feel about him. Why not, since he knows that hundreds of other girls, girls who don't even know him, worship him?'

She had had to accept the fact that she was not to see him as often as she had expected. Bray kept his engagement book and made appointments for him, both business and social, but Gail knew that these had to be dove-tailed into one another with meticulous care, leaving Kip little spare time. She solaced herself with the very real delight she took in her small home, which daily became dearer to her.

Priscilla Grant came to see her, the two somewhat shy of each other at first, both of them wary of the introduction of Kip's name into the conversation, but Gail soon discovered that her first feeling of jealousy of Priscilla had no grounds for she had a husband and a small boy, of both of whom she was devotedly fond.

She met John Leith, a pale, studious, rather delicate man who adored Priscilla, and Jacko, who was seven and a cherub.

So her jealousy of Kip's leading lady was a pricked bubble, and the Leiths became almost her closest friends, their house a refuge on the few occasions when even her flat failed to satisfy the restless craving for something different. They did not discuss Kip, however. Had he meant less to Gail, she could have talked of him, but she had no intention of letting anyone else, even Priscilla, share the secret she hugged to her breast, and she felt she could not have talked of Kip without revealing it.

On the evening of the day of her talk about reviewers with Kip, she suddenly decided she would see his play again, and asked Paul Bray for a ticket.

'What will you have?' he asked her. 'Not much to spare tonight, but I'll find out from the box office,' and later on he told her that he had been able to do nothing better than a spare seat in a box.

'Will the other people mind my butting in?' asked Gail doubtfully.

'No. They have paid for only half the box seats so they will not expect to have it to themselves. You'd better wear something rather nice. People do at Mr. Delaney's theatre in the boxes.'

She thanked him for the tip, and amused herself by dressing in her one evening dress, not a survival of the old days but an inexpensive, charming little frock of jade green lace which she had worn on the one or two occasions when she had acted hostess for John Chives' guests.

She found herself enjoying the play much more than she had done on the first night. She was not now suffering agonies of apprehension, nor that foolish fear lest someone should let Kip down.

She was entertained, too, by the two people with whom she shared the box, a middle-aged couple who felt that Kip would do better to go back to his gay musicals and his former leading lady.

'Though of course they do say she was no better than she ought to be,' said the lady. 'Then I don't suppose any of these stage people are.'

George grinned.

'Perhaps not, my dear,' he said, 'though one never hears anything unpleasant about Delaney.'

'No, poor dear. That's so,' she agreed comfortably. 'It was such a tragedy about his wife. On their honeymoon, weren't they? People say he's never looked at a woman since. Terribly sad. They say she was such a lovely girl, that I suppose nobody else has ever had any attraction for him, poor man.'

'Ssh, May. The curtain's going up again.'

Gail's attention wandered a moment as she thought of the wife whom Kip had loved.

Just before the end of the last act, the attendant brought her a note.

'Miss Marlin?' she asked, and when Gail nodded, the girl said: 'I was to wait for an answer.'

She ripped open the envelope on which her name had been scribbled in Kip's writing.

Let me drive you home [he had written without formal beginning]. The car will be waiting round at the back, outside Crespin's garage. Will you get in it and wait for me?
K.

All her world grew lovely and filled with radiant light.

'Just say Yes,' she told the girl, and at the end she slipped away quickly, and found the long grey car, and a few minutes later Kip came to join her, slipping into the driving seat beside her with a smile and a little pat of her hand.

'Good girl,' he said. 'Bray told me you would be there, and I don't like your going home alone.'

'It's such a little way,' she pointed out.

He smiled and started the engine.

'Would you rather have gone alone?'

'Of course not,' said Gail.

'Then don't raise objections to whatever I try to do for your comfort,' he told her, but she heard the friendliness in his tone and was utterly content.

A semi-circular courtyard made it possible to draw cars off the road at Albery House.

'I suppose this is good night,' he said, and her heart gave a little jump at the incredible suggestion.

'Will you—come up, Kip?' she asked.

He sat still and looked at her as she leaned forward towards the door handle. There was a strange expression on his face, an odd, unsmiling look.

'I ought not to, Gail,' he said. 'It's very late. Better ask me in the daytime.'

'I never see you in the daytime,' she said, 'except when you're too busy to bother about me. Please come up, Kip. Just for five minutes.'

His answer was to switch off the engine and put the key in his pocket.

They tiptoed to the lift, a noisy hydraulic affair which refused to keep secret any arrival or departure in the flats, but Gail had no care. Her whole being was centred on the joy of having Kip there, all to herself, in her own home.

The little flat threw out a welcoming beam of light as soon as she had unlocked the door and found the switch, and she opened the door of the sitting-room for him and switched on that light too.

He looked round approvingly.

'You've made a delightful little nest here,' he told her. 'I like your curtains, and old Chives' things look really well here. This old cupboard is a nice piece. Glad you picked that out. I must remember you've got that. I may want to borrow it if I put on those old Sheridans.'

He was talking for the sake of it, and they both knew it.

Gail was busying herself in her little hall-kitchen, heating coffee and milk, setting out cups and saucers of old delft, and tiny, sweet biscuits. She had bought those biscuits and kept them tightly tinned, though she disliked them. They were Kip's favourites, and a supply was kept at the office for him. She had refused to admit to herself her reason for buying them to keep in her flat.

'Light the gas fire, will you, Kip?' she asked him through the open doorway, and when she wheeled in the little trolley she found him stretched out in her easy chair and looking so completely at home there that she caught her breath sharply.

She talked feverishly, looking anywhere rather than at him, but at last he set down his empty cup, took hers from her, and drew her to her feet, holding her hands.

'My dear,' he said, and she had never heard that note in his voice, even on the stage. 'I've got to leave you. Do you realise why?'

Tell me—Kip,' she said in a whisper.

'Because—if I stay—I shall kiss you, Gail.'

'Don't you want to?' she asked him very softly.

'More than anything in the wide world,' he said. 'That's why I'm not going to, Gail. Because I want it so much,' and he loosed her hands, and she did not move until the last sound of the lift had died away and she knew he would not come back.

Then, from excitement and frustration and longing, for love of Kip, she cried herself to sleep and woke in the morning with a headache and a fierce anger at herself.

Why be such an idiot because he had not kissed her? There would be other times. Last night he had kept from that embrace only by the almost superhuman strength of his will. He would not always and forever be so strong.

She did not see Kip until the afternoon, when he popped his head into her room and, finding her alone, came in and closed the door.

If she had expected him to show some memory of last night, she was disappointed, for he looked just as usual, his smile neither more nor less friendly and impersonal.

'Gail, I've got a royal command for you. Mrs. Delaney wants you to have tea with her and I accepted for you. She's such a great invalid that we let her have her own way in most things, and she apologises for not having been able to see you before. She's had a bad time lately.'

Gail had risen from her desk.

'Mrs. Delaney?' she asked uncertainly.

'If I don't come for you myself, Ethel will fetch you and show you the way. Two minutes to four precisely – and make yourself look nice,' and with another smile and a nod, he was gone.

Mrs. Delaney? She had no idea his mother was even alive, but there was no connection at all between the offices and the rest of the flat save by the double doors which only Kip used, so she had had no means of knowing anything about life on the other side of them.

She speculated about this unknown mother, of whom he had spoken as if she were an autocrat and the real ruler of the establishment. It would be strange, she thought, seeing Kip subservient to anyone else's will, Kip taking second place in any gathering, possibly even slightly eclipsed!

By five minutes to four, she was ready, her face powdered but not otherwise made up. She knew that Kip disliked makeup off the stage.

Ethel came for her, but on the other side of the double doors, Kip was coming down the corridor.

'Alright, Ethel,' he said. 'This way, Gail,' and he led her to another double door leading into a little ante-room where a middle-aged woman with a grim, unsmiling face was sitting with her sewing. She wore a nurse's starched grey and white uniform, her sparse grey hair neatly banded beneath the white cap.

Kip smiled at her and her features relaxed a little.

'Martha,' this is Miss Marlin, who is helping Mr. Bray. Gail, this is the real ruler of my household, Martha Halett, and none of us ever dares to disobey her. We're going to tea with Mrs. Delaney, Martha.'

'Yes. She told me,' said Martha. 'She's ready for you.'

'How is she this afternoon?' asked Kip.

'She's had a sleep this morning, and the new doctor, Dr. Blair, is coming at six.'

Kip nodded, went across to one of the two doors opening from this ante-room, and knocked softly, opening the door without waiting for a reply.

Gail, going in before him as he held the door open for her, had the impression that she was entering a garden, for the whole place was filled with flowers and perfume, was softly lighted and very warm, and lights had been so cunningly arranged that, even on this blustering March evening, the room seemed filled with sunlight, yellow and dappled with tiny points of shadow.

Then, going to the other side of the huge, embroidered screen which guarded the door, she stood quite still, speechless, petrified by shock.

The woman in the elaborate gilt bed, propped up with orchid-coloured cushions to match the satin eiderdown and the hangings of the room, was certainly not his mother! The hair was golden, the skin fair and smooth, the lips delicately chiselled, the eyes, perhaps the most lovely thing about this whole lovely face, for they were the blue of hyacinths growing in a wood, and the long lashes made a deep, dark fringe about them, accentuating their exquisite blueness.

All this she saw in an instant, that amazed instant between rounding the screen and hearing Kip's voice beside her.

'Darling, I've brought Gail to see you,' he said, and there was a softness in his voice, a special tenderness, which brought a lump to Gail's throat.

But Gilda Delaney was speaking to her, smiling, holding out one delicate hand on which exquisite rings sparkled, matching the jewels at her throat and in her small earlobes.

'How nice of you to come, Miss Marlin,' she said in a sweet, cultured voice. 'I do sincerely apologise for not having asked you to meet me before, but I have not been very well lately, and Kip did not think it wise for me to see strangers. He bullies me dreadfully, you know,' setting Gail's hand free so that she could slide her own into Kip's and draw it against her cheek in an infinitely tender, appealing little gesture.

'You're not exactly strangers, you two,' said Kip, keeping his hand there and rubbing it gently against Gilda's cheek.

Kip bent and kissed her hair.

'Will you sit here, Miss Marlin?' – indicating a chair near the bed.

'It would sound much nicer if you called me Gail,' said the girl shyly, finding her voice at last.

Gilda smiled.

'Well, we'll see. I expect I shall. Ring for tea, Kip, will you? It's a minute past the hour already.'

Gail heard the imperious note of the spoiled child there, but who could wonder if Kip and everyone else spoiled her?

Before he could reach the bell, a smiling maid had arrived with a laden tea-trolley, and Kip produced from a corner a specially constructed tray which enabled the invalid to manage her meals in considerable comfort. Gail realised that she was completely motionless from her waist downwards, and her heart was torn with the tragedy of it. So young, so utterly lovely, and doomed to a living death!

Gilda surveyed the assortment of tiny sandwiches, cakes and biscuits and frowned.

'I asked for strawberry cake, Dorothy,' she said.

'Cook is very sorry, madam, but she could not get strawberries anywhere, so she has made you some of the little honey cakes you like.'

'Honey cakes? I'm sick to death of them,' said Gilda, pushing aside the tempting plate the maid was offering her. 'I don't know why someone could not have got me strawberries, even if it is March, do you, Kip?'

'I expect Cook did try, darling. She always makes a great effort to get you what you fancy,' said Kip. 'Have one of these little jiggers. They look good.'

'I don't really fancy anything, since I can't have strawberry cake,' said Gilda peevishly, but when persuaded by both her husband and Dorothy, she contrived to eat an excellent meal.

Gail could not eat. She was still suffering from the shock of discovering Kip's wife to be alive, and she was relieved when, very soon, Kip suggested that she should return to her work.

'We mustn't keep you from more important affairs, Miss Marlin,' said Gilda sweetly. 'Goodbye. It has been so nice of you to come. You must come again when I am well enough for visitors, though I am afraid it is not a very attractive proposition for a girl in health and strength to come and sit by the bedside of a useless cripple.'

'I shall be glad to come whenever you like, Mrs. Delaney,' said Gail gently. 'If I can do anything at all for you, you have only to let me know.'

'Thank you, but there is really very little that anyone can do for me, I am afraid,' said the invalid with a little sigh, and the next moment Gail found herself outside the overheated, perfumed room and breathing the fresher air of the corridor.

Martha Halett gave her a searching glance as she went through the ante-room without responding to her smile, and Gail wondered briefly why the woman had taken a dislike to her.

Kip followed her out and went with her to the office wing.

'It was nice of you to go, Gail,' he said very evenly, without looking at her. 'It is dull for her, lying there year after year. She has marvellous courage and scarcely ever utters a word of complaint.'

Gail hesitated, and then spoke in a low voice.

'I had no idea your wife was still alive, Kip,' she said.

He gave her a startled, surprised glance and held open the door into her room.

'You didn't know?' he asked. 'But—I thought everybody knew, and—well, I assumed you knew.'

'I thought she had died then, after the accident,' said Gail.

'No, though perhaps, as she says, that would have been the better way,' said Kip almost harshly.

He came into the room with her and shut the door, and for a moment or two they could find nothing to say. Then Kip spoke quietly.

'You realise now, don't you, Gail, why I—ought not to have come into your flat last night?'

She looked at him.

'Was that the only reason why you were sorry you came, Kip?' she asked.

'Yes,' said Kip, and again they were silent.

Gail's whole being was rising in passionate resentment of what Fate had meted out to her, bringing this man within reach of her, letting her believe that he might someday belong to her, and then snatching him back, showing her the one impassable barrier which neither he nor she nor anyone else could pull down.

'Will she—never get better?' she asked at last.

'I'm afraid not. I have done everything, spared nothing in trouble or expense. Every surgeon of note in the world has been asked for opinion or advice, and none of them gives any hope. It seems that the nerves have been destroyed, and nothing can recreate them, but she is otherwise quite strong and perfect – heart, lungs, all the vital organs functioning perfectly – but she cannot move from her bed and never will be able to move.'

'And she may live to be quite old?'

'Yes,' said Kip, and again they were silent.

At last she moved a little and laid a hand on his arm.

'I'm so dreadfully sorry,' she said, her voice quivering. 'I wish I could do something—say something—'

She could not go on. What, indeed, was there to say? The thing was tragic beyond words, beyond thought or imagination, and in her feeling for him, she could for a moment forget herself and what this meant to her and must always mean.

He covered her hand with his own.

'I know, dear, but there isn't anything. Don't try. I'm sorry you didn't know about it. It didn't occur to me. Shall we—just forget and go on? Or do you want to leave me, Gail?'

'Oh no, Kip! Not that!' she said, and he smiled at her look and tone of horror.

'Alright, then. Back to the beginning,' and he smiled again as he used a phrase now familiar to her. 'By the way, I forgot to give you a message. Priscilla wants you to go there tonight. We don't play on Tuesday nights, you know. Gives everybody a rest. John has to work late, and Priscilla has to stay with the boy. I told her you would ring her up if you were not going.'

'I'll go,' said Gail, and then Paul Bray looked in to speak to Kip, and outside life absorbed them both again.

That evening, sitting in the quiet room, Priscilla in a house frock looking very different from the glamorous stage star, darning Jacko's stockings, Gail spoke of Kip's wife.

'Do you know, Priscilla, I thought she was dead. I'd no idea until I went to tea with her this afternoon. When Kip spoke of a Mrs. Delaney, I thought it was his mother. I had a shock.'

'I suppose we all took it for granted that you knew,' said Priscilla, threading her needle again. 'It's a terrible tragedy for Kip, especially as he is still so completely in love with her. I don't think he's ever looked at another woman. He centres his life round her. I don't suppose any woman has ever been so much cherished and beloved, and all to no purpose. She can never be a wife to him, and Kip's the sort who definitely ought to have a wife and a family.'

'A family? Kip?' asked Gail, trying to visualise Kip as a father and failing completely.

Priscilla smiled.

'There are many sides to him,' she said. 'Kip's not the sort to wear out his heart over something he knows to be unattainable. He makes his life out of the things he can have.'

'You know him well, Priscilla, don't you?' asked Gail a little enviously.

'Fairly well. He's always been my good fairy. He pulled me out of the chorus years ago and told me I ought to be doing serious work, and when this chance came I'd have died rather than disappoint him.'

'I think that's how Kip gets on so well,' said Gail, glad to talk about him, as is the inevitable way of a lover. 'We'd all die rather than disappoint him, so as he expects a lot from us, he gets a lot. I'd do anything in the world for him. I'm so thankful and happy to be working for him.'

Priscilla gave her a keen look as she rose to put away her mending.

'Don't fall in love with him, though most of us go through that stage,' she said lightly.

'Even you, Priscilla?'

She smiled.

'Even me—though actually there's never been anything serious in my life except my old John.'

'And you think there will never be anything serious for Kip except Gilda? Do you know her, Priscilla?'

'Oh yes, I've been taken in to see her. I've been several times. She always likes to inspect us all, you know, and I feel she must have been greatly relieved at sight of my plain, unromantic countenance,' with a smile.

'Nobody could ever think of you as plain,' said Gail fervently, and the older woman's smile deepened.

'I think, fortunately for me, Mrs. Delaney does,' she said.

'You mean she's jealous? Afraid of Kip falling in love with somebody else?'

'Well, naturally. He's her whole life, and so far no one has ever come between them. Perhaps he is not really the type. I sometimes think he gets rid of all that sort of energy in his plays, writing them and acting, so that women don't matter a lot to him. Still, Mrs. Delaney cannot be blind to the fact that he is a most attractive man, and growing more attractive with the years, whilst she is just a useless log.'

'She's very, very lovely,' said Gail.

'Yes,' said Priscilla briefly, and Gail thought, 'She doesn't like Gilda. Why? She was perfectly charming to me this afternoon,' but Priscilla did not pursue the subject.

Chapter Five

The weeks that followed Gail's first visit to Gilda Delaney were uneventful ones, except that every new day seemed an adventure to the girl, whose heart was definitely in her work.

Several times she was summoned to what she called in her own mind the 'state apartments' to take tea with the invalid, and though her own feelings for Kip's wife did not grow appreciably warmer, Gilda evinced an interest in the girl which was almost affectionate, an interest which she made very apparent to Kip.

'She's a nice child, this Gail,' she said to him on one occasion, Gail being present and embarrassed. 'Why don't you take her out, Kip? Give her a good time? She must live a very dull life in this little flat she tells me about. Is it as charming as she believes it to be?'

'How should I be expected to know what Gail's flat is like?' he asked her. 'Here's Martha, looking stern, which means we have outstayed our welcome. Come along, Gail. I want to have a look at those contracts before you go,' and she had an idea that he was glad to get her out of the way.

There was little intimate communication between them during this period. Gail could not rid her mind of Priscilla's definite statement that Kip was still in love with his wife. She had watched them together and listened to him with the sharpened ears of love, and her heart had sunk, for everything seemed to prove the truth of Priscilla's words.

One day Gilda had shown Gail her jewels.

When the visitor had been ushered in (no one ever went except by invitation) Gilda had been playing with a string of pearls which she had taken from their white velvet case, letting the beads slip through her delicate fingers one by one like a rosary, and Gail had a strange impression of something rather terrible in the way Gilda handled the pearls, looked at them, almost fondled them.

Her eyes were very bright and her lips soft and moist.

'Aren't they lovely?' she asked, when she had greeted her visitor. 'Kip has just given them to me. He always gives me something, generally a jewel, out of the proceeds of a new play. Lovely, aren't they?' and she held them against her cheek, and again Gail had that impression that inordinate love was being given to these inanimate objects.

'They're marvellous,' said Gail, and put out her hand to touch them. Gilda jerked them away instantly out of her reach.

She flushed a little, but the other made no comment, merely asking if Gail were fond of jewels.

'Yes. What woman isn't?' asked Gail. 'Not that I possess any or am ever likely to.'

'I have wonderful jewels,' said Gilda, her voice soft and almost cooing. 'I'll show them to you if you like. They're in a little safe let into the wall over there. Do you see? It looks like a picture frame with a Van Dyck in it. Here is the key,' feeling under the pillow and producing a small key on a gold chain. 'It goes three to the left and two to the right.'

Gail found the keyhole with some difficulty, and made an involuntary exclamation when the door came open to reveal a small lighted safe which was a veritable Aladdin's Cave.

One side held a stack of leather and velvet cases of varying shapes and sizes, whilst on the other side were fitted trays of rings, brooches and bracelets.

'The trays first, one at a time,' said Gilda, a note of excitement in her voice, and when Gail had brought them, carrying them with a feeling of awe to the bed, where she had first had to spread a black velvet cloth, the invalid tipped them out in disorder and then began to sort them out, one by one, lovingly, a caress in every touch, sliding the rings on and off her slender fingers, fitting on the bracelets.

She was soon tired, and left Gail to put the trays back in the safe, and replace the key under her pillow.

But Gail never forgot the sight of those small, clutching, caressing fingers. They had left a disagreeable impression on her mind, quite apart from the jealous thought of how much Kip must love her, to pour out the wealth of a king's ransom on her like that.

It was just about this time that she first met Phillip Westing.

A certain amount of clearing up had remained after Mr. Chives' estate had been settled, and the executors had decided to publish his unfinished book on Period Costumes, and Gail had been asked to undertake the necessary arrangements. It was in this connection that she met Westing, chief clerk for the firm of Bradey & Sons, who were reproducing the engravings.

He was a man in the middle thirties, thin-faced, with an intelligent brow, thick brownish hair and attractive grey eyes.

Gail, to whom the procedure was new, was glad to be able to leave the arrangements in what she recognised as capable hands, and Phillip Westing made no secret of the fact that he enjoyed handling the job, and handling it for her.

She was feeling very lonely at the time. Now that Kip seemed definitely unattainable, she had begun to realise how little there was in her life besides him, and that if she were not to develop into a dull, unimaginative automaton, she must enlarge both her interests and her circle of friends, and Phillip Westing was only too glad of the opportunity offered him in that second capacity.

He was a good talker, and if his choice of subjects was limited, they were new enough to Gail to be of sufficient interest to her, not to bore her.

Westing was a professed and burning socialist, and the fact that Gail Marlin had had Jeremy K. Marlin for father encouraged him rather than deterred him in his talk of the crime of malting money without earning it by the sweat of one's brow.

She talked about it to Kip, who laughed and told her not to go Bolshy on him, and raised her salary.

Westing was scornful when she told him about it.

'That's just what these wealthy men do. They think they can buy anyone with an extra few bob a week, and that they've only got to pat you on the head and tell you everything will be alright for you to sit down for another hundred years or so as slaves.'

Gail laughed. She never took him quite seriously.

'But Kip doesn't treat us as slaves,' she said. 'He pays us all decent wages, and has an almost feudal regard for those who work for him, even in the humblest capacity, last week he sent away the wife of a scene shifter to a sanatorium and is paying all the expenses himself, and sends him down in a car every Saturday night after the show so that he can spend his Sundays with her and come back for the Monday night show. That isn't treating him as a slave.'

'No, but don't you see. If that man had a proportionate share in Delaney's undertakings, there would be no need for him to take anybody's charity, and Delaney would not have to offer it. The man could pay his own expenses.'

'But Dobb thinks he is adequately paid,' said Gail.

'Only because his overlords for generations have made him believe that a mere pittance is good pay. The working classes of this country have had their noses ground to the earth so long that they can't see beyond them.'

'But, Phillip, Kip wouldn't grind anybody's nose,' she protested.

'You will make everything personal,' he said. 'Who's talking about your precious Delaney?'

'You are. We both are. Oh, don't let's quarrel! Why should we over a subject on which we both really feel alike?'

He smiled grudgingly. He was a dour man, not given to smiling, though to Gail he had shown a side of himself which was usually deeply hidden beneath his constant grudge against a life which, after all, had not treated him too badly. He had a safe and reasonably good job, with a pension at the end of it, made possible by the firm he so often derided as task masters, nigger drivers and capitalists, referring to himself and his fellow workers as 'wage slaves'.

But when they were not arguing about the social system, he and Gail were good friends, on her part largely because she lacked the initiative to make many friends, and because there was something in Phillip Westing which roused her compassion, that pity which is supposed to be akin to love.

In her capacity as one of Kip's confidential staff she met a good many men, but they were mostly of a kind with whom she had nothing in common. Their quick wit terrified her. She could not keep up with them. She found herself examining everything she said before saying it in case it could be turned to some other and often ribald meaning, which is the surest murderer of conversation. Some of them wanted to make love to her, and from these she fled in disgust. She did not want love-making. She wanted friends, wholesome contentment, and she could not find them amongst the men who frequented the business part of No. 1 The Close.

So, gradually, almost unconsciously, her friendship with Phillip Westing grew until it became of importance in her life.

Then one evening he told her more about himself than so far he had volunteered.

It was a warm August evening, and she had gone with him to watch a cricket match in which his firm was taking part, though he himself was not playing.

'Not good enough, I suppose,' he had told her when she asked him why, and she divined that the bitterness hid disappointment.

He would have been glad of a chance to shine in front of her.

So they had sat instead under the trees, apart from other spectators, and he had spoken of himself.

'You don't know much about me, Gail, though I know everything about you,' he said. 'Like to hear?'

'Very much,' said Gail honestly.

'Well, shall we leave out all the part about being born of poor, but honest parents?' he asked. 'I didn't have a very thrilling childhood – council school education, with a couple of years at a commercial school, and then out into a cold, hard world to earn a living and all that. Did my bit in the war, of course, not that that made any difference since I was not even a temporary gentleman!' with that bitterness with which he seemed to infuse everything.

'However, that's going too far,' he said. 'When I was young, not much more than twenty, I made an ass of myself. Usual thing. Married a girl because I thought I couldn't live without her and then found it damned difficult to live with her, especially when the kids came along.'

'You're married, Phillip?' she asked, surprised.

'I was, but she died,' he said. 'Don't waste tears on me, Gail. We didn't hit it off. She wasn't my type, and—well, I was damned unhappy and jolly glad to get into the army and out of it all for a bit. She died two or three years ago.'

'And the children?' asked Gail, trying to readjust her mind to this new view of him.

'Two. Joyce is twelve now and Hugh's ten.'

'Who looks after them?'

'A woman. A housekeeper person, one of a long line of 'em, mostly thieves. Poor kids. I don't have much time to give to them, so they just have to rub along as best they can, though sometimes I think—'

She did not ask him to go on. She knew what he was thinking, that he ought to give the children a mother.

She was quiet and thoughtful, and when they parted she went back to her flat and sat by the open window with her hands idle in her lap for once.

Kip was away. Once a year, whilst the theatre was closed, the Delaneys made a tremendous trek to the sea, Torquay as a rule, Gilda travelling in a special ambulance, whilst the many gadgets constructed for her comfort and convenience were removed to the house on the seafront and a room made ready for her reception as if royalty were expected.

The staff had their holiday at this time, all except Martha Halett, who in all these years had never spent an hour away from her mistress. Bray had gone off somewhere on his own, and Gail was going to clear up some arrears of filing and listing and then she, too, would be free for three weeks, though she had made no plans.

On the evening before he left, Kip had asked her what she was going to do, and she had told him she didn't know.

'You ought to get away to the sea, Gail. What sort of holiday do you really like?'

'I don't think I'm keen on going anywhere particular, Kip,' she said listlessly.

'Nonsense. Of course you must get away. Everybody ought to have a holiday and I know I work you all damned hard. What would you like to do? Like me to fix up a cruise for you somewhere? What about Madeira? Or Norway? Let me pay for it, Gail. After all, I owe you that much.'

But her face had flamed and she had drawn herself up.

'Of course I shouldn't dream of letting you pay for it. You pay me my salary.'

'Not enough to go cruising on.'

'I'm not keen about cruising.'

'Well, here's an idea. The Millers always take a bungalow or cottage or something at Salcombe, in Devon, and they must be going about this time. They always have room for extra people, especially if they can pay their whack. Why not go with them?'

'But, Kip, they haven't asked me.'

'Don't be silly. What does that matter?' and in spite of her half-hearted protests, he had made inquiries of Cora with the result that Gail was to go down to them as soon as she had finished in London. There was no reason why she should not go down tomorrow.

But tonight she was preoccupied with thoughts of Phillip Westing.

She felt certain that it was in his mind to ask her to marry him.

She probed her own mind, knew that to no one else in the world was it possible for her to give what she had given, and could give, to Kip, and yet she could not visualise herself living single all her life because she could not marry the one man she wanted. She was fearlessly honest with herself. She wanted to be married, to have a normal life as wife and mother. Most girls in their hearts do desire marriage. There are few who deliberately choose to remain single.

Why then close her mind against the thought of other men, the thought of Phillip Westing in particular?

Of the men who had asked her to marry them (and they were not so many, after all, who were prepared to go to those lengths to get her) she felt herself to be most in tune with Phillip. There was something in him which was wider, deeper, more enduring, she felt, than anything she had discovered in these other men. She felt herself to be akin to Phillip Westing in many ways, and deep in her heart was the thought that, if she could not give him the wild, passionate adoration which would have been Kip's, she could give him loyal and devoted friendship and service, and mother his rather pathetic children, whom she had not, of course, met.

Surely she had enough to give Phillip Westing? She was definitely fond of him.

With her mind still drifting about uncertainly, she went down to Salcombe the next day.

'You won't mind sharing a room with Ethne, Gail, will you?' Cora asked. 'We have to arrange it that way as we have only three bedrooms. When Kip comes, we put him into Rex's little room and take Rex in with us.'

'Yes, and Dad snores all night like a BBC Symphony Orchestra,' remarked Rex.

'Well, isn't it worth it to have Kip here?' asked his mother, who endured the snoring uncomplainingly every night for love of the snorer. That's the way women are made – and some men too.

'Every time,' said Rex.

'I didn't know Kip was coming down,' said Gail. 'He didn't say anything about it.'

'Torquay isn't very far away, and if they are there when we are here, he usually pops over for a day's fishing and stays the night,' said Cora comfortably.

Gail's spirits had gone to boiling point as soon as she had heard Kip's name, and realised that she might see him here before they returned to town. Had he intended that when he had arranged for her to be here? Had he? *Had he?*

The holiday mood possessed her. She forgot everything in delight of being here, with this charming, happy family, and if she thought of anything at all, it was of Phillip Westing rather than of Kip. When the thought of him came up in her mind, she pushed it back. Kip must not matter, could not matter to her.

But when, a week later, they moored the Saucy Sue by the wall of the Salcombe Hotel to betake themselves to their more humble lodging, and found Kip's tall form at the top of the steps, Gail knew that he had actually never been far from her thoughts.

She stood up to wave to him, and his eyes seemed to come straight to her.

For this type of holiday, scrambling in and out of boats and over rocks, slacks were the only wear, and to her workmanlike navy blue she had added a gay striped jersey, scarlet and white and blue, with a twist of the same stripes round her hair, which had lost its London neatness and blew about round the scarf in little bobbing tendrils. She was burnt almost as brown as Rex, and Kip caught a flash of white teeth when she smiled. He had never seen her look so happy or so radiant, and he told her so when, a minute or two later, they had scrambled out of the boat and up the steps.

'You look a holiday girl whom nobody could possibly mistake for Mr. Bray's Miss Marlin,' he told her. 'Feel fit?'

'Marvellous,' said Gail, and he linked his hands in the arms of the two girls and walked back with them to the cottage, where Cora hung over the gate waiting for them.

'How long are you staying, Kip?' asked Ethne happily.

'Oh—two or three days, if you'll have me,' he said.

'Of course we'll have you!' said Ethne. 'Won't we, Gail?'

'Naturally,' said Gail, and again she knew that Kip was looking at her and that she was nice to look at, untidy and sea-stained though she was, her feet in old sandals, a lump of rope swinging from one hand.

'What do we do tonight, Cora?' he asked, as he helped them to dispatch a huge tea.

'Take me somewhere in the car, Kip, somewhere restful and quiet,' she said.

'Does that mean we can't go, Mum?' grumbled Rex, who hated to be parted for one moment from his hero.

'Yes, it does,' said Kip, who realised that Cora was tired, and knew that whilst they had all been enjoying themselves she had been toiling for them in the heat and difficulties of a cottage kitchen. Granted that she chose to do so and really enjoyed it, she was human and none the less tired. 'You kids can stop in tonight, or go and make mud pies, whilst your betters go for a nice quiet run to some nice quiet pub, have a nice cool drink and come back in the nice, peaceful moonlight.'

'What about Gail?' demanded Rex. 'Is she a kid or a better?'

Kip looked at her, his eyes softening.

'I don't know. What do you think, Gail?' he asked, and because she knew it was what he wished her to say, and that her turn would come, she chose to stay with Ethne and Rex, and presently they were left with the washing-up whilst Kip, with Cora beside him and George in the back, drove off in search of their nice, quiet pub.

She and Ethne had gone to bed before the car returned.

Ethne talked a little while from her corner of the room.

'I do love Kip,' she said dreamily. 'I wonder if there's any other man in the world like him? Someone a bit younger and not married? If ever I find him, I shall stick to him like a limpet until I've married him. Isn't it a shame that Kip's got to stay married to Gilda?'

'Do you know her?' asked Gail.

'I can just remember her before they were married. She's a very lovely person, isn't she? I really don't wonder Kip fell so badly for her.'

But there was just something in the girl's voice which made Gail ask. 'You didn't like her, did you?'

'No. Mum lectured me when I said afterwards she wasn't good enough for Kip, because, of course, she came of a good family and her people were socially above Kip's, or I suppose they were, and Kip was potty about her and she seemed potty about him, but—well, I just didn't like her. Of course I don't know what she's like now.'

'Kip still seems to be in love with her,' said Gail quietly.

'I know. Queer, isn't it? But then Kip's not like anybody else in anything. That's why I love him so. I'm sleepy. Goodnight. See you in the morning,' and in another few seconds she was asleep.

Gail lay awake until she heard the car come in, heard the whispered goodnights of the Millers to Kip, and then he went to put the car away in one of the difficult garages built into odd places in and about the precipitous little town with its narrow streets and sharp corners.

Later he came back, walking very quietly up the stairs to the room next to the one she shared with Ethne.

Leaning forward, she spoke softly through the closed door.

'Goodnight, Kip.'

There was a little pause. Then: 'Goodnight, Gail,' and silence.

It was enough. She could be content with so very little, just to know him under the same roof, was enough. In the morning she would see him, and there was no business to keep him from her, no hordes of friends and sycophants, no theatre, no—Gilda.

And in the morning Kip showed himself in holiday mood, dressed in an ancient pair of shorts and an old blue sweater, as irresponsible and hare-brained as Rex himself, swimming and boating and fishing and climbing with them, and in the evening taking them all packed into the car to some queer, lovely old inns in forgotten corners of Devonshire, where they drank golden cider from great pewter tankards and were very quiet and sleepy going home and wanted nothing more than to tumble into their beds.

But on his fourth, and last, night with them, Kip gave Gail her reward.

'Look here, urchins,' he said to the Miller children, having obviously squared the Miller parents beforehand. 'You can amuse yourselves tonight. I'm going to take Gail out somewhere on her own, and it's no use arguing because it won't make any difference. What shall we do, Gail? Where would you like to go? In the car? Up the estuary? Out to sea? Not in the *Saucy Sue*, I may add.'

'Why not? She's a fine craft,' said Rex in swift defence.

They did not argue against Kip's fiat. They had long ago learned the futility of it.

'She may be,' agreed Kip with a grin, 'but I'm not man enough for her, so we'll hire old Matt's. How about it, Gail?'

'I'd love that, Kip,' she said quietly, though her heart was racing.

So presently, with the calm of the evening settling down over the little town, with the old salts leaning over the seawall smoking or chewing, with holiday makers coming in to bed, to dinner or to supper according to age and social status, Gail and Kip stole out across the quiet water in old Matt's boat, the engine chugging away in less crazy rhythm than that of the *Saucy Sue*.

'You want to be careful coming back over the bar, Mr. Delaney, sir,' warned the old boatman before they started. 'There'll be a strong tide running out later.'

'Aye, aye, skipper,' said Kip.

Old Matt was the only one in Salcombe beside his immediate circle who knew that he was there, and Kip had dared the Miller children, with dire and awful threats, ever to speak his name above a whisper.

Old Matt was to be trusted.

They did not speak as they ran smoothly out and towards the sea, through the silver channel of the estuary, deep held between the steeply sloping sides of tree- and bracken-covered rock which towered above them until they ended abruptly in the long ridge of rock known as The Dragon's Back, from its fiercely prominent crags.

Then Kip set the tiller and dropped down beside Gail, one hand loosely guarding it, the other, after a moment's hesitation, going round her shoulders.

'Just this one evening, snatched from the miserly hand of the gods,' he said. 'You're glad to be with me, Gail?'

She caught her breath sharply. It was so much more wonderful, so much more poignant a moment than even she had anticipated.

They were rocking gently, almost imperceptibly, on the bosom of a sea deceptively calm and sweet, and the silver path of the moonlight led across to the rocky coast and bathed it in a glory which hid its cruelty, its menace, its treachery.

'Glad? Do you have to ask me that, Kip?' she said, and his arm closed about her more tightly, and she could feel his cheek against her own.

'Life deals out a good many very poor hands,' he said. 'What are your cards going to be like? I've got a good many of the honours in my hand, but I'm afraid I've got to make up my mind to miss the best tricks. You mustn't miss them, my sweet.' She turned a little in his embrace.

'I love you, Kip,' she said.

'I know, my dear. I ought not to have let you.'

'You couldn't have helped it, Kip. Nobody could. It was just bound to happen, from the beginning. I wish—you loved me.'

'What makes you think I don't, Gail?'

His voice was very quiet, very gentle, very steady.

'Oh, my dear, if you only would!' said Gail, her voice breaking.

She hid her face against his shoulder, and he held her there, stroking her head gently. He knew he ought not to have come, ought not to have been so weak – for her sake, not for his own.

'Gail – my little sweet thing – there can't be any talk of love between us. That is really why I brought you out here, to get you to myself, to have this out with you. Now I realise I have asked too much of the high gods – to have you here – and not make love to you. Gail, darling, let me kiss you.'

She lifted her face to his and gave him her lips. They were cold, and the salt had left a tang on them, but they warmed beneath his own, and he knew that they were the lips of a woman, a woman who was seeking her birth right, demanding the love he dare not give her because he loved her too much.

When he released her mouth, she sat up, laughing, triumphant, glowing.

'Now nothing else matters!' she cried. 'Nothing you or anyone can say can alter things. You love me! You love me, Kip! And I love you— love you—love you. Isn't it wonderful? Isn't the world a heavenly place? Oh, Kip, kiss me again. Put your arms round me.'

'And let the boat drift anywhere?' he asked with a smile. How beguiling she was! Vibrant, full of life, eager for fulfilment, a woman to be desired, to be possessed, to be worshipped.

'Let it go to the bottom. What does anything matter even if we died tonight, together. Kiss me. Hold me very tightly. I—oh, Kip, I believe I'm going to cry.'

'I hope you're not,' he said, and let the tiller go and gathered her into his arms and kissed her until she was breathless, spent, lying against his breast in an ecstasy of pain and joy.

Presently he put her from him and resolutely made for the glimmering lights of the harbour mouth again.

As they went, he talked to her, remorse holding him, and Gail sat and listened, but nothing he could say could dim the glory in her soul just then.

'Gail, my sweet, this can't go on. It mustn't go on. I knew I ought not to have come to Salcombe the very moment I saw you, standing up in the old boat with your gay little jumper and your hair blowing, and your eyes looking for mine. I knew before then that I ought not to come, but I couldn't keep away, knowing you were here, and then I was weak again and brought you out here tonight, knowing this must happen, knowing that we were aching for each other and that at the first contact we should be in each other's arms. The blame is all mine. I'm a lot older than you, Gail – older and wiser in the ways of this daft old world where everything is topsy-turvy, and human beings have taken what God gave them and twisted it all out of shape until there is no meaning or reason in life any more. Gail, are you listening?'

'Mm,' said Gail dreamily, and she was listening with her ears but not with her mind.

'Dear, you've got to listen. You've just got to understand. This is— the end. We can't go on like it. I'm bound by much more than honour. You see—it was really my fault that Gilda is like this.'

'Your fault? *Your* fault, Kip? But it was an accident. The train was wrecked.'

Her mind was alert now, taking in all he said, trying to form a future out of it, a future for herself and Kip and their love.

'I know. I didn't cause that, of course, but Gilda had a premonition, a sort of hunch, about that train. She wanted to come home by air. We were on our honeymoon, you know. I hated air travel, still do, and I wouldn't let her have her own way, made her go on the train with me – and that was what happened.'

'But, Kip, it's absurd to put the blame on yourself!' said Gail. 'Surely Gilda doesn't do that?'

'Can you blame her if she does? She's living a ghastly life, Gail, and had I given in to her all this would have been saved.'

She was silent. She could see that argument would not avail her. Rightly or wrongly, Kip chose to hold himself responsible, and she had to accept it.

When she spoke again there was a different note in her voice, and he knew that she had released the argument.

'Do you still love her, Kip?' she asked.

'Do *you* ask me that, Gail? In a way, I suppose I do. I loved her madly when I married her. She could send any man crazy, and she simply had me dancing on a bit of string. She was so lovely, so utterly, unbelievably lovely. But—now? Dear, I am a man, and Gilda now is no more than a beautiful doll. I love her for what she is, but—it isn't any longer the way a man loves a woman. How can it be?'

'If—if she ever got better, Kip, would you love her like that again?'

'I don't think so. That's over, dead, a memory. I was young when I married her, only five years younger in point of time, but twenty years in experience and the things that matter. She would not satisfy me now.'

'And you'd never leave her, Kip?' asked Gail in a low voice.

'No, my sweet. That's why up to now I've cut women out of my life, never let one matter to me – until you came – and I couldn't help myself. You had to matter to me, Gail. But—there's nothing for us, my darling, ever.'

There was a faint touch of bitterness in his voice, the first she had heard in it, and it brought her nearer to him, her head against his knee, her hand finding his free one and holding it between her own.

'I'm still glad I love you, Kip,' she said in a low voice.

'I'm not. It isn't fair to you, Gail, and I want you to try to forget it, to look at life as if we had never met, to realise that there are other men in the world, other sorts of happiness than the only one you can see at this moment. I ought to send you away from me, and if I think it's being too hard for you, or for me, I shall have to.'

'No, Kip, no! Let me go on working for you!'

'I want you to. I'm hoping it's possible for us to be sensible people, courageous people, but I'm not going to let you spoil your life for me, Gail. You were made for all the sweet and lovely things of life – home and husband and children – all the things I can't give you. Find them for yourself, my sweet. You're so young – and life's so damnably long—'

His voice shook, and Gail laid her lips against the hand she held.

'Oh, Kip, I do love you so utterly,' she said brokenly.

He did not reply. There was nothing he could say, though he was blaming himself bitterly. Why had he not had the strength, the decency, to leave things as they were?

He had negotiated the tricky business of getting the boat over the bar against the swiftly running tide, and now they were running down the estuary, passing the lordly yachts at their moorings.

Gail turned misty, pain-haunted eyes to Kip's, and he bent and laid his lips swiftly on hers to shut out the look.

'Don't, Gail,' he said. 'Don't my sweet. You make me feel like a murderer.'

'Oh, Kip—'

'No, darling. No more kisses. I daren't. Let me go, my dear,' and he disengaged her clinging arms very gently and set the engine running swiftly and so back to the quay where old Matt was waiting a little anxiously for the return of his boat.

They walked to the cottage hand in hand, stopping at the gate involuntarily to look into each other's eyes.

'You run up to bed now, my darling,' he said unsteadily. 'I'm going to have a last smoke here – and I'm clearing off early in the morning.'

'Kip.'

He wished she would go in, not make things so damnably hard for him, but he could not turn from the appeal in her eyes,

'Dear, it's so much better to let me go,' he said.

'Kip – you'd marry me if—if you were free, wouldn't you?' she asked.

'You know I would, Gail.'

'Then—then, Kip—I haven't get anybody belonging to me. It doesn't matter to anybody what I do. I'd be content with so little, Kip—'

He laid his fingers swiftly over her lips, pain in his eyes.

'No, my dear. Don't say the words, though don't think I'm not— loving you for your thoughts and honouring you above all women for what you would do for me. It can't be, sweet. Not that way, a cheap and unlovely thing.'

She gave a little sob. In her heart she had known he would not take what she was so ready to offer.

'Kiss me again,' she whispered.

'Best not,' he said, and turned away, and Gail went swiftly indoors.

Chapter Six

Gail found, to her chagrin and sorrow, that Kip meant what he said.

As far as their love life was concerned, everything was at an end, and that enchanted hour at Salcombe might never have been for all the awareness he showed.

Life went on its former course, except that he had started on a new play and, whilst still giving his perfect, polished performances in *The Roundabout*, he threw all his energies for the rest of the day into his new creation. He worked alone for some hours, with Bray and Gail sentinels at his door, refusing all corners, keeping his telephone quiet, and presently he would come to Gail with an incredible stack of papers covered with his purposeful handwriting.

'Transcribe these for me, Gail, will you?' he would ask with the same smile he would have given anyone.

Since he seemed determined to avoid any personal issue with her, Gail was thankful to be kept busy, remaining far into the evening so as to be sure that each day's work should be finished and ready for him the next morning. She did not know whether he was aware of the long hours she put in. If he did, he never mentioned them, but she felt sufficiently rewarded if, on seeing her neat, careful typescript, he smiled at her and said: 'Very nice. Good girl.'

She was seeing less of Phillip Westing at this time, partly because of her lack of time, but also because she did not want matters to be brought to a point at which she must make some decision. As the days went by, however, and all slipped rapidly into weeks, and the chill of autumn helped in the overlaying of that bittersweet memory of the summer, Phillip came to mean more and more to her, his friendship comforting to her loneliness, his persistent, though as yet unspoken admiration for her a balm to the spirit constantly wounded by Kip's ignoring of her as anything but a machine in his service.

Phillip raged to her about the length of time she put in for her employer.

'It's scandalous,' he said. 'What time did you start this morning? Nine?'

'About that,' said Gail, who had been at her desk half an hour before that.

'Nine o'clock, and now it's half past eight – nearly twelve hours a day, and you don't even go out for meals—'

'I have a very good lunch sent in to me,' she protested.

'Yes. A sop to keep you from taking an hour off!' he scoffed. 'And I don't suppose you get a penny overtime, do you?'

'We don't expect it, Phillip. Kip pays us well, and during slack times we work far less than the agreed hours a day—'

'Well, I haven't noticed you working any less since I've known you …'

'But, Phillip, that's why Kip pays us so well. Instead of getting extra money when we work longer hours, we get extra money all the time without always doing the long hours.'

'Rot. He gets as much out of you for as little as you'll take, and so do they all. That's your capitalist system for you. You must know what he's worth financially. Whose money is that? Yours and all the niggers' slaving for him …'

She had to laugh at that. The picture of Kip as a man with a huge whip lashing them all to work for him was irresistibly comic, and since by this time they had reached the place where they had decided to go for a meal, the subject was dropped for the time being.

They ate at cheap, crowded restaurants where the cloths were not always clean, and the china was thick and chipped and the waitresses too busy to give anyone proper or courteous attention.

Gail had forced herself not to mind, or assured herself so often that she did not mind, that she had almost come to believe it.

On this occasion she suggested rather diffidently that she should be allowed to entertain Phillip, or at least to pay half the bill.

'I wish you'd let me, Phillip, just this once. I'd like to, really,' she said.

'Well—alright, if you feel like that about it,' he said, and ordered a glass of beer on the strength of it in place of the water he had decided upon before.

Gail chid herself for wishing that he had not accepted with such alacrity. After all, why make the suggestion if she had not intended it to be taken?

'What shall we do now?' he asked.

He seldom brought a ready-made plan for their hours together, and as a rule it was Gail who suggested the means of filling them in, choosing to walk, or to go for a bus ride out of consideration for his pocket, though she would have liked more stimulating entertainment now and then.

'Could we go to the pictures for a change?' she asked him.

'Scarcely time to see the programme round now,' he said.

'We should see the whole of one picture,' she pointed out.

'And pay for the whole show? You young plutocrat,' he said. 'That's bad economy. Another night we'll start earlier, perhaps have a spot of food before we meet and go straight to the pictures. What about a bus ride? We could go out west somewhere and come back on the same bus.'

It was a chilly evening with the dankness of autumn in the air and Gail thought longingly of the warm comfort of her flat, but hesitated to take him there. However, the buses were full and a fine drizzle of rain had begun to fall, so she made her hesitating proposal at last.

'Would you like to come to my flat for a cup of coffee and a warm?' she asked.

'Can a duck swim?' he replied instantly. 'Here's a bus,' and they ran across the road to board one going in the direction of Albery House.

'Jolly nice little pitch you've got here,' he remarked, making himself at home in the sitting-room whilst she made coffee for them.

'Yes, it is nice, isn't it?' she agreed. 'Don't forget that I owe this to Kip too!' with a little teasing laugh, though at once she regretted having mentioned that name again.

She listened in silence to another tirade against a system which kept the rich rich, and the poor poor, by the efforts of the latter.

Presently, however, when she had cleared away the cups and saucers and refused to join him in a cigarette, he did the very thing she had feared, bringing the conversation to a personal issue.

'Aren't you lonely here, Gail, all by yourself? It seems to me only half a life for a girl.'

'I work hard and I like the quiet when I've finished,' she said.

'You work too hard,' he replied.

She smiled.

'Well, don't let's go into all that again,' she said.

'Agreed. I think you know what I'd really like to say to you, if it weren't such darned sauce on my part, don't you, Gail?'

'I—I don't think I want you to say it, Phillip,' she replied, nervously.

'Don't you? Well, I might as well, in spite of that. Would it ever be possible for you to think of marrying me, Gail? I know it's a cheek. I said so at first, didn't I? I don't seem to be offering you much, but I'm very, very fond of you. I think you know that. I don't go running about after women, and I've never wanted one before in the way I want you. I'm not a romantic sort of chap. I can't wrap it up in flowery language, but I mean every word I say, and if you'd only marry me, Gail, and take us all under your wing, I'd never let you regret it. Everything I have or am, such as it is, would be yours to do what you liked with. What do you say, Gail?'

He could see her distress.

'Oh, Phillip, I wish you hadn't!' she said. 'I—I don't know what to say. I feel it's asking more of me than I could undertake, not because I wouldn't be willing, but because I really don't feel capable. You see—there are the children—'

'They're nice kids, Gail. You'd like them. Why not meet them first? I suppose I've been a blundering ass in the way I've put things, but that's me all over. Look here. Forget what I've just said. Pretend I never said it, and have a look at the kids. We could all be so jolly happy together, and heaven knows they need something better than I've been able to give them since their mother died. What do you say, Gail?'

And because his friendship had become something on which she had come to rely, something real and solid amongst all the shifting sands and evanescent bubbles of her life with Kip, she caught at the opportunity to keep it as the one bit of security beneath her feet.

'Alright. I'd like that,' she said.

'Good. Friends again, then, Gail?'

'Haven't we always been that, Phillip?' she asked with a smile.

For one moment of fear she thought he was going to kiss her. A light had leapt into his eyes and he had taken a step towards her.

Then something in her own eyes must have warned him, and he offered her his hand instead, a strong hand with a good grip.

'Yes, thank the Lord. You don't know what it means to have someone like you in my life, Gail, even if there is never any more than friendship between us though I shall hope there may be something more.'

After he had gone, her spirit sank into a morass of despairing thought. What, after all, was there for her in life? It was unthinkable that she should go in indefinitely as she was now, merely working for the man whom, with all her heart and soul, she desired in love. Yet she had to face the facts. Kip had told her quite plainly how things must stand between them, and he had never varied one iota from that since. She was certain that he never would vary. Why, then, not make up her mind to take the second best? Whilst she might have hesitated, and even refused to marry a man to whom she could give nothing because the real love of her heart was not hers to give, to Phillip Westing she could give a great deal that counted. He was a lonely man and one whom, for some reason she could not yet understand, life had embittered. His home life must be a mere travesty of comfort and her heart was always tender to the thought of motherless children. Yes, she had much to give a man like Phillip Westing, and he had made no extravagant love assertions, no suggestion that he either sought or wished to give passionate ardour. After all, he had been married, had had children, must have lost or buried most of his young allusions. Companionship, loyalty, a sincere affection and sympathy with many of his aims and beliefs and hopes – surely these were things which would count for far more in the end, with a man like Phillip Westing?

And then came the Saturday afternoon that was to prove the turning point in her life.

Kip liked her to regard Saturday as her free day and seldom made demands on her that day, but on this particular morning she had gone to her office for an hour to finish some work, and he had heard the sound of the typewriter and, after a moment's hesitation, had gone in.

She looked up in surprise, unable to disguise the gladness in her eyes at sight of him though a moment later it was gone.

'You here? This morning?' he asked.

'I wanted to finish this,' she said.

'Leave it and come and have a coffee with me,' and though she knew it was worse than folly, she was not able to resist the temptation. It was so long since he had spoken like that, looked like that.

In the little coffee house where they could sit more or less alone in the old-fashioned high-backed settles which divide it into separate compartments, and where they had often been, he stretched his hand across the table for hers.

'We can't go on like this, can we?' and she saw the haunted look in his eyes, the look which brought an answering look of pain into her own.

'No,' she said. 'Kip—do you want me to leave you?'

His hand gripped her own. It would have hurt her if she could have felt any physical pain at that moment.

'Is there any alternative, my darling? We can't either of us take it much longer and it isn't fair to you. I've made my life, for good or ill, and there's nothing I can do to alter it, *nothing*.'

She knew what he meant, that there was no possibility of release from Gilda, being as she was, and he would never seek it. She nodded her head without meeting his eyes.

'Yes, I know,' she said.

'But you've got all your life in front of you. I've said all this before, but it hasn't got us anywhere, has it? Now—'

She knew what that unfinished sentence meant and by her bent head, by the pitiful drooping of her whole body, he knew that she did.

'Gail—'

'Alright, Kip,' her voice stopping him. 'You need not go on. I know I must leave you. You'll let me have a little while—to make my plans—'

Her voice was low and sad and hopeless.

'Of course, my darling. You don't think I want you to go, that I shan't miss you every hour of every day?'

'Don't let's talk anymore, Kip. I can't bear it,' and she rose from the table and left him sitting there.

And as if Fate had at last determined to make her take the road mapped out for her, when she met Phillip later in the day, she saw at once that he was in trouble.

'Tell me what's wrong, Phillip?' she asked.

'Oh, a lot,' he said. 'We're in the devil of a fix at home. My beautiful housekeeper has done a bunk and taken with her everything she can lay her hands on, and we haven't got anything in the house for tomorrow, and don't know where anything is—'

'But, Phillip, what a rotten thing to do,' said Gail hotly. 'Who is with the children now, at this moment?'

'Oh, they're alright. Joyce is used to managing,' he said.

'But she's only a child,' said Gail pitifully. 'Look here. Let me come with you this afternoon and I can at least fix you up with something to eat and so on.'

It was what he had intended, but he did not make the mistake of jumping at her offer too quickly. The result was the same, however, and presently they were in the Underground and going out to the cheap suburb which was unknown territory to her, but which she in no way disdained, being no snob in spite of her upbringing.

She found the house a tiny one in a row of exactly similar dwellings, their flat fronts close to the street, an iron railing and a few dilapidated shrubs setting them back by only two or three feet. The inside consisted of a parlour, obviously unused, and a kitchen-living-room, with a scullery behind it, whilst upstairs (this she discovered later) were two bedrooms, the larger one with two beds in it for Phillip and the boy, whilst a double bed in the smaller one had served for Joyce and the now vanished housekeeper.

It was all something of a shock to Gail, who had only imagined such houses without ever having been inside one, and though it looked clean and reasonably neat, the absence of comfort, but above all of beauty, appalled her.

However, she did not waste time and thought on that, but made the acquaintance of Phillip's children with considerable interest.

Joyce was a pretty little thing, with fair fluffy hair and pink cheeks. Hugh was a less attractive child, with a small, solemn face and huge spectacles and that look of abnormal cleanliness which Gail, knowing Rex Miller, recognised with sympathy.

He would be glad to get his clean collar off and be comfortably grubby again.

She had an easy manner with children, never making the mistake of talking down to them, and when she had briefly made their acquaintance she left them to take stock of her and form what opinion they liked of her, wondering if they knew of their father's hopes and intentions.

With her few months of experience at the flat, doing her own cooking and cleaning and her bits of intimate laundry, she felt able to tackle the present situation with some measure of assurance, and when it was ascertained that the departed Mrs. Syme had left no food of any description in the house, not even a loaf of bread or a drop of milk, she forgot her own affairs in Phillips'.

A detailed survey of the house revealed to her furious anger that Mrs. Syme had removed from the house every scrap of bed linen, except that on the beds, grey with use, every towel and cloth, and even the children's winter clothes, now made necessary by the increasing cold, had gone from cupboards and drawers. Many household treasures had vanished, and some explanation of it was found in the stack of empty gin and whisky bottles in the cupboard of the room which Joyce had shared.

Gail and Phillip made a list of the missing articles, and whilst she found and washed some personal linen for him and the children, he went out to make a round of the pawnshops and to discover, if possible, what articles were still redeemable.

Gail worked with a will, helped by Joyce and rather more shyly and awkwardly by Hugh, and in the evening, with the children in bed, she and Phillip sat in the stuffy little parlour and looked at each other.

'Well,' he asked rather bitterly, and suddenly her heart melted to softness for him. He was so forlorn, so helpless, and her compassion over-rode all meaner considerations.

Here was a job ready to hand, a niche she could fill, people who really needed her.

'Phillip—my dear—what is it you feel for me?' she asked. 'Do you love me? Or is it just—another housekeeper you want?'

'I love you, Gail. Now that you have seen us as we are, our poor little place and wretched plight, it seems a damned cheek to go on asking you to marry me—but I do, darling. Gail, will you? I believe we could be happy together, all of us, and God knows I haven't had much happiness in life up to now. If you'll take me, Gail, I swear I'll never let you regret it. How could I, seeing what I'm asking you to take on?'

It was sweet to her to be wanted, to feel there was something she could do in the world. She loved Kip and he loved her, but of what use was their love to them or to anyone else?

Since Kip was definitely and forever out of her life, surely this was the next best thing?

So, sweetly, gently, she told Phillip, she would marry him.

There was no immediate reaction on his part, for which she was glad. She did not intend to withhold herself from him. If she gave at all, she would give royally, without stint, and without thought of that paradise whose gates could never open to her now, would never have opened to her even if she had not given her promise to Phillip Westing.

They talked of their future, and she felt herself kindle to the idea of that useful, busy life with a man who most obviously was going to adore her. Yes, she was doing the right thing. She felt sure of it and when, as she rose to get her outdoor things, she knew he was going to kiss her, she had no such feeling of revulsion as she had feared. It was as if his lonely spirit called to hers, and her body gave response.

But as his lips met hers, she was aware of not revulsion, but of a faint fear. Of what? Of Westing? Of herself? She did not know, but when his first almost hesitant kiss had been given, his arms tightened about her and his mouth clung feverishly to hers so that involuntarily she struggled for freedom. She was not ready for passion yet, and had scarcely realised that there had been passion in the kisses she had given to Kip. He had sensed so much a part of her and she of him and there had been none of that feeling of invasion of her privacy as she felt now. She had not consciously given to Kip because of the wild joy of receiving, but with Phillip Westing she knew she was giving and had the primitive urge to give only of her own free will.

He laughed a little and let her go.

'Not ready for me yet?' he asked her. 'You're shy of me, aren't you?'

Her answering laugh was shaky.

'I think I am,' she said. 'You were a bit—fierce, you know.'

He smoothed her hair with a hand that trembled. She realised that he was holding himself strongly in check, and the woman in her felt a prick of excitement at this, almost the first, evidence she had had of the power that can make a strong man weak.

'Darling, what a lot you've got to learn,' he said tenderly. 'It's going to be wonderful teaching you what love means. Don't be afraid, Gail. I shall be very gentle with you. I'm not an ignoramus in these things, and perhaps you'll be better off with an old hand who knows the ropes than with a clumsy young fool who thinks more of himself than of you. Don't worry, darling. Old Phillip will take care of you. We're going to be so happy, dear—so happy!' and his eyes kindled and his mouth grew soft and he kissed her again, but gently this time, and her fears were lulled so that she lay peacefully in his arms for a long minute and told herself that she was at rest.

He went with her to her bus.

'I can manage alone,' she said. 'You stay with the children,' but he would not have that.

'They'll be alright,' he said. 'They're used to it. Besides, they're asleep,' and when the bus came along he got into it with her.

'I'll come to the corner,' he said. 'I can walk back from there if there isn't a bus coming,' and when the conductor appeared, he tendered sixpence.

'Two, please,' he said.

'Mine's more than that,' said Gail quickly, but apparently he did not hear her, or the remark did not sink in until the conductor had gone.

Then he looked at the two white tickets in his hand and made a little sound of annoyance at himself.

'Look what I've done,' he said. 'Of course you want a sixpenny, don't you? I must get you another ticket before I get off,' but he forgot to do so.

A straw in the wind? Perhaps. But Gail did not see it. She was telling herself she was going to be happy. She was going to give happiness. She had done the right thing. Beyond shadow of doubt, she had done the right thing.

She had a little way to walk from the bus stop to Albery House, and unconsciously her footsteps lagged a little, as if reluctant to return to even the outward shell of the life she was leaving.

And when at last she reached the steps leading to the outer door, a tall figure detached itself from the shadows and came towards her.

'Kip!'

'Gail, I had to come. I had to see you.'

'No. You should not have come,' said Gail, her voice wrung with the utter certainty of her words.

'I couldn't let you go like that, not knowing what you were going to do, where you were going—anything about you.'

She realised the time. It was only ten o'clock.

'Kip, the theatre!' she said.

'I know. I sent a message. Carter's gone on for me. I had to see you.'

She was silent. He was so conscientious about his work. As soon as possible he gave his understudy a good chance on tour, but in London he never missed a performance. And on a Saturday night too!

He put a hand beneath her elbow and turned her back from the steps.

'Let's walk a little way, Gail. It's early yet, and I want to talk to you.'

She could not resist him, though her pride, her common sense, her new loyalties bade her throw off his hand and go her way without him.

'Darling, I've got to know what your plans are,' he said, and they were divinely conscious of each other, body and spirit, so that nothing, nothing, could prevent that lifting of the heart in contact with each other.

But she must be sane, must not now jeopardise her new-found sense of wisdom and contentment, comparative though the latter must be.

'Must you know, Kip? Need that matter now?' she asked. 'We've got to go our separate ways. Leave me to go mine. Please, dear. It's the only thing you can do for me.'

'But, Gail, what will you do?'

'I shall be alright.'

She felt how difficult it was going to be to tell him, if tell him she must, about Phillip Westing. He might not understand. Did she completely understand herself why she was doing it?

'Have you got anything in view? How will you set about finding another job? What sort of job do you want? Gail, don't withhold yourself entirely from me in this. Let me at least have what satisfaction I can get out of seeing that you are alright as far as that's concerned. I want to give you some money, too, to carry you on. Don't wriggle. That's your *legal* due, since you are leaving me without my giving you proper notice.'

'I don't want anything from you, Kip,' she said proudly.

'I know your silly little rag of pride, my dear, but you're not going to wave it in my face,' he said, and before she could prevent him, he had taken her bag and stuffed something in it, refusing to return it to her, but holding it in his other hand away from her.

'I shan't use it, Kip,' she said.

'Never refuse good money, my dear,' he said, half serious, half in jest. 'It'll stand your friend when everybody else fails you,' and she heard in his voice and words an echo of Jeffrey Templar, that good friend with whom Kip, so utterly different, had so much in common.

He returned to the main issue, which was her future.

'Let me help you over a new job, dear,' he said. 'I've been exercising my mind about you all day, and it occurs to me that you ought to be able to turn your talent for dress design and colour into money. Why not take a course at a good art school and specialise in it, and then try to get attached to one of the famous fashion houses? I might help you there as well, and you'd like that sort of thing. Does the idea appeal to you? If you won't bite my head off, I'm going to suggest something else as well, which is that you go on living in your flat, so that you'll only have your food and classes to pay for – and I've designed my cheque to cover that for the time being, anyway. Don't be too proud to take from me, Gail. There's nothing else in the wide world that I can do for you now, but at least you don't have to worry about money.'

She had listened to him with only half her mind, knowing that his idea was a good one, but knowing too that she could not accept it. Even without Phillip Westing in the background, she could not have done so. The only possible way in which she could reconstruct her life was by cutting herself adrift from Kip, and how could she, if she were living as he suggested, within a stone's throw of him, and actually being supported by him? It was not her pride which refused. She knew that the link between them was too deep and real for anything as shallow and false as money pride. It was the knowledge that no middle course was possible for her. Where Kip was concerned, it must be all or nothing.

'Well?' he asked her, as she was silent.

She looked back at him, steadily, with a world of complexities in that look.

'Thank you, Kip, I appreciate all you say – all you have been thinking out to help me, but—I shan't need it. You see—I'm going to be married.'

It was out, just the stark truth, unadorned, and even in her own ears it sounded fantastically grotesque. She, who belonged to Kip, talking of marriage, to another man?

He was stupefied for a moment, and she felt his arm grip her own fiercely. Then the grip relaxed and she knew he had himself under control.

'That's—unexpected news,' he said quietly. 'Want to tell me about it?'

She told him of Phillip, unemotionally, but showing him the secret places of her mind as she could not have done to any other living person, for Kip knew her and would understand.

He did understand. She blessed him for that. He did not worry her with a lot of questions. He was weighing up what she had told him, and her chances of happiness.

'Well, I'm not going to pretend it makes me glad,' he told her at last. 'How could it, when I want you so desperately myself? Still, we're not going into all that again. You're the one to be thought of now, Gail, and only you. I wish I knew Westing. He doesn't sound to me the right sort for you, and he's too old, and I don't like the children complex, but only you can decide that sort of thing. I know the maternal instinct in you is strong, but I want to warn, you, Gail, if it isn't too late. Don't confuse pity with love. I don't suggest that you think yourself in love with Westing, not in the way you and I think of love. But I know there are other kinds of love, and that the grand passion is not a thing which usually finds its way into a workaday world and life.

'I play enough of them on the stage, these tremendous affairs, and I think—mind you, I only say I think—they might not be tenable in real life. I love you, Gail. You love me. If you like, it's the grand passion. We won't discuss that, but keep our private view of it. The thing is, I believe that something quieter and more gentle and practical is possible to most people, and I think that is what is going to give you a real chance of happiness with some other man. But is Phillip Westing that man, Gail? How much do you know of him? You tell me he is a socialist. That means all sorts of things in practice, but is he a socialist at heart? Does he really believe in absolute equality? Absolute personal freedom? The right of the individual, as such, no matter what the sex or age or social status? That, to my mind, is real socialism, but I have yet to find the professing socialist who does not make certain reserves especially in his own home circle.

'Is he going to give you personal freedom, Gail? You're going to give up a lot for him. You're prepared to be poor in this world's goods.

You're going to undertake responsibility for other people's children without the urgent force of actual parenthood. You're going to have to work with your hands. You're going to enter a social sphere quite different from anything you've so far known. Speech will be different. Manners will be different. Everything will be strange to you. You are going to be terribly dependent on this man's capacity for creating happiness for you.'

Gail was deeply grave. Kip had never talked to her like this before. She had not known him capable of it, and yet how could he have created a play like *The Roundabout* without deep thought of and for his fellow creatures, deep knowledge of them?

'I'm not afraid, Kip,' she said at last. 'I think I've reckoned all these things, and I believe that Phillip and I can find happiness, working together for it.'

Kip gave a sigh. This was the end of so much that might have been glorious and so much that might have dragged them down into the slough of misery and regret. If only Gail were not contemplating a marriage which seemed to him so inadequate. She had so much to give, her youth, her beauty, her intelligence, her warm heart and fresh and lovely mind, her sympathy, her tolerance – everything, it seemed to him, that woman had to give to man. He hoped this Phillip Westing was going to be worthy of it, but his heart was heavy for her.

'My dear—my dearest—I hope so,' he said with that sigh. 'My God, Gail, if he isn't good to you, I'll murder him!'

Almost unconsciously they had turned back and were walking towards Albery House again, as if accepting the turning point in their lives, and now they had reached the steps and Gail must go in.

He held her hand tightly.

'Must it be goodbye?' he asked her in a strained voice.

'You know if must, Kip.'

'And I'm never to see you again?'

Her heart was breaking.

'How can we, and still go on living decently?' she asked. 'I've made up my mind about Phillip. You have Gilda. Let's be true to our own selves in being true to them, Kip. I'm going to make Phillip a good wife, and, I think, a loving one. I do love him – not the way we love, but that sort of thing just doesn't come true in real life. He loves me sincerely, but of course I am not his first love either, so perhaps we shall not expect too much of each other. You won't see me, Kip, though perhaps sometimes, later on when it won't hurt so much, I shall be able to see you. I shall creep in now and then, probably in the gallery, and watch you and—remember—oh, my darling!' and her control broke, and she leaned her head against his shoulder and clung to him, but there were no tears. She had vowed that there should be no tears. So much she could do for both of them, and with amazing strength she kept them back though her heart seemed to be weeping tears of blood.

He held her closely, his face a white mask of despair. None of his devotees would have recognised their hero at that moment, but there was none to see.

'Sweet—my very own—I shall know if you are there. Something will tell me, and you will know that every word of love I speak, every tender look, every throb of my heart, is for you—not for the puppet thing on the stage, but for you, my love—my love.'

For a few moments they clung together. Then Gail raised her head to smile at him. He could not guess what that smile cost her.

'Now, my darling,' she said.

He gave her her bag mutely and turned away, and Gail walked blindly up the steps and let the heavy door swing behind her.

Chapter Seven

Gail was married to Phillip Westing on a June day months later than they had anticipated or than he, at any rate, had desired.

There had been several contributory factors to the delay, the chief of which had been the financial one.

Phillip had admitted at the outset that he had no money put by.

'I'm sorry, dear, but it just hasn't been possible,' he said. 'The children's mother had a long illness which cost me no end, and someone had to be paid to look after them, and then I had that succession of housekeepers to rob me. It's been just one damned expense after another, and of course I work for a firm which believes in keeping wages to rock bottom level.'

Gail had been sympathetic. Phillip had been quick to learn that it was easy to play upon that string, and Gail's thoughts flew at once to possibilities of helping him.

The chief trouble was that they could find nowhere to live. It was manifestly impossible for them to start their married life in the little house where he was living, for two bedrooms would not accommodate themselves and the two children now that Joyce was growing bigger, though Gail suspected that had her predecessor lived, they would have had to manage. The neighbours, with whom she became casually acquainted in the months of her engagement, lived in that fashion and thought nothing of it, their families crowded together without regard for age and sex or comfort.

Housing problems were acute and there was nothing to rent, except at exorbitant figures, and houses were fetching prices far above their value or Phillip Westing's means, even if he had any capital for a nucleus.

He was in despair, longing to marry Gail, and she, now that her future lay clear before her and she had resolutely turned her mind from the past, was scarcely less anxious.

She had not told Phillip the real reason for her leaving Kipling Delaney's employ, allowing him to believe that the job had been a more or less temporary one. She had remained at the flat in Albery House for a week or two, relying on Kip's promise not to try to see her, but the strain was too great whilst she was so near him, and she gave up her tenancy, moved her furniture into two rooms in a quiet Bloomsbury house, and decided to get a job until her marriage.

Kip's cheque was for a hundred pounds, and though her first thought had been to refuse it, in the end she put it into the savings bank, knowing that it was foolish and hurtful to him to reject his help.

She could not bring herself to offer it to Phillip in order to get their much-needed house, however. She could not lay the foundations of their home with Kip's money, so she said nothing about it to him, so that he thought she was as penurious as he himself appeared to be.

In the end she went to Jeffrey Templar.

'Jeffrey, will you be a dear?' she asked, not beating about the bush, going straight to the point as she knew he preferred people to do. 'Will you lend me a thousand pounds?'

He stared at her and blinked a little.

'Good lord, what on earth for?' he asked her bluntly.

She told him.

'We shall never get married unless we can get some money from somewhere, and I want to get married, Jeffrey. We've found a little house. It needs a lot of inside decorating, but Phillip and I think we can do that ourselves as the outside's alright. Will you, Jeffrey? I'm keeping on at my job (I told you I was working for Hannam's, the antique dealers, in the galleries), and we think that between us we could pay you back at the rate of three or four pounds a week until we have reduced the mortgage to an amount which Phillip could meet at building societies' rates out of his own salary.'

'I see. Well, if you're really sure you want to marry this man, and if the house provides reasonable security, I might,' said Templar. 'Give me the address of it. I'll send someone to see it, a surveyor I know, and if it's alright and won't fall to pieces in a few years, you can have the money.'

'Oh, Jeffrey, you *are* a dear,' said Gail gratefully.

'I don't know so much about that. I'm not at all sure I'm doing the right thing in making it easy for you to marry Westing, but as you seem set on it, I suppose you'll find a way somehow, and at least I can see that you start off comfortably.'

The house was surveyed, the report satisfactory, and Gail was told that she and Phillip might go ahead with the arrangements to purchase it, and the money would be forthcoming when they wanted it.

Westing was in the seventh heaven. The house was a modest enough little place, one of a row of similar suburban villas, with small, prim bow-fronted windows, a tiny garden keeping it back from the road, a square of grass surrounded by flower borders at the back. To Phillip, however, it was luxury beyond his wildest dreams compared with the comfortless, insanitary little house which so far had been the limit of his attainments, and though the two rooms and tiny kitchenette downstairs and the three bedrooms and bathroom upstairs were badly in need of repair, that was a small matter to his enthusiasm and energy, especially with Gail keen to help him.

One little rift arose over the title of the property.

Jeffrey Templar had had the transfer and mortgage deed made out in Gail's name, so that 5 Reedsdale Road would be ostensibly her property.

'You'd better let your young man see these before you sign, Gail,' he said, handing the deeds over to her. 'They're in order, of course, but he ought to see what you're doing. You can bring them back this afternoon and sign them here, if you can get hold of him at lunchtime.'

That was when the rift became apparent, for, to her amazement and a little to her dismay, Phillip took strong objection to the deeds being in her name.

'I didn't think there was any question of it,' he said. The house is always in the husband's name and, after all, I'm going to find the money for it in the end, whoever pays for it now.'

Gail wrinkled her brow.

'Well, we shall be paying for it between us,' she said.

'I shall have to find the bulk of it. I thought the idea was for you to stay at your job for a year, when we hope to have paid two hundred off the mortgage, and then you leave and I pay the rest as and when I can afterwards. That is to say, I shall still be responsible for more than half the value of the house, when you haven't any longer an income. That being so, the house should be in my name.'

'Does it really matter, Phillip? I mean, what difference can it make, since we shall both be living in it? I think Jeffrey's idea is well—that, if anything happened to you, the house is there for me. He is talking about you taking out a life policy to cover it, to make me safe.'

'I wish, Gail, you'd get out of that habit of referring to men by their Christian names – first Kip, and now Jeffrey. I don't know that I like it.'

She laughed a little. It was so unimportant.

'My dear, I know it's a disgraceful habit, but everybody called Mr. Delaney, Kip, and I somehow slipped into calling Mr. Templar, Jeffrey, but of course I won't if you don't like it.'

'I don't like it,' said Phillip definitely. 'However, about the house. I can't oblige you to have it put into my name, of course, and if you take these things back to Templar and sign them, I must put up with it. But this is how it seems to me – either you trust me to do the right thing by you and look after your future, or you don't. And if you don't trust me, what's the good of going on together? It strikes at the foundation of things. It is the foundation of things, mutual trust.'

He had sounded the right note, as he knew. It was a bold note, for he had not the slightest intention of losing Gail or letting her lose him, but he told himself that a man who is not master in his own house is a poor thing, and how can he be master in a house which is not his, but his wife's?

Gail was quiet for a little while, fingering the deeds in their long envelope. Then she smiled and slipped a hand through his arm.

They were walking along the Embankment, enjoying the brief winter sunshine.

'Alright. I'll put it to Jeff—Mr. Templar. I want everything to be right between us, Phillip. You know that.'

He squeezed her arm. That was how it should be, and he was glad to realise she was to be so amenable because, of course, anything else between husband and wife was unthinkable.

'Good. You won't regret trusting me, dearest,' he said.

'What shall I say about the life insurance, Phillip?'

'Tell him to mind his own business,' he said, and then, quick to note the change in her face, he turned the words aside with a laugh. 'I didn't mean that, darling. I was only pulling your leg. Of course I shall take out a policy. I should do that without your Mr. Templar's advice. I know the right thing to do. That, as well, you can leave to me. I won't let you suffer. What is he afraid of?'

'I don't know that he's afraid of anything, Phillip, but he has always taken an interest in me and my welfare, having been my father's friend as well as his solicitor, and—well, that's all. I shall have to go now, dear. See you same time tomorrow?' for they had fallen into the pleasant habit of meeting after lunch for a stroll on fine days.

Gail was thoughtful, however, as she went back to the Oxford Street galleries where she had been lucky in finding a job she liked and could do well, combining as it did typing and shorthand with interviewing prospective buyers and occasionally going with them to advise them on furniture tapestries and decorations in period style. Though her work for John Chives had been for the most part limited to costume, she had gained considerable knowledge of furniture and decoration at the same time, and Hannam's were glad of her services, and paid her well.

She was sorry that the little altercation about the house had arisen. Look at it as she might (and she was very ready to look at it from Phillip's standpoint) the thing had left a nasty little feeling in her mind. Why had he been so insistent about the house? After all, Jeffrey lending the money on her account not on his, and though he was correct in saying she did not propose to pay anything like half the cost of it, she would be earning part of it and should at least have a share in it. However, what did it really matter? When two people married, they shared more than a bed, and surely questions of mine and thine did not arise?

So she rang up Mr. Templar and explained Phillip's point of view in some detail, conscious that the voice at the other end was somewhat silent.

He made the very point she had anticipated.

'The money is being lent to you, Gail, and for your comfort and convenience. Why should I care a hang about Westing's?'

'I know, Jeffrey, but Phillip sees things differently from some people, and he—well, to be honest, I think he will get a great kick out of owning a house, even if it's only nominal ownership, and if you don't feel you must absolutely insist on the papers going through in my name, I'd really rather they were in his.'

'Suppose he isn't good to you? Marriages do go wrong, you know, and then he'll stand possessed of the house that is meant for you.'

She laughed.

'This marriage isn't going wrong,' she said.

'I seem to have heard that one before, too,' said Templar grimly. 'Well, what did he say about life insurance?'

'Oh, he's going to do that, anyway. He said so.'

'Alright. Since he's promised to do that, you should be alright. I can see it's going to make you unhappy if I don't give in about the house, so I'll have the deeds altered into his name. Better give me his full name and how he describes himself, and his present address.'

Gail gave the information, and that incident was closed.

They owed a thousand pounds for their house, but the deeds were in the name of Phillip Westing.

That over, nothing seemed to remain of the slight rippling of the waters, and they set to work with tremendous ardour to get the house ready.

Here they were on safer ground than when the spiky furrows of high finance had to be negotiated, for they were working with their hands and their brains, with all their energies, with bright hope, with good comradeship, in the tangible medium of paper and paint, of hammers and tacks and screws, of spade and fork.

A temporary housekeeper had had to be found for Phillip until such time as he and Gail could marry and make more permanent plans, and a kindly, comfortable woman had arrived to take charge, more or less competently, of the little household, though Phillip spent all his free time at 5 Reedsdale Road, merely going home to sleep, and not always that on Saturday nights.

This was the period of their joint lives when Gail was the most consciously happy.

Her work for Hannam's was pleasant without being arduous, and she had a good deal of free time, and now that she had a means of filling every moment of it, she not only ceased to dream by day, but her nights, too, were unmolested, for when she went to bed she was too tired for anything other than dreamless, unbroken sleep.

With great enthusiasm and courage but little knowledge, they had undertaken the interior decoration of the whole of the house, had chosen their wallpapers and paint with complete accord, bought a collection of unfamiliar tools, and Phillip picked the brains of all his associates to glean information as to their best use.

During this time, Gail's admiration for him as a workman and a craftsman stood him in good stead. He was an excellent worker, methodical, painstaking, thorough in everything he did, and only the best was good enough for him. If he had an unfailing eye for the defects in Gail's work, he did not spare his own, and when eventually she became the paper-hanger and he the painter, she found herself surveying her handiwork through his eyes, watching for the least variation from the vertical, the smallest air bubble, the most minute failure to match the pattern at the joins.

They were queer, unreal weeks, busy, physically tiring, but strangely happy weeks. Gail, with little opportunity for thinking of Kip, spending all her free time with Phillip, told herself that she had been wise in taking this course. She could never have been anything more than a hidden grievance in his life, whereas she could not but be aware that she was everything in Phillip's.

The days he did not see her (and they were few), he wrote to her, letters of love and hope and promises and assurances to which it was not in her warm nature to feel no response. If there were some secret place, deep within her heart, to which Phillip Westing had no key, he held the rest of it. The future was his to make or mar, Gail his to possess forever if he knew the way to hold her.

And in case it appears that she was too ready for a second loving, too quick to replace Kip whom utterly she had loved, let it be remembered that her love for Kip had been something idealistic, never brought to that fruition which would have bound her to him in refusal to any other man. In his watchful care lest he spoil her young idealism, Kip had been almost too reticent, too delicate in his love-making, and there had been so little of it that, in the presence of Phillip Westing's more robust demands on her physical response, that other became rather the figment of a dream, an exquisite, fragile memory, the mere ghost of what Phillip gave and roused in her. She was ready for a woman's response to the call of a mate, and Phillip called her.

So she came to her marriage, on that sweet day of June, with a heart that was glad, a mind that had freed itself from all that might have shackled it, a body warm with the human urge that keeps the rhythm of the world.

She was married at Heatherley, from the Millers' house, and Cora gave a reception for her in the tiny back garden, bright with flowers.

Gail wore blue, a flowery, fluttering gown of georgette, with a picture-hat of flower-trimmed lace.

Cora, always romantic, had wanted her to wear bridal white, but Phillip put his veto on that before Gail had had time to reply one way or the other.

'Oh Lord, no. We don't want all that flummery,' he said. 'A lot of fuss and show and expense, and besides, I can't afford the kit I should have to get to go with it, morning coat and all that rot, and never an occasion to wear it again. Wear something that'll make me alright in a lounge suit, Gail,' and since at that stage she was only anxious to please him in all things, she abandoned her half-formed visions of bridal satin and chose the blue georgette in which she looked like a flower herself.

She had wanted Jeffrey Templar to give her away, but this he flatly refused to do.

'No, Gail. Sorry. I've never given a woman away in my life and I'm not going to start it now, or on you. Besides which, you're not mine to give away, and if you were, I shouldn't give you to Phillip Westing.'

He could not get over his antipathy to Phillip, which he was willing to admit had very little grounds, and was more instinct than anything. When they met, by Gail's arrangement, Jeffrey was very pleasant, but she realised with a little chagrin that he wore what she described to him afterwards as his 'grand' manner, and it had the inescapable effect of putting Phillip's back up and convincing him that the kindly, generous-minded and completely unsnobbish lawyer was a striking example of that particular brand of 'bloated capitalists' whom he detested and despised – possibly through jealousy.

So Jeffrey neither gave her away nor went to her wedding, though he sent her a handsome present and a telegram of good wishes.

Kip did the same, and Gail had a few bad moments over the case which came to her a few evenings before the wedding.

There was a card enclosed, a formal one which said 'With Mr. and Mrs. Kipling Delaney's good wishes', but there was also a note for Gail herself, sealed in an envelope and sent separately.

I want you to have something of intrinsic rather than just sentimental value (he had written, without conventional beginning or ending). I should like to have sent you jewellery, pearls for preference, so that it might be personal and always realisable, but I think it might embarrass you, so I am sending you silver instead. Heaven bless you, Gail, and give you happiness for ever.

K.

She read the note many times, extracted every breath of sweetness from it, had a moment's terrific revulsion from what she was doing, appalling fear of the future, and then tore the note into tiny pieces and burnt them.

Kip had sent her a case of solid antique silver, exquisite in design, beautiful to handle, perfectly matched.

Phillip had been inclined to be amused over it.

'Queer idea to send old things for a wedding present,' he said. 'Might have coughed up something more modern. Why, the pattern's almost off this one,' balancing a spoon in his fingers.

Gail took it from him and replaced it in its velvet partition.

'They're much more valuable than new silver would be,' was all she said, but she was glad of the excuse afforded her never to bring the silver into use. She knew what had been in Kip's mind, that someday she might be hard up and that each separate piece of the silver had its own value, which would not lessen with time, though she felt she would rather starve than part with one fork, one tiny, exquisitely wrought spoon.

But on her wedding day she did not think of Kip.

She woke to find a fugitive sun darting in and out of her window with its magic fingers, and went to the window and knelt there, looking out over the quiet country scene.

'O God, let me make them happy,' she found herself praying, though she had never had a religious urge, and had not said prayers since she was a child. 'Let me be kind and loving and patient and, above all, understanding. Let me be tolerant of things which are different. Give me imagination and wisdom. Don't let any of them ever be sorry that Phillip has married me.'

It was in that mood, both humble and exalted, that presently she drove to the church with George Miller, found Phillip and an office colleague waiting for him, made her vows to him, received his.

The marriage service meant a lot to her. She had read and re-read it, seeing beauty in its simplicity, its directness, which found an echo in her own heart. She would be all these things to Phillip – loving, tender, faithful, yes, even obedient, though she could not conceive of husbands any longer ordering their wives about!

Phillip's hand stole into hers as they stood there waiting for the final blessing, and she held it tightly. He was feeling as she did, she told herself. Of course Phillip had been married before, had made these same vows to another woman now dead, but she was only too ready to believe him when he told her that that other love, that other mating, had been such a feeble, flickering thing of his boyhood, and this the full light and strength of his manhood.

Presently Gail changed into her travelling clothes, grey with a jaunty little scarlet hat, a grey travelling coat over her arm, and the last of the confetti was thrown over them, the last goodbyes said, the last old shoe tied to the back of the car, and they were off to London for their train to the village and the little seaside farmhouse where they were to spend their honeymoon.

They had time to spare at Liverpool Street, and Phillip suggested that after they had retired to the respective cloakrooms to remove all the confetti they could find, they should meet in the buffet for a cup of tea.

He was waiting for her when she returned, and she felt a glow of pride in him. He had no claims to good looks, but his face was clever and keen-eyed, he held himself well, and was always spotless and well-groomed. He might despise the rich, but he adopted their views on personal appearance, and his clothes were good and well-kept.

They sat at one of the marble-topped tables, and Phillip ordered two cups of tea.

'Our first meal, Mrs. Westing,' he said, and she coloured and smiled.

The place was crowded, and the waitresses had far too much to do, but their train was not due for over half an hour so they had plenty of time, but as they waited for the tea to be brought to them, Gail was surprised to see Phillip's brow heavy and his eyes stormy, whilst he drummed irritably on the table with his fingers.

'What's wrong, dear?' she asked him.

'Well, why doesn't that girl bring the tea? It's a quarter of an hour since she had the order,' he said.

'Darling, it isn't!' protested Gail cheerfully. 'We've only been in here five minutes.'

'I say we've been here quarter of an hour,' he said, and she flushed crimson at his tone and the flat contradiction of what she knew to be the truth.

'Phillip, it was quarter to when we came in, and look at the clock now,' she said.

He gave her a look which amazed her.

'Are you suggesting I am telling a lie?' he asked, and then, as at that moment the harassed girl brought the two cups of tea: 'Why the hell have you been such a long time? Think we've got all day to sit here?'

The girl looked unperturbed.

'Sorry, sir, but I was as quick as I could be,' she said.

'Then you're damned slow,' said Phillip. 'Give me the bill or I suppose you'll keep me waiting another half-hour for that.'

Gail choked back her dismay. What on earth had possessed him to speak to the girl like that? One of her earliest lessons had been that in no circumstances should one be rude to a servant, whose position made defence impossible.

Phillip, now that he had his tea, seemed unconscious of offence.

'Sugar, darling? Oh no, you don't take it, do you?' and he helped himself and smiled across at her. 'What's the matter? You look very solemn.'

There were other people at the table with them. She would not enter into an argument with him before strangers. She had learnt by experience that the presence of others did not deter him from any desired line of conduct, so she preferred to let the matter drop, though she could not at once forget it.

It was unpleasant, to say the least of it, and she hoped it was only part of the extraordinary happenings of one's wedding day, which cannot be considered as a normal day nor one producing normal reactions to trifles.

But she was to see other evidences of that swiftness of his to see and combat offence where none had been intended.

They had had to decide on a cheap honeymoon, money always being short, but Phillip had been assured, in the letter from the proprietor of the farmhouse guest rooms, that for the price he was asked to pay he would be given 'a nice room with a view', though at the time he had rather derided the thought of the view as being quite unnecessary for one's honeymoon.

'I shan't bother much about the view outside, darling,' he had said to Gail. 'All the view I shall want will be inside, with the blind down. What do you say?' and she had felt embarrassed, but expressed the opinion that the view did not much matter anyway.

But when they were taken upstairs and shown into a room which overlooked the fields and moorland rather than the sea, he expressed himself as dissatisfied.

'I understood we were to be given a room with a view of the sea,' he said with that touch of arrogance which was always surprising to Gail, in view of his frequently expressed belief in the equality of man.

The good woman smiled apologetically.

'A nice view, sir, but I don't think I promised a sea view,' she said pleasantly. 'We have only two rooms facing that way, and we have to charge more for them than you wanted to pay, but this is quite nice. You can see right over the moors from this side, and some people really prefer it, especially at this time of year with the broom in flower—'

'Well, I don't,' said Phillip, interrupting her pleasant flow of words. 'If you had meant there was no sea view, you should have said so.'

She coloured and bit her lip.

'I'm extremely sorry, sir. It was a misunderstanding. If you really wish to have a room with a sea view, I might be able to arrange it—if you could wait whilst I see whether—'

Gail, realising that she felt at a loss, came to the rescue.

'You know', dear, I think I'd rather be on this side of the house,' she said. 'If there's any wind in the night, the sea might be disturbing, and I think the view of the moor is lovely—so quiet and restful.'

Phillip turned to her.

'Well, my dear, of course if you would rather we kept this room, that's a different thing,' and he turned back to the woman. 'Very well,' he said in that lordly way. 'My wife wishes to remain here, so we will make it do. What time is supper?'

The woman told him and left them together.

Gail, who had rather dreaded the first moment she should find herself in a bedroom with a husband, found that that moment had passed in a quite unexpected fashion, and she took off her hat and threw it on the bed, shaking her hair free as she always did at the first opportunity.

'Well, this is this,' she said, with a jauntiness intended to cover her slight embarrassment.

Phillip was standing playing with the lock of his suitcase, which he had carried upstairs himself though Gail had casually left hers to be brought up by someone unspecified in her mind. She had never had to carry her own case upstairs.

Phillip looked up at her.

'Gail,' he said.

'Yes?'

She was fishing in her handbag for a comb.

'I hate to have to ask you this, but did you give the girl at the station, the waitress at Liverpool Street, some money?'

Gail brought her mind back with a shock of surprise.

'Yes, I did,' she said. 'I saw you'd forgotten to give her a tip, so I gave her some coppers. Why?'

'I had not *forgotten* to give her a tip. I hate the whole system of tips, which is degrading to the worker, but in her case she had not earned it, which was the precise reason why I did not give her one. You, of course, chose to negative my deliberate action by giving her money.'

'My dear, I don't suppose it was her fault if we were kept waiting. She had too many tables to attend to. I felt sorry for her.'

'If she is overworked, she has the remedy in her own hands, like all other workers. Since she chooses to allow herself to be exploited by her masters, that's no reason why I should be expected to pay my hard-earned money to help make up the wages they ought to be paying. Please allow me to decide that sort of thing another time. And another thing. Just now, when Mrs. Best was going to give us another room, you butted in and said we would stay here. Please don't do that sort of thing. It doesn't look well from a wife.'

Gail stared at him, the comb suspended above her head. Was he serious? Or was this one of his rather heavy and laboured jokes? He had not a very lively sense of humour, though with Gail he had laughed more than he had done for years, probably in his life.

'You—you aren't serious in all this, are you, Phillip?' she asked incredulously.

'I'm afraid I am,' he said, with tight lips, and she let the comb drop on the dressing-table, and went to the window and looked out with unseeing eyes at the view she had chosen.

What did one say in answer to that sort of speech? Nothing? Just accept it is yet another of the day's strange happenings?

Something hurt her horribly, but she plucked the thought away before she let herself recognise it. She was here with Phillip. Phillip was her husband. They were starting a new life together here and now. This was the first hour of it, the start of that lovely, vital, strong, happy thing which was to be their married life.

All the sweetness of her, the tolerance, the charity, rose to combat the thing which was hurting her, and she turned blindly and put her arms about Phillip, and laid her cheek against his.

'Darling,' she said, 'what's all this about, anyway? We're on our honeymoon. We're married, Phillip. Isn't that the thing that matters most? More than these silly trivial things? Kiss me. I'm your wife.'

His arms came about her, everything swept away but that divine truth. She was his—his own—utterly and for all time.

'My dearest, forgive me,' he said unsteadily. 'I'm a clumsy brute. I ought to be shot.'

'Do you love me, husband?' she asked.

'Do I? Darling—darling—oh, Gail, I want you, all of you, forever,' he said, his voice thick, his eyes bright, his mouth hot on hers.

'Well, haven't you got me?' asked Gail as for a brief second she withheld her lips, tilted her head back and looked at him with eyes dreamy with the passion he consciously, excitingly, evoked in her.

They were very late for supper.

But there were other little episodes, trifling in themselves, which marred the perfection of their companionship during that fortnight which should have been all enchantment, a quiver full of unforgettable memories with not one shaft of regret.

The first was when, at the end of the first few days, there was a letter for Gail, excitingly unfamiliar in its superscription, 'Mrs. Phillip Westing,' though it was in Priscilla's well-known scrawl.

Gail slit it open at the breakfast-table, read it with shining eyes but without comment, and put it into her bag.

Afterwards, when they were strolling down to the beach for Gail to decide whether or not it was warm enough for her to bathe, Phillip threw a too-casual question at her.

'By the way, who was your letter from?' he asked.

She looked faintly surprised, as one does not ask that question.

'Priscilla Grant,' she said, without vouchsafing any further information.

It was a tender and very private letter Priscilla had written her, saying that, a little to their regret just now, she found she was going to have another baby. Priscilla was essentially a maternal woman, and Gail knew that she had intended to have a companion for Jacko, but Priscilla had some wise, very gentle comments to make on the advisability of having an intentional rather than an accidental family, and Gail knew that they were meant for herself as much as for the writer. Priscilla knew that Gail meant to go on with her work at Hannam's for at least a year, and the advice she gave her was both practical and wholesome, as well as being delicately worded.

But Phillip could not leave it at that.

'Well?' he asked.

'Well what?' asked Gail, not understanding.

'The letter,' he said.

'I don't know what you mean,' she said truthfully.

'I want to see it.'

She gave him a look of astonishment.

'*You* want to see *my* letter? What on earth for?' she asked.

From earliest times her personal liberty and privacy had been respected, and though she had as a rule shown her schoolgirl letters to her father, he would never have dreamed of asking to see them, and during the past six years there had been no one to be sufficiently interested in her correspondence.

'Because I have a right to know what people have to say to my wife,' said Phillip.

She could find nothing adequate to say for the moment. Then she said quietly: 'I don't think we should talk about rights, Phillip. In the ordinary way I should have no objection to your reading letters which I may receive, but there is such a thing as personal liberty of action, and the choice should be left with me as to whether you read my letters or not. I should never dream of asking to read your correspondence.'

'I never have any private letters,' he said self-righteously.

'My life is an open book. I have no secrets from you and you should have none from me.'

'This isn't a secret,' said Gail.

'Then why not show me the letter?'

'Because I don't choose to do so,' said Gail.

'I suppose there's something in it you don't want me to see? You've been discussing me with your friends behind my back? This is the reply, I suppose? Chewing me over after a week of marriage with me?'

He was lashing himself into a fury, and Gail saw red lights herself. She would not have minded him seeing the letter, though she felt that it was a woman's letter to and for a woman, and that Priscilla had not intended it for his eyes, but in the face of his determination to invade her privacy she was determined he should not see it.

'You're being perfectly insane, Phillip, but if you really want to have a row with me, and it seems you must do to provoke a quarrel like this, for heaven's sake try to find something a bit more important than a silly letter.'

'Such as?' inquired Phillip with a politeness meant to be maddening to her and succeeding in its intention.

'Oh, I'm not going to argue with you when you take such a tone,' she said. 'I don't know what's the matter with you. I've done nothing, said nothing, and here we are having an all-fired row just because you can't get your own way. You're like a spoilt child, and I'm not going to pander to you. You can go down to the beach by yourself and perhaps an hour or two of your own disagreeable company will bring you to your senses.'

She turned and marched the other way, but before she had gone more than a few yards, he had come back, was slipping a hand through her arm, suddenly afraid that she meant it and that he really would have to spend the day, or at least the morning, by himself.

'Don't quarrel with me, Gail,' he said. 'I can't bear it.'

'Well, I don't want to quarrel,' she said. 'I loathe quarrelling with anyone, and if we can't get through a fortnight without having rows, what are we going to do for the rest of our lives?'

'Sorry, darling. Really. Forgive?'

She was more than ready to do so. At times like these all the bottom seemed to be dropping out of her life and leaving her to look into a yawning pit of emptiness – or worse.

'Alright. Let's forget it. I snapped too. I don't think I want to bathe. Too cold. Let's go up on the moors and knock a ball about. I'll get the sticks.'

When they were tired of their extremely hazardous golf, played with a golf ball and two hickory walking-sticks, they sat down in the bracken, and after a moment's hesitation Gail produced Priscilla's letter.

'Here. Read it if you like, though it wasn't meant for you to see, and if you laugh at my dear Priscilla, I shall never forgive you,' she said.

He took the sheets of closely written paper from her and she saw the quick gleam in his eyes and at once regretted that she had given him the letter. He had meant all the time to get hold of it!

Lovers' tiffs? Perhaps – but deep in her heart Gail was growing afraid. The tiffs were about nothing and were soon over and the making-up was sweet, but that 'nothing', when analysed, had its foundations in the very root of things. He wanted utterly to dominate her. He could not bear that she should have any individual life, any freedom even of thought, let alone of action. He wanted to build a wall about her, and set high spikes on top of it – a prison wall, so that she could not get out and no one could get in.

He called it loving her. Was it love of her? Insidiously, surely, the little serpent of doubt was creeping into her thoughts of him.

Love of her? Or only of himself?

There was the occasion, too, when another of the guests in the house said that the vicar had agreed to open for his inspection some old records which were kept in an ancient chest in the vestry.

'I wonder if they would interest you, Mr. and Mrs. Westing?' he added, and Phillip at once said that it would, without reference to Gail, with whom he had already arranged to go on the bus for a picnic to some woods.

She made no demur, not caring either way, though she rather wished he had shown her the courtesy of consulting her, and when they reached the vestry they found several other young people there, a hiking party whom the vicar had invited inside.

The old books were interesting, but Gail had seen so many of them, much more ancient and amusing, in her work for John Chives, and when she had seen as much as she wanted of them, she retired to a seat and shared a newspaper with one of the girls of the hiking party, who had brought one in with her. Gail and Phillip had not bothered about the rest of the world whilst they were on their honeymoon, and a newspaper was a novelty.

'Did you ever see such sights as we are going to look this winter?' showing Gail the fashion page, with its extraordinary caricatures of the human form divine.

Gail laughed, her crisp laugh ringing out in the quiet of that ancient, musty place smelling of dampness and decay.

'I rather fancy myself in the poke bonnet,' she said, indicating the most bizarre of them. 'Or what about the one with the feather?'

She had left Phillip completely absorbed in some of the old accounts, for he had never seen such things before, and he was working out for himself the rates of pay which had obtained in that dark age of husbandry. He was perfectly happy, and Gail had been quite content to wait for him. The company of a girl of her own age was attractive, too, after nearly a fortnight of unadulterated husband.

At her laugh he looked up, frowned, and then stood up, closing the book with a little dusty bang.

'Thank you,' he said to the vicar in an unnecessarily loud voice. 'Very interesting, but my wife is obviously bored, so we will go. Come along, Gail,' and he stood in the doorway of the vestry, his face like a thundercloud, waiting for her to get up from her seat and join him.

There was silence in the room, the old vicar slightly flustered by something he did not quite comprehend, being a little deaf, the girl hiker openly amused, the others watching the little drama in the discomfort people always feel at having to witness a domestic altercation which does not concern them.

Gail hesitated. Then, a patch of crimson in each cheek, her head very high, she rose and stalked out of the place, nor did she pause or slacken her pace until she had gone up the road, through the farmhouse garden and up into their bedroom.

Phillip followed her, his face grim and determined, and when he had closed the door, she faced him like a tiger cat.

'How dare you—how *dare* you treat me like that?' she stormed. 'In front of all those people, strangers at that, speaking to me as if I were a servant, or a child in disgrace! I've never felt so humiliated in my life. I hope you're prepared to apologise to me, Phillip.'

'*I* apologise to *you*. I like that! You're the one who ought to be apologising,' said Phillip harshly.

'What for?' asked Gail, her anger at fever heat so that she did not know what to say to him. There were no words to express what she was feeling.

'I thought we went there to share a mutual pleasure. You wanted to go. I only went to please you, and as soon as we'd got there, instead of looking at the things we'd gone to see, you go off and gossip with some girl you've never met in your life before, and I find you reading a newspaper!'

Phillip's anger was cold and biting. Gail's hot rages could not contend with it. He could bring her to boiling point more quickly than anybody else she had ever met, could goad her by a word or a look where with anyone else she would long ago have laughed and forgotten.

'Why the devil shouldn't I?' stormed Gail. 'As for it being my idea, it was yours. We were going to the woods for a picnic and you changed the plans without even asking if I minded. I went because you wanted to see the things. They weren't any novelty to me, but I was quite content to sit and wait till you'd had enough of it, and the newspaper was there, so I looked at it. Any harm in that? Or isn't your wife allowed to read a newspaper anymore?'

'Don't be childish, Gail.'

His voice was like a whiplash across her own.

'I'm not childish. It's you who are mad,' snapped Gail.

'Not at all. I told you when we first decided to get married that the only way to make a success of it is to pull together, and that means going the same way, wanting to do the same things, liking the same things. Alright. If you can't like the things I like, then I must find something you like and do that with you instead.'

She was mad with exasperation.

'Phillip, really! Two people don't merge into each other by just getting married. They remain two people – two in sympathy with each other, but still two people.'

'They can't be in sympathy if they have separate interests,' persisted Phillip, his tone the judicial one of conscious rectitude and superiority to a delinquent. 'As I say, if you cannot pull the same way, we shall never get the boat anywhere.'

'What you mean is if I don't pull your way all the time,' said Gail. 'It comes to this. Either I give in to you in everything, large and small, and totally submerge my own individuality, or we are going to spend our life in these petty quarrels. Is that it?'

'Certainly not,' said Phillip, who had appeared willing enough to defer to her opinion and her wishes in every way before they were married. 'If and when I think your way is the right one, I shall take it with you. If, on the other hand, I know it to be the wrong one, I shall expect you to give up your ideas without hesitation or question.'

'And who are you to be so sure that you know who is right and who wrong?' demanded Gail. 'Have you got a special dispensation for perfection from God, or what?'

'You needn't be insulting,' said Phillip in that maddeningly judicial, superior tone of his. 'If there is any question about the right and wrong of a thing, I, as the man and therefore the master, have the right to decide, which I shall certainly do. Understand?'

'Understand? Yes, I understand I have married an intolerable prig and a bully and a self-righteous, pompous ass,' Gail cried, and tearing open the bedroom door, she ran downstairs and out across the garden and did not stop until, high up on the moor, she threw herself down amongst the bracken and sobbed with a breaking heart.

Mind and spirit were quivering from the contact with that special sort of intelligence which was Phillip Westing's, and for the first time she saw him for what he was and what she, in her unthinking wrath, had called him – self-righteous and a bully.

There was no getting away from that. She said the words over and over to herself. That was the man she had married, the man who was so utterly blind to real things, so callous of her hurt, so completely wrapped up in himself and the business of achieving his own ends that her desires and her happiness and her pleasures were to count as nothing in their lives. 'I—I—I' – that was all that counted with Phillip Westing, that she should go his way, fall in with his wishes, utterly abnegate herself for him and subjugate her life and her personality to his will.

She sat up at last, her aching head in her hands.

'What have I done?' she asked herself tragically. 'What have I done to my life now?'

She could not bring herself to go back to the farm, to face the other guests who by this time knew that she and Phillip were on their honeymoon.

What could she do? She had run out of the house with neither hat nor coat, and, what was worse, without money. She could not get away from here.

At last, shaken, her legs trembling from very exhaustion after that nerve-storm, she began to walk down towards the farm, and stopped short, in a panic, when she saw Phillip coming towards her, waving.

She turned to run, but realised that it was hopeless, and instead she stood still and waited for him to come to her. She felt drained of everything, a ghost, a shadow. She did not care what he said to her, what he did. She felt no more fight left in her.

But when he reached her, she could see that he had been suffering too – not as she had done, for he was a man of very different temperament and could not give himself, even to grief and sorrow, as she had done.

But he had been feeling something too, and his hands came out gropingly towards her, and she saw that he was afraid she might repulse him.

'Gail—Gail—'

He could not speak beyond her name, and then, somehow, they were in each other's arms, and her tears were flowing again, and she did not know whether she were relieved or more wretched at his coming.

Her body responded to the warmth and comfort of his, to the passion which the very touch of her never failed to arouse in him, whilst her spirit knew itself to be withdrawn, wounded, shrinking.

'I love you, Gail. You're everything in the world to me. Don't leave me. Don't draw yourself away from me. If ever I lost you, I should die.'

I—I—I! The same insistent ego! The thought was swift in her mind before she could check it.

'Gail, don't push me away from you. I want you. I need you. I should do away with myself if you left me. Gail—speak to me. Look at me, Gail. Kiss me.'

And because she was unutterably tired and did not know what to do nor where to turn, because this was her husband and she had chosen life with him, and there in London their home and their friends waited for her to come back with him, because the children waited for them, Gail left herself limp in his arms, felt his kisses on her lips, eager, compelling, seeking – always seeking.

That terrible, relentless ego!

He began to talk to her again, sitting with her in the bracken, his arms about her, his relief showing in every word and movement, relief that she had not gone away from him.

'I'm jealous, darling,' he said in extenuation and excuse, though she had not again accused him, had said nothing at all, submitting to his caresses without consciously feeling them, certainly with no response. 'I always have been and I always shall be. That's at the root of it. I love you so much that I want you to myself, all of you, exclusively, not shared by anyone or anything.'

She roused herself to some response. If only he would not talk! If only he would give them time, both of them, to pass this bad spot, to get round the corner and look for something better beyond.

'That's the sort of thing that can make us both very unhappy, Phillip,' she said. 'It isn't a thing I really understand very well. I thought jealousy meant jealousy of another man or another woman, not—not of just things—everything—oh, Phillip, don't let's go on talking about it. What's the use? It doesn't get us anywhere—and I'm so tired—and cold—'

She was in a thin dress without a coat, and she was shivering.

Phillip jumped up, pulled her to her feet, chafed her hands a little, and then began to walk her down the hill.

'Come on, darling. Let's get back to the house. I ought to have had more sense. Of course you're cold and tired, my poor little love. Come along. Let's hurry, and when I get you in you'd better go straight to bed. I'll get Mrs. Best to give you a hot-water bottle, and I'll bring you up some supper. Hurry, darling.'

She was grateful to him for his care and comfort. She would have been grateful to anybody, and it just happened to be Phillip. Also she was glad that he himself had suggested that she need not appear in public again that day. It saved another possible argument, and she was too utterly tired and worn for further struggling.

He smuggled her upstairs without being seen, brought a hot-water bottle, returned presently with supper on a tray, sat with her whilst she ate, was tender, solicitous, lover-like.

Later, surrendered to him, she tried with an almost fierce intensity to make of this phase of married life the overmastering, all-conquering ecstasy which it seemed to be to him. Never had she given her body more wholly, and yet never felt her mind so far withdrawn.

'You do love me!' he exulted. 'Now I know you love me! Oh, darling—darling—isn't love the most wonderful thing on earth? The only thing worth having? I love you, you love me, and nothing else matters, nothing!'

But long after he had fallen asleep in the easy fashion of the satiated male, Gail lay awake, staring into darkness with eyes that held the world's sorrow in them, the martyrdom that only a woman can know when, lying beside the man who has sworn to cherish her, she asks herself again and again that futile question: 'What have I done? What have I done?'

Chapter Eight

Life at 5 Reedsdale Road settled into an orderly routine with amazing speed, and at least outward success.

Joyce and Hugh had no doubt about the success. To them it was unqualified by any regret. The house was nicer than anything they had dreamed of living in; their new mother, who preferred to be called just 'Gail', was more like a jolly elder sister than a person put in authority over them, and the little girl quickly developed a passion for someone who bought her dainty clothes, let her mess about in the kitchen when they were both at home, and never scolded her; the new housekeeper, who came in every morning but left when Gail came home in the evening, was kind and gentle with them; the food was good and plentiful, and well cooked; and, more amazing than all, their father seemed a changed being, brighter, less inclined to find fault, even having little jokes with them and allowing them to play mild practical jokes, though his temper had always been so uncertain that they were a bit careful about the last-named.

Now that the idle, difficult days of the honeymoon were over Gail found things easier and Phillip better to handle. They had their own jobs which kept them occupied most of the day, and there were still many little things to be done at home, small carpentry jobs inside the house and out, and the garden to be worked.

It had been decided, after some discussion, that few of the things from Phillip's former house were suitable for the new house. They were old-fashioned and ugly, besides having been badly used for the most part, and Gail had had little difficulty in persuading him to let her own home, the few good pieces which she had brought from John Chives' house, form the nucleus for their home together.

She bought one or two pieces from Hannam's, or from sales which she had to attend on their behalf, but the furniture for the living-room and the children's bedrooms was new, inexpensive but attractive.

'If we give them anything valuable we shall be on thorns it they don't take care of them, whereas if we buy new, cheap things and they damage them, we can always replace them,' she said, so Joyce's heart had been gladdened by pale blue-and-white enamelled wood, with bedstead to match, whilst Hugh had a more masculine suite in deal, stained to look like oak, with an iron bedstead which would not suffer if he used it as a private gymnasium.

Gail had loved furnishing her home, and though she had had to use a little of the money Kip had given her when she left him, she had not the same feeling about using it to make her home beautiful as she had when it was a question of buying the home itself where she and Phillip were to live.

Their financial arrangement seemed to be working comfortably.

The original idea had been that Gail should send Templar a monthly cheque when she received her salary from Hannam's, and that Phillip should give her the same amount, namely, three pounds a week, for the housekeeping, to include light, coal, gas, and the wages of Mrs. Brigg. Gail had smiled secretly to herself at the idea that the family could be maintained and Mrs. Brigg's wages paid out of three pounds a week, but as Phillip had said that was all he could possibly afford to contribute, she had accepted it and gladly made up her mind to supplement it out of her own salary, which was a good one, and would allow her to do so even after Jeffrey had had his three pounds.

In actual working, however, Phillip quickly suggested it would be more sensible if he sent his cheque to Jeffrey Templar each month whilst Gail put her stipulated three pounds into the housekeeping.

'It comes to the same thing,' he told her. 'It's really rather silly for you to pay your money to Templar and then for me to give you the money to pay the bills here with.'

'It doesn't make any difference as far as I can see,' said Gail, but when after a few months Hannam's entered a bad patch of business and had to reduce her salary, she found it difficult to continue the housekeeping on the scale on which it had started and decided to ask

Phillip if he could help. Considering things carefully, and knowing what he earned, approximately, she had come to the conclusion that she was bearing too large a proportion of the burden of supporting a household which, after all, was more his responsibility than hers. She never had anything for herself, she needed winter clothes which she had not bought in her trousseau, and she had had to over-spend on the children so that they should be warmly clad.

'Darling, let me talk high finance to you,' she said one night, producing her small account book.

'Must we?' he asked. 'I rather wanted to get on with this as it has to go back to the library.'

Once she would have snatched the book gaily away from him and insisted, but she had learnt caution in her dealings with him.

'It won't take long,' she said persuasively. 'This is the position. I have put it down here. The housekeeping, children's clothes, laundry, and all that sort of thing is on this side, and on the other side what I'm putting into the house, and you'll see they don't balance—'

His quick mind, trained to figures for years, was able to take in at a glance the two sides of her account, and he smiled and pushed the book back into her hands.

'Dearest, I don't want to know how you spend your money,' he said. 'I trust you absolutely. You know that. You don't have to account for it to me.'

'But, Phillip, that isn't the point, quite. I can't afford to run the house as I hoped, and I want—'

Still he waved her away, gently inexorable.

'My dear, your money is your own to do what you like with. I don't want to know how you spend it. It's your very own, to do what you like with.'

'I know, but—'

'Gail, don't let's start an argument,' he said. 'Not about money, anyway,' and once more he tried to get back to his book.

'Phillip, you don't realise that I *want* you to take an interest in it because it's being spent on you and your children—'

His face wore the look she had come to hate and fear.

'That's enough, Gail. If you don't want to go on managing the house, I'll take it over from you. I've done it once. I dare say I can do it again.'

'Don't be silly, Phillip,' she said, exasperated. He was a pastmaster at making the conversation take a quite different turn from the one intended, and she felt sure that he knew what she was trying to get at, which was a more equitable distribution of the family expenses. 'I don't want you to take over my job. Why should I?'

'I don't know, but if you can't manage it—'

'I can manage it,' said Gail, who had felt rather proud of herself for having been able to take on a ready-made family and cater not only for its suet puddings and orange-juice, but also for its clothes, cough mixture and pocket-money.

'Alright. Then don't come running to me,' said her husband.

Gail gave it up and waited for another opportunity, but found it was always the same. Phillip simply would not listen to her when it was a question of the household expenses, and gradually, as she struggled more and more deeply with the increasing expenses of the winter, with coal and boots and medicines and chilblains and extra blankets, she became harassed and careworn, with the inevitable reaction in frayed nerves and a sharper tongue than she had known she possessed.

Phillip's best-liked line was the indulgent assertion that her money was her own to spend exactly as she liked, and that he had no right or wish to exercise any authority over her spending of it, but when this gradually wore thin, and she told him openly that he must help her with the weekly expenses, he replied with a flat refusal, told her to cut down her bills, and accused her of being thriftless when she said she could not do so and yet give him all the choice foods he liked to eat. He grumbled at the cheaper cuts of meat, however appetising they were made, pushed aside on his plate with a look of disgust any re-dished remains from the previous day, and encouraged Hugh, who disliked suet puddings and milky foods, to complain about the food.

Finally, he went over the housekeeping accounts with her and marked the items he said could be cut out. They were all special things she got for the children, oranges, eggs and a somewhat expensive cereal which she found Hugh would take when porridge revolted him.

It made her angry.

'Phillip, the children need these things. They were undernourished. They have chilblains, and Hugh is a lot underweight.'

'Then cut down on your own clothes,' he said, looking at the simple woollen dress she was wearing. 'You need not have bought that.'

'I had to. I interview customers, and was not respectable. It only cost four pounds, and you have just paid over ten pounds for a new suit, and bought yourself two sets of new underwear though your others were perfectly good, and I told you Hugh has no overcoat.'

'Doesn't it occur to you that I, too, have to keep up an appearance?' he snarled at her. 'Besides, the boy's got an overcoat.'

'Not one that he can wear. He's grown out of it, and it's dreadfully shabby.'

'Teach him to be more careful with his clothes.'

'Why did you buy those expensive underclothes? I mended your others, and they would do quite well this winter.'

'I hate mended clothes. They irritate me, great bulges everywhere.'

It was a libel on Gail's mending. She made darns of exquisite neatness, and he knew it. He had no justification for his extravagance, but would not admit it and thereby earn both her forgiveness and respect. He preferred to put up fictitious justifications.

'Well, we've got to cut the expense somehow, Phillip. We can't stand it.'

'Well, *I* can't do anything about it. I give you what we agreed, and if it isn't enough, I can't help it,' he said churlishly.

'You spend too much on yourself,' said Gail, snapping at him in a way that would once have been foreign to her but which now came far too easily. 'You smoke all day long and half the night.'

'That's right. Take away my one pleasure and relaxation,' he said.

'The welfare and health of your children should come before pleasure and relaxation for yourself,' said Gail. 'You have no right to smoke so many cigarettes unless or until your children are properly fed and warmly clothed,' said Gail with spirit, though she could see he was either not listening to her or pretending not to.

Suddenly he got up from his chair and began to pace the room, holding his head with both his hands.

'Oh God—my head, my head!' he cried wildly. 'Will it never stop? Round and round and round—the maze—the maze!' and suddenly he crumpled up and fell on the floor at her feet, his eyes closed, his body motionless.

Gail was alarmed. He was ill, and she had been badgering him like this about money!

She ran upstairs like a mad thing, brought down sal volatile and smelling salts, pausing only to put water on the gas to heat.

She knelt at his side, supporting his head on her knee.

'Phillip—oh, darling, I'm so sorry, so sorry!' she said, everything forgotten in her pity for him, her blame for herself in not having known that he was ill.

Gradually he yielded to treatment, opened his eyes, gave a feeble moan and recognised her.

'Feel—so—ill,' he said.

'I'd better get the Paxtons to telephone for a doctor,' she said anxiously. 'Do you think you could get up to bed if I helped you, dearest?'

'I—I'd rather—stay here—few minutes,' he managed to murmur. 'Not—doctor.'

'Nonsense, Phillip. If you're ill, of course you must have a doctor,' but he pulled at her skirt and kept her there.

'No. Be alright—soon. Nothing—really. Stay with me, Gail. Don't—go away. Don't—leave me.'

She heard the water boiling in the kettle, and called upstairs to Joyce, who was in bed but not yet asleep.

'Joyce! Come down, darling, and fill a hot-water bottle for me. Don't be frightened. Your father's not very well,' she added, as the child, who must have been at the top of the stairs to have got there so quickly, came into the room with her fair hair in pigtails and her red dressing-gown wrapped about her plump little form.

She stood for a moment looking at her prostrate parent with a strange, unnatural expression on her face, and then, at Gail's repeated injunction, scuttled away into the kitchen to return a few moments later with the hot bottle.

Gail took it from her and, making sure that it was not too hot, put it against Phillip's feet, from which she had taken the shoes.

'The rug from the couch, Joyce,' she said, and wrapped him up in it, the child still standing looking at them with that strange, inscrutable expression on her piquant little face.

In a little while Phillip murmured weakly that he felt better, and Gail helped him to his feet with difficulty, and sent Joyce back to bed.

'Keep yourself warm, darling,' she said. 'I'll come and tuck you in again presently, but I must see to poor Daddy first.'

Gradually, painfully, step by step, she got him upstairs, he leaning most of his weight on her, but at last she got him into bed, gave him some of the precious brandy which she was hoarding for emergencies, and sat for a moment on the edge of the bed, holding his hand.

'Better now, dearest?' she asked him, all her tenderness called out by his need of her, his helpless weakness, whilst she blamed herself bitterly for having been at least a contributory cause of his collapse.

'Yes. Better now,' he said, like a tired, comforted child. 'Not angry with me anymore, are you darling?'

'I wasn't angry, my dearest,' she said. 'I'm sorry about all the things I said to you. Forgive me?'

He stroked her hand.

'Always forgive you, dear—always—always,' he murmured, and as he seemed about to drop off into an easy sleep she stole away, remembering Joyce and wondering if the little monkey had tucked herself well in to avoid waking with cold feet, as she did so often.

But the blue bed was empty, and Gail tiptoed to the other bedroom, wondering if the child had felt scared at sight of her father's collapsed form and had crept into her brother's room for comfort.

She listened at the door, which was not quite shut, to hear if they were asleep, and to her astonishment titters of suppressed laughter were mingled with the whispers of both children.

'What did he look like?' asked Hugh.

'Same as usual, all stark and spoke in jerks,' giggled Joyce.

'Did she fall for it?'

'You bet she did! She's such a sport that I almost told her, but I thought I'd better not, not whilst *he* could hear, anyway.'

'Golly, you'd have caught it hot!' said Hugh. 'He'd have leathered you.'

'She wouldn't have let him. You should have heard her, though,' and the little minx gave a faithful representation of Gail's own voice as she had spoken words of comfort and compassion to her husband.

'She'll rumble him. She's cute,' said Hugh. 'He won't put it over on *her* for long. I wish I'd seen him, though. You always get all the luck.'

'I'll call you next time they have a row, and then if he puts on the fainting act, we can both see,' promised Joyce.

Gail, sick and horrified, went back into hers and Phillip's bedroom and left the child there. Better that they should not know what she had overheard.

She looked at Phillip.

She could have sworn that when she came into the room, somewhat unexpectedly, he had his eyes open, but now they were shut, and he was breathing stertorously and as if in pain.

Was it possible? Was this just an act, put on to get himself out of a disagreeable situation? To end in reconciliation and kisses one of these soul-destroying quarrels which she hated, but which he seemed always to be courting?

'Phillip,' she said sharply, and he started up, looked at her with wide, staring eyes, and slipped back on the pillows again.

It was so well done. Was it possible that it was only pretence?

She undressed and got into bed, and lay for a few minutes staring into the darkness, not knowing whether she would be more angry than amused if she ever proved that it had been a trick, all that business downstairs.

Suddenly Phillip moved, flung an arm above his head, and groaned.

'Money—money—money!' he said in a deep, moaning whisper.

Gail lay quite still, and very soon he spoke again, but more in his normal voice.

'You asleep, dear?' he asked.

'No,' she said.

'I—did I disturb you?'

'No,' said Gail again.

'Was I talking in my sleep?'

Now she knew.

She did not speak for a moment. Then she said quietly: 'No, Phillip. I wonder why you thought that? You never talk in your sleep, dear.'

Poor Phillip! What a strange mixture he was! – part man, part spoilt child, always ready to quarrel with anyone who would quarrel with him, even Gail, with whom he need have had no quarrel, or perhaps chiefly Gail for the very reason that every day, every week, he knew himself to be more deeply in debt to her, not only for material help, but for sympathy, service, tolerance, charity, and the care she gave his children, who turned more and more to her and troubled less and less about him.

Poor, unhappy Phillip! So sure that the world was his enemy, whereas he, and he only, was his enemy.

They did not refer in the morning to his 'seizure' of the night before, neither did Gail return to her discussion on the housekeeping bills. Somehow she must find a way to meet them without his help. For both their sakes, if she were to retain any respect for him at all, there must be no repetition of such scenes.

What could she do for him? A divine and all-conquering love might have saved him from himself, but he had not the ability to call it forth from any human being because he could not give it, and Gail's sympathy and honest striving were not enough. His self-pity and insensate jealousy were eating like a canker at his heart and at their married lives.

He seemed to her to be determined to find a cause for complaint against her, and his long bouts of sullen silence, sometimes lasting for weeks at a stretch, were reducing her to a state of nervous strain which reacted on both of them. Questioned, he would give her no explanation of his apparent grievance against her, at the most merely hinting darkly that she 'knew quite well what was the matter,' though she had not the least idea, and did not realise at the time that the only thing wrong was his own bad temper.

Occasionally he found some ridiculous peg on which to hang that resentment of her.

There was the time when, pressed by a despairing, miserable Gail to explain what he had against her, when he had maintained for three weeks his sulky silence, he had flung at her an accusation which amazed her.

'If you would only tell me, Phillip, what's wrong,' she had insisted. 'We can't go on like this. It's hell for me, and if I don't know what I've done wrong, how can I put it right? I thought we agreed that there should be complete honesty between us?'

'Honesty?' he repeated with a sneer. 'You're not exactly the one to prate about honesty!'

'What on earth do you mean?' she demanded hotly, though she had determined not to let this turn into a quarrel, as the slightest variation of opinion from his was prone to do. 'What have I done that isn't honest?'

'You should know,' he said meaningly.

'Well, suppose you tell me,' said Gail curtly.

'I will. You're receiving letters and hiding them – letters from men.'

Nothing could have amazed her more. Whatever she might have expected, it was nothing like that, for her life had been an open book and no man but Phillip had existed for her since her marriage.

'I think you must be mad,' she said. 'When have I ever done such a thing? And who is supposed to have written the letters? And where have I hidden them?'

'I don't know who wrote them, but I saw you slit open an envelope addressed to you in a man's writing, and you did not take out the letter. You just looked into the envelope without more than a glance inside, and then put it in your pocket to read later, when I was not about. You need not try to look so innocent. It was a grey envelope with a crest at the back. One of your grand friends for whom I'm not good enough, I suppose,' with another sneer.

'I think, as I have said, that you are quite mad,' said Gail. 'I have had no letters from men, crested or otherwise, but it seems useless for me to deny it. However, if you wish to look in my desk, you can,' and she took out her keys, flung open the top of her bureau, and watched him whilst, without shame, he went through the little stack of things she kept in there, triumphantly pouncing at length on just such an envelope as he had described and flinging it down before her.

'There you are. Perhaps you can explain that,' he snarled.

Gail, puzzled, picked it up and took out of the envelope – the printed circular of a famous toy shop from whom she occasionally bought things for the children. She had recognised it and not bothered to look at it at the time, had put it away in her bureau for future examination and forgotten all about it!

She showed it to Phillip, her lip curling but her heart sick. What was going to happen to them if he could behave like this?

'You'd better look at what you based your quite unjustifiable accusation on,' she said. 'This is what I've been suffering over the past three weeks – toy trains for Hugh.'

He glanced at it, but was not at all discomfited.

'Well, you should have shown it to me at the time,' he said morosely. "That would have saved any unpleasantness. You have a nasty habit of being secretive, Gail.'

'And you have a nasty habit of being suspicious, Phillip. Are you going to apologise to me for your behaviour over this?'

He glared at her.

'Apologise to you? What on earth for?' he blustered. 'If there's any apology due, it's from you, not from me,' and he turned his back on her and marched out of the room.

Gail tore up the circular slowly and threw the bits into the basket.

Undoubtedly they were living in too narrow a circle, simply reacting on each other until the tiniest incidents became magnified into drama.

She had felt the lack of friends since her marriage. Her circle had never been large, but the few friends she had were good ones whom she did not want to lose. Phillip, she discovered, had no friends. He was fond of parading his lack of them as a virtue, telling her that he made his home circle fill his needs and did not divert from his wife, and children any of his interests. Since he had no use for friends himself, he did not expect Gail to need any, and she had yielded, in the early, lovingly submissive days of marriage, to his dislike of having other people in the home, if only for an hour or two. Not even Priscilla or the Millers had been to Gail's home, and she knew they must think it strange.

She decided that Phillip would be better if he could get outside himself by meeting other people, hearing their views and being stimulated by their presence.

Priscilla Grant had more than once suggested their spending an evening at Kensington with them, but Phillip had always refused to go, and Gail now decided to try the experiment of having Priscilla there for the weekend. She could not accommodate John as well, and in any case someone had to stay with Jacko, and Priscilla, who was now some six months pregnant with her second child, would probably appreciate a quiet change.

She suggested it to Phillip.

'Joyce wouldn't mind sleeping downstairs on the couch for one night,' she said, 'and Priscilla could have her room. She won't be very presentable, but she'll take you for the old experienced married man you are and won't feel too embarrassed. You won't mind, Phillip?'

In spite of her breezy beginning, her last question tailed off rather anxiously. Phillip could be so difficult when he liked, and she had found that he usually did like.

However, on this occasion she took a grant for signifying that he did not mind, and it was arranged that Priscilla should come on the Saturday afternoon, meeting Gail and her husband in town and travelling down on the suburban line with them. John and Jacko would come to tea on the Sunday and take her back with them.

Gail was radiant. She was proud of her home and the children, and she was proud of Priscilla, and she sincerely hoped Phillip would allow her to be proud of him, though when they went up to town together on the Saturday morning he was not in the best of humours.

'Don't forget we're meeting Priscilla at ten past one at the bookstall,' she said.

'Alright,' he said. 'I haven't forgotten.'

His tone was sulky and ungracious, and Gail looked at him in exasperation. Why on earth could he not be pleasant for once?

Priscilla was charming to everyone, and on the few occasions she had met him she had been particularly nice.

She slid a hand through his arm, contemptuous of herself for the attempt to propitiate him which should have been unnecessary but which his sour humour made advisable if she were not to be humiliated before Priscilla.

'Be nice, dear,' she said. 'I'm so much looking forward to showing Priscilla our home.'

'I don't know what for,' he said. 'We don't want other people messing about. When I do get a few hours of free time I want to spend them as I like.'

Gail withdrew her hand and walked along the platform with him, her anger and indignation against him rising. Was she to have no liberty of action? No pleasure chosen by herself, even so simple a one as the entertainment in her own home of her woman friend?

'No one is preventing you from doing so, Phillip,' she said. 'The weekends are also my free time, however, and I have a right to some little pleasure too.'

He did not reply, but gave her a sulky glance and strode ahead, pushing his way through the barrier and giving a haughty glare at a man who inadvertently knocked against him in the general crush. That arrogant stare which Phillip invariably gave to anyone who dared to brush against him in passing had once amused Gail. By this time it had become an infuriating thing to her, suggesting as it did that Phillip felt himself to be above mortal clay, a superior and untouchable being, whilst he still loudly declared himself to be a socialist.

She turned and went her way, which diverged from his at this point, and when later in the morning she met Priscilla she hoped he would have recovered

At her first sight of him coming towards them, however her hopes saw their doom, for his brow was dark and his whole face sullen and unsmiling, nor did it relax into the barest courtesy of a smile when Priscilla gave him her friendly greeting of: 'Hullo, Phillip. How nice to see you again. I do think you're charming people to let me come to you this weekend.'

He did not reply, merely raised his hat perfunctorily and strode on in front of them, leaving them to follow meekly to the front of the train, where there was often an empty coach.

After two or three stops they had the compartment to themselves, and Gail, infinitely embarrassed and ashamed of Phillip's surly silence, was very chatty and bright, describing to their guest what they had been doing to the garden and what they hoped to do.

'I'm trying to get hold of a shrub the Millers have at Heatherley,' she said. 'I've almost run it to earth, but if I don't they will give me some cuttings.'

Phillip had not spoken at all, sitting opposite them ostensibly and very rudely reading his paper, but now he lowered it and spoke suddenly, his lips curling.

'In case you've missed the point before, you will by now have been left in no doubt that my wife is a very wonderful woman,' he said in a tone of biting sarcasm.

Priscilla went scarlet and bit her lip. The insult to Gail was unmistakable and utterly uncalled-for, and she was hurt to the very soul for the warm-hearted and kindly girl.

She had seen little of Gail during the six months of their marriage, but on the few occasions on which she had seen her friend she had been unhappy at the change in her. The brightness which had characterised Gail had been dimmed, as if the fires which lit it had been quenched. There was a look of strain about her, a hurt, puzzled look in her eyes, and Priscilla had realised that all her spontaneity had gone and that she seemed to be watching herself, guarding every word she spoke. Why?

Now she understood. Phillip Westing was draining her of joy, of comfort, of belief in herself. What grudge had he against this girl to whom he owed so much? Priscilla did not know how much, but she had seen the children, and knew that they were happy with Gail, and surely that alone, even if there was nothing else, should have earned her their father's appreciation.

Phillip's gratuitous insult stung Gail to swift reply, though as a rule she left such things unanswered in the presence of others.

'And you are leaving her in no doubt that you are an ill-mannered boor,' she said, and at once regretted, too late, having descended to his level by such a remark in front of a guest.

Fortunately the next station was theirs, and they left the train and made the short journey on foot to Reedsdale Road in silence, Gail carrying Priscilla's small case in spite of its owner's protests, Phillip striding in front of them.

Gail felt sick with humiliation and dismay. What a start to their happy weekend!

The children made a welcome diversion, shyly adoring Priscilla.

In the afternoon they went into the wintry garden, and then for a walk, Phillip remaining at home by his own choice, and when they returned he was sitting hunched in a chair, buried in the inevitable paper, nor did he address one word to anybody, except to grant 'good night' in response to the children's timid good nights.

It was a ghastly evening for Gail, and no less so for Priscilla, who was shocked and troubled, for her own John was the soul of courtesy and hospitality, and she knew how bitterly Gail must be feeling her husband's boorish conduct.

It was a relief when Priscilla said she would like to go to bed, though it was still only nine o'clock. Gail went up with her, but did not mention the state of affairs until Priscilla, very gently, said: 'Dear Gail, I think it would perhaps be better if I went back home in the morning. I can telephone to John from the station to meet me.'

Gail swallowed hard, clenching her hand on the bedrail.

'I'm so sorry,' she said in a muffled voice.

'Don't worry, dear,' said Priscilla. 'I really ought not to have come. Men are strange creatures. They have their funny ways, even John.'

She spoke lightly, with a smile which was meant to soothe poor Gail's hurt, but the girl wished she would not be so kind. She could stand anything but kindness just then.

'I cannot imagine John insulting a guest in his own home,' she said harshly. 'I'm sorry, Priscilla. I ought to have known better than to ask you. I ought to know Phillip better by now. He's just a surly, unmannerly beast. I apologise for my husband, Priscilla, but am quite sure he would never apologise for himself nor even admit that any apology is due. He is a law unto himself, and serenely sure that he has every right to behave as he likes and to whom he likes. He is Phillip Westing, omniscient, omnipotent!'

Her tone was bitter. She felt vindictive. Her sense of humiliation was intolerable. Nowhere in the world, and by no other human being, had she been treated as Phillip Westing treated her. Outside this house she was respected, liked, treated with the honour due to any woman, especially to a gentle and intelligent woman, but the one man who had sworn to love, honour and cherish her never ceased to try to humble her to the dust.

Priscilla laid a hand on her arm.

'Darling, don't get bitter,' she said. 'It isn't worth it. Don't let other people, no matter who they may be, spoil your sweetness, destroy all the nice things about you. Have the courage and the belief in yourself to keep these things. They're what we love you for. They're you yourself.'

'I think I hate my husband, Priscilla,' said Gail in a low voice of concentrated feeling.

'No, Gail. Don't say it, my dear, or allow yourself to think it. It's just a phase. Something has upset him, and it was most unfortunate that I should come just at this weekend. It will be alright when I have gone. You'll see.'

'Oh yes, it'll be alright then,' agreed Gail bitterly. 'That's what he wants. He hates me to have anybody here, to go anywhere, to have any interest or thought that is not exclusively for him and his wellbeing and pleasure. That's what I exist for – the pleasure of Phillip Westing! I've no doubt at all but that when you've gone he will be all over me, kissing me, making protestations to me of his love to me. Love! That's what he calls the hateful thing that only humiliates me further. He calls it loving me, this ministering to his own beastly lust. He insults and humiliates me before my friends, before his children, and then when he gets me to himself he thinks all will be right again if he can lay his hands on me and satisfy the needs of his body by kissing and mauling me …'

She stopped and covered her face with her hands, appalled at what she was saying, at what she did not even realise had been her thoughts, but which now she recognised. She had felt like this for weeks, possibly months, but had not known the depths to which her self-respect had been dragged until now, when she found herself putting into words all the bitterness and humiliation and disgust Phillip Westing had brought to her.

Priscilla did not speak. She did not know what to say nor how to say it.

Gail recovered herself, stood upright, dropping her hands. Her face was like a white mask.

'Sorry,' she said very quietly. 'Yes, you'd better go in the morning. There's no need for you to get up early, because Phillip never gets up till lunchtime on Sundays, so I'll call you about nine and bring you some breakfast.'

'I can come down, Gail.'

'No, don't. I'll give the children theirs first as they like to be up and doing, and when I've seen to the lunch I'll go with you to the station. Good night, dear. No—don't kiss me, if you don't mind. I—I don't think I could bear kindness tonight,' and she left the room abruptly, hesitated on the landing, and then, since no privacy was possible to her in this little house, with Phillip in one room downstairs and Joyce asleep in the other, with Priscilla and Hugh in the bedrooms, she had no alternative to going to bed in her own room, in the double bed which she shared with Phillip. Before they were married he had laughingly but none the less firmly set his face against any suggestion of two beds, and since the room was small and Gail had then been in love with the idea of marriage, she had agreed and bought the double bed.

She pretended to be asleep when Phillip came up, keeping her eyes closed, but he did not speak to her, and soon she knew by his snores that he was asleep.

He was still asleep when she woke in the morning, and tiptoed to the bathroom with her clothes over her arm. First she paused and looked at him as he lay there, his character revealed in sleep as it was not always revealed in consciousness. She saw the lines of meanness and cruelty about his mouth, the full, sensual lips whose significance had escaped her inexperience before their marriage.

It was a hard face, a cruel and selfish face, but it was also the face of a bitterly unhappy man.

Gail slipped away. There was no compassion in her for him. If he were unhappy, it was a condition of his own making. His life held all the ingredients for happiness, and Fate had been kind to him. He had had good, hard-working parents who had denied themselves for him; Gail had by now had ample evidence that his first wife had been a good woman, industrious, kind, affectionate, though she had not been able to go on loving Phillip Westing, who must have treated her even worse than he did his second wife, for she had been sickly and had lacked Gail's youth and spirit; he had nice children who caused him no sort of anxiety physically or morally, and who were doing well at the elementary schools which were the best he could afford, or so he said; and in Gail herself he had found a woman who was kind, loving, and careful of his children. No, viewing it from all angles, he had no quarrel with life except his own determination to see himself as a hardly used martyr, and to seek ever-fresh grounds for self-pity.

When she had seen Priscilla off at the station, having first telephoned to John on her behalf, and felt the stab of his unconcealed delight in the prospect of getting his wife back a few hours earlier than he had expected, Gail returned to 5 Reedsdale Road and finished preparing the lunch. Mrs. Brigg did not come on Sundays, but left food partially prepared for Gail to finish off.

The children were quiet, sensing trouble, and when Phillip came down, unshaved and in his dressing-gown, at one o'clock, Gail did not speak to him.

'Where's Priscilla?' he asked, looking at the four places at the table.

'Gone home,' replied Gail shortly, and the meal proceeded in deathly silence, broken only by Hugh's whispered request for more pudding and Joyce's later request that they might get down.

She sent them out for a walk, washed up the dishes, and then went into the sitting-room where Phillip, shaved and dressed now, was preparing to be amiable.

'I want to talk to you, Phillip,' she said abruptly, shutting the door.

'I suppose I'm going to be called over the coals for yesterday?' he asked aggressively.

'No,' said Gail, 'though I am glad you realise I should have some justification for doing so. I'm not going to bother with that. I'm leaving you, Phillip.'

He stared at her, open-mouthed.

'Leaving me?' he echoed. 'Bui you can't do that. You're my wife.'

'I know, unfortunately,' said Gail, determined not to have an open quarrel with him, but to keep herself well in hand. Tears were her enemy, they and her quick temper. Phillip's cold, biting sarcasm could always set her at a disadvantage, put her in the wrong when she knew, and he also knew at heart, that she was in the right. There must be no tears and no temper now. 'I am not your slave, though. You have tried to treat me like a delinquent servant, humiliated me in every way your bitter mind can devise, exploited my earning capacity to rid you of your responsibilities and give you more to spend on yourself, and now you have insulted my friend and driven her from the home which I help to maintain, just as you drive away anyone who comes here to see me. I have come to the end of it, and I am leaving you. You can do what you like about it. I am in no way dependent on you. I am sorry for the children, but they must lay the blame on you. I am going to Heatherley, to Mrs. Miller's, until I can make fresh plans, but for your own sake, I advise you not to come down or try to bully me there as you do here. There will be a man there, and I do not fancy George Miller would hesitate if you force your way into his house or insult a guest there. Goodbye Phillip. I hope I shall never see you again,' and she turned and walked out of the room, leaving him speechless now with rage, though he had tried again and again to interrupt her carefully prepared speech, and she had had to resort to the indignity of raising her voice above his interruptions.

She went upstairs and packed a bag, but when she came down again he was standing in the hall, barring her way. She could see that he was in a towering rage, and felt frightened, for he could always frighten her, and she knew that he had great physical strength.

'Please let me pass, Phillip,' she said, controlling her feeling of panic.

'No. You're not leaving my house,' he said between set teeth.

'I am leaving it, Phillip, and if you prevent me tonight, I shall go tomorrow. You cannot keep me chained up, you know.'

'You're not going out of this house today,' he said doggedly, an ugly look on his face.

Gail knew the terrible impulse to murder. She could have killed him as he stood there with that look on his face, a half leer, his cruel mouth set in a grim line in spite of that travesty of a smile, his eyes mocking her. She could quite understand hot-blooded murders of such men as Phillip Westing by women over whose misery and helplessness they gloat.

Gripping her suitcase, she turned and ran out of the house through the kitchen, through the garden, out into the narrow passage which divided it from the garden opposite and, on the mad impulse to escape, hid in a fenced garden whose gate had stood ajar, and remained there, scarcely daring to breathe, whilst Phillip searched for her, and finally returned, concluding that she had escaped him in the main road.

Feverishly she made her way to the station and to Heatherley, the trains difficult and slow on a Sunday afternoon in winter, but eventually, by early evening, she had made her way to the Millers' house and into the motherly, comforting arms of Cora, who asked no questions but held the girl to her breast as if it were her own Ethne coming to her for comfort.

Chapter Nine

Gail sat on the edge of her bed in Ethne's room and re-read Phillip's letter.

It was a fortnight since she had run away from him, and the kindness and love she had received in the Millers' home had done much to soothe and restore her. At first Cora had been seriously alarmed for her. The girl had seemed distraught, almost beside herself with fear and the dreadful loathing which had replaced her once real love for Phillip Westing, or for what she had believed him to be.

But gradually the peace of that home had its effect on her, and she was able to talk.

'It's a vicious circle, Cora,' she said. 'He says he gets bad-tempered and morose because I don't satisfy him physically as a wife ; I loathe him to touch me at night because he has treated me to his temper and insults and humiliations all day, and because of that, *because of that*, Cora, I can't bear him to touch me; he reacts to it by further tantrums and surliness; and so we go on, acting and reacting on each other's nerves until any sort of married life is impossible for us. I can't go on with it. I can't live with him again, ever. He can't expect me to.'

Cora understood better than Gail realised. She had had her own difficult path to travel when she and George were young, before the children came. She had had to teach him what so many men fail to realise, which is that a sensitive, intelligent woman can be reached physically only by the appeal of the mind, and that where her spiritual affections are set, there will her woman's body follow. George had loved her enough to learn that lesson, but how could it be taught to Phillip Westing, who truly loved only himself?

She spoke of tolerance, charity, great forbearance, but knew that Gail must work out her own salvation, and possibly Phillip's, though her heart was sore for the girl and deeply angry with the man who had not known the treasure that had been put into his hands.

Phillip telephoned, but she put the receiver up. He wrote to her and she sent the letters back unopened. He waited for her outside Hannam's shop, and she let herself out by a back door and fled from him. He waited for her on the station, and she saw him and went down to Heatherley by a different route. He came down to the house and asked for her, but George Miller, stalwart friend, denied him entry.

They had set a bulwark about her to protect her, but she knew that she could not remain behind it forever, and when at last she had opened a letter in a strange handwriting and found it to be from Mrs. Brigg, enclosing one from Phillip, she knew she must come out of her hiding-place and take up life again.

> *Dear Madam [Mrs. Brigg had written], I think I ought to inform you that Mr. Westing is very ill, and I feel you ought to be here. I enclose a letter which he has written you in the hope that you will read it.*
>
> *Yours respectfully,*
> *Sarah Brigg.*

So, at last, Gail had read what Phillip had written, in pencil and in a shaking hand, and lacking his usual flowing style.

Briefly, affectionately, he told her that he knew he had been greatly to blame, and that in different circumstances he would by now have given up all hope of her forgiving and returning to him, but that, things being as they were, he dared to write again and humbly to hope that she could find it in her heart to forgive him.

> *I am very ill, dear [he had then said]. I must have been ill for a long time without realising it, and this must have caused me to behave as I have done to you. I don't urge that in extenuation. I merely state facts and leave judgment to you. I was taken ill in*

the office some days ago, and they sent for a man up there, who sent me on to Lockson of Harley Street. I had a shock. He did not beat about the bush. I have no more than two years at most, and possibly not that, of active or useful life. It's rheumatoid arthritis, and nothing, he says, can stay it. Great care, a quiet life and rigid diet will help to stave off the final complete rigidity of the limbs, but he cannot give me more than two years at the outside.

I dare not ask you to come back to me, Gail, and it is only for the children's sake that I venture to write to you at all, since you have decided so definitely to cut me off. Don't visit my sins on their heads, my dear. They love you and have not deserved to lose you. I love you, but have deserved to lose you. All I can do now is to throw us all on your mercy. And so, even if it be for the last time, let me sign myself.

Always your devoted and loving husband,
Phillip.

When she had read and re-read it until she felt she knew it by heart, Gail replaced the letter in the envelope and locked it in her case.

What was she to do? Everything within her shrank from going back to him and to the home which he had made so unhappy for her, and yet she was his wife, she had accepted responsibility, and, now that he was ill with this terrible threat hanging over him, had she any right to her own separate life?

The thought of the future appalled her. Married to him only six months, and very soon, within two years at most, she would find herself responsible for the maintenance of a permanently helpless man and two children not her own.

But she must go back. There was in her too strong a strain of personal responsibility to refuse this burden. At whatever cost, it was hers, and hers alone.

She went down to Cora. She could not show her Phillip's letter, which, in spite of her new hardness of heart, had touched her.

'I'm going back home,' she said briefly. 'Phillip is ill—very ill. I can't do anything but go.'

Cora saw the lines of strain and trouble back in the girl's face, but she made no attempt to deter her. She, too, felt that Gail's duty lay with her husband and her home, and she did not despair of their finding a new happiness after this separation. It was hard for her to believe that a man could not find happiness with Gail, who gave so much to life.

She did not send any message to Phillip. She merely walked in that evening, put her hat and coat in their usual places, and went back to the sitting-room where the children were doing their homework and Phillip was sitting in an easy chair by the fire.

She had expected to find him in bed, or at least in the outward guise of an invalid, but except that he looked pale and worried, he was much as usual.

She gave him her hand.

'I hope you're feeling better, Phillip,' she said.

'Thank you—thank you—yes, I shall be—alright again now that you're back,' he said, stammering, actually stammering, in the relief of having her here again, and then he seized her in his arms and buried his face in her neck, regardless of the curious eyes of the children.

'Oh, Gail—darling—dearest—you've come back to me! You've come back, to me!'

She stood him in her arms, her eyes looking out above his bent head, an inscrutable look in them. Since she had decided to come back, to take up life with him again, it was undoubtedly better that they should be on affectionate terms, and yet she knew her heart and mind and body to be untouched by his demonstrations. Once he had been able by his touch, his kiss, to rouse in her instant, glad response to him. Now there was no response. She felt cold, aloof, an outsider, listening to the repetition of a well-known speech.

She roused herself. There must be no half measures. Since she had decided to come back to him, she must come back in her entirety, generous, holding back nothing.

So she smiled, and when he lifted his head she kissed him and made no attempt to free herself from his clinging hands and strongly enfolding arms.

That night their reconciliation, as far as Phillip was concerned, was complete, but Gail, not witholding herself, knew that something had been lost to them irrevocably, that he embraced the hollow shell of what had once been a living, loving woman. She was no longer his mate. She was just his chattel, giving her body, but having no more to give.

In the morning she discussed his health with him.

'I'm glad to find that you're better than I expected,' she said, when she had taken his breakfast to him and watched him eat heartily of the poached eggs, coffee and toast which he said he was allowed to have.

He was not to go back to work yet, having a doctor's certificate releasing him.

'Did the specialist give you the certificate?' she asked him.

'No. I was so bad one morning that Mrs. Brigg called in Dr. Penning, and he gave me one, but I told him he need not come again. What's the use? I know the verdict, and Lockson gave me my diet—at least, he told me what I could eat and I wrote it down. You'll find it in the kitchen somewhere. I gave it to Mrs. Brigg.'

Before she left for Hannam's she waited to see the housekeeper, and studied with her the list of foods allowed to Phillip, which filled her with dismay.

'That's the worst of these specialists,' said Mrs. Brigg. 'Money's nothing to them, and I suppose they live on these things as a general thing, but I'm not going to manage them out of the housekeeping, madam.'

She had expressed no surprise at seeing Gail back, but had greeted her as if nothing unusual had happened, for which the girl was profoundly thankful.

She re-read the list. How was she going to manage it?

Chicken, fresh salmon (preferably Scotch), sole, turbot, oysters, eggs in any form, fresh fruit, cream. Nothing re-cooked. Nothing tinned.

'He forgot the champagne,' remarked Gail with a touch of scorn.

How could people in their position afford to keep a man indefinitely on such expensive luxuries as were on that list?

'I ordered a chicken today, madam, just for Mr. Westing, and the children and I are having shin of beef stew with vegetables. Will you have some of that tonight, or some of the chicken?'

'Heavens, not the chicken, Mrs. Brigg! How much was it?'

'Ten-and-ninepence. I could not get one less, and there's next to nothing on it, and Mr. Westing doesn't like stuffing, or that would help it out.'

'Well, we must manage,' said Gail, and ran off to catch her train, but in the evening she spoke to Phillip about it as he made a good meal off the remains of the chicken, and she could see that there would be nothing there for him the next day and he must not eat a re-hashing of the chicken carcase.

'Diet's an expensive business, my dear,' she said brightly.

'I know. Brutal, isn't it? Still, whilst I'm having those things I'm not having anything else.'

'I shan't be able to afford it without help from you,' she said diffidently, knowing with a feeling of sick fear how these discussions on money always ended, no matter how delicately she handled them, nor how willing she was to shoulder more than half the burden.

He gave her a deprecating smile.

'My dear, what can I do?' he asked. 'I'm helpless. I'm in your hands. I've only got so much, and I can't spend it twice. You know you can have everything I've got, but you can't have more than I've got.'

It sounded so well! Gail had heard it so often before.

'Then we must ask Mr. Templar to let us get behind with the house repayments,' she said helplessly.

'No, we can't do that,' he said at once. 'The house is all that stands to you for security if anything happens to me, and whilst I am able to work I must pay off all I can there.'

'There—there would be your insurance, if—if anything happened to you,' she reminded him reluctantly, feeling that it was brutal to speak to him of his own death.

He smiled again and spread out his hands.

'Sorry, dear, but—' and his gesture suggesting impotence finished the sentence for him.

She frowned.

'You took out that life policy, Phillip, didn't you?' she asked. 'The one you promised Mr. Templar you'd take out before we were married?'

'Matter of fact, I didn't. I couldn't. I spent a lot on this house, one way and another, what with paper and paint—'

'I paid for half of that,' she reminded him.

'You thought you did, but I never told you the full extent of the cost,' he told her, and she wondered about that. If he had not told her, it was quite unlike him. She let it pass, however. What was the use of doing anything else?

'You could have saved the premium up and taken out the policy when you had it,' she said.

'Perhaps I could, but I didn't. It's very well for Templar to jaw about saving and life policies and so on, but he's a rich man and hasn't any children.'

'So if you died, Phillip, there's nothing at all for the children and me?'

'No,' said Phillip sulkily. Gail let it drop. She saw, though, that he was right about the payments for the house. They must go on at all costs or she and the children would be homeless, whether Phillip lived or died, since in two years' time he would be a helpless invalid on her hands.

She returned to the original point.

'Well, we've got away from your diet. If you can't possibly help me, what are we to do? If you have to live on chicken and Scotch salmon and cream and all those things, what are the children and I going to live on? My salary is small now, as you know, and I have Mrs. Brigg to pay out of it.'

He patted her hand.

'Don't worry your head about it anymore,' he said. 'Tear up the diet sheet. Let me have the same food as you and the children, and forget the rest.'

'But, Phillip, the specialist said—'

'I know, darling, but if we can't do it, we can't—and after all, if the thing's got to happen, why wait two years for it? Why not let it come now? I don't mind. Life isn't so sweet for you with me alive,:' and he broke off with a sudden twist of pain which brought her to his side.

'Phillip, can I do anything for you?'

'No, dear. Nothing. I shall be alright in a minute,' he said, and he was.

But she did not renew the conversation about the diet and when two delicate fillets of sole were served for his supper the next evening whilst Gail had bread-and-butter and cheese he made no comment.

Still, on the whole things were better. She did not refer to the past, nor did she make any attempt to invite another friend to the house, whilst he seemed to exert himself to be more entertaining, to talk to her on the very restricted subjects which evoked his interest, namely the office and politics, and to describe in detail events in his army service which invariably redounded to his credit and suggested that the final triumphant end had been possible only through his efforts.

His talk of 'my men' and 'my chaps' and what he had said to the Colonel and what the Adjutant had said to him led Gail on one occasion to ask innocently, 'What *was* your rank when you left the army, Phillip?' – expecting that he had been at least Captain, if not Major, Westing.

He hesitated, cleared his throat, felt rather than saw the solemn eyes of his daughter Joyce on him, and then said airily.

'Well, of course, I was doing all the work of the sergeant-major towards the end, but I was never listed as more than corporal – well, of lance-corporal, I should have said,' as Joyce's eyes became more and more fixed on him. 'You'd better run up to bed, Joyce,' he added sharply. 'Past your bedtime,' and the child, with a small, infuriating smile, slipped past him and upstairs to bed.

She had heard those tales so many times, and each, time they had a little more embroidery worked into them!

He began to excuse himself to Gail when they were alone.

'I had such a lot of responsibility in the war which was never recognised. I didn't wear the right sort of tie to be handed a commission!'

She laughed.

'Lord, I don't mind whether you were a general or a private,' she said. 'Why should I? It's such ancient history now,' and she marvelled that he should think it important enough to bother about, let alone try to deceive anyone over.

But affairs along the kitchen front were becoming difficult, and as Phillip seemed so well she began to wonder whether it would not be possible to relax the rigidity of his diet so as to enable her to get more suitable food for the children, who were growing visibly and had enormous appetites and needed more nourishing food than she could get for them whilst spending so much on Phillip.

Rather than re-open with him a subject which caused so much trouble, she decided to take matters into her own hands, and one afternoon left Hannam's early in order to see Lockson, the Harley Street specialist to whom Phillip had referred.

She had spoken to him first on the telephone.

'I'm not coming as a patient,' she said. 'My husband saw you some months ago, and I'd like to talk to you privately about him, but I can't afford to pay you another fee. Can I come to you without your charging me, or am I asking something which is never done?'

He liked her frankness, and like all sincere men of his profession, considered the patient of more importance than the fee.

'Come by all means, and on those terms,' he told her with a laugh. 'What did you say your name is?'

She spelt it out to him, adding. 'You saw my husband in January, but I don't know the exact date.'

'I'll have him looked up before you come,' he said.

But when she was facing the quiet, grey-haired man in his comfortable room, he gave her a surprise.

'You know, Mrs. Westing, I'm afraid you must have made a mistake, I have no record of anyone of your husband's name, and most certainly did not see him.'

She looked nonplussed.

'But—I'm sure it was your name he said. Otherwise how should I know you? He was taken ill at his office, and the doctor who was called in sent him to you.'

'And what did I diagnose?' asked the specialist with a little smile.

'Rheumatoid Arthritis. You specialise in that?'

'I certainly do,' he said, the smile now turning to a puzzled frown. 'What is his firm?'

'Bradey & Sons, of Lithower Street.'

He consulted his records again, found a card and studied it.

'I was certainly in touch with that firm in January,' he said. 'One of their women cleaners had had an accident and arthritis was feared, and I advised in the case, but it was not a man and not your husband.'

'You gave him a diet and told him he had only two years of active life to live,' said Gail, producing the diet and handing it to him.

He read it and gave it back to her with a smile.

'I'm sorry, Mrs. Westing, but do you know what I think? I think your husband has been having a little joke at your expense, playing a little trick on you. You go home and tell him you have rumbled him, and get your own back on him,' and he took her to the door, shook hands in his friendly fashion with her and watched her go down the street before returning to more serious patients.

Gail was in a maze. What was the real solution to all this? Could it be possible – but it *couldn't* be possible that he had fooled her again? Made up the whole thing to play on her sympathies and get her to return to him?

She remembered the 'faint' he had staged, and the ribald laughter and comments of his own children which she had overheard. And afterwards he had pretended to be talking in his sleep, in order to show her that her insistence on their money problems was eating into his mind even whilst he slept.

And now he had had to devise something bigger, something desperately serious, since no mere faint or temporary indisposition would have made her come back to him – threatened permanent invalidism, all that horror she had endured at the thought of the responsibility it would thrust on her – and his choice foods, specially cooked, rigidly kept for him, and him alone, whilst she and the children had had the cheapest of everything, even gone short of food when poultry and salmon and oysters and cream had been dearer than usual.

She felt bitter. How easily she had been duped! No wonder he had made a fuss of her when she came back! He must have been so pleased with himself.

She went home intending to have it out with him.

There was a roast fowl for him, a macaroni pie for herself and the children.

She left the macaroni in the kitchen and carried in the fowl and set it at her own place, though as a rule she left Phillip to carve for himself.

'Shall I bring in the other things for us, Gail?' asked Joyce.

'No, dear. I think we'll all have chicken tonight, for a little treat. I'm sorry there will not be enough vegetables for us all, but I brought home some potato crisps and we'll make do with those.'

Phillip looked surprised, but made no objection.

'That's right,' he said with unnatural heartiness. 'Let's celebrate. All share the old man's chicken, eh? You going to carve, Gail?'

'Yes,' said Gail, and did so, sharing equally, a little of the breast on each plate, a leg each for Phillip and Joyce, another joint for Hugh and another for herself, until there was nothing left.

'There won't be anything for Dad tomorrow,' said Joyce, somewhat scandalised, though her plate looked inviting.

'That's alright,' said Gail. 'We share with him today and he will share with us tomorrow. That's fair, isn't it?' and no one said any more about it, though it was a silent and somewhat strained meal for all its opulence.

After the children had gone to bed Gail asked Phillip a quiet question. She wanted to give him a chance to get it straight with her. She hoped he would tell her the truth, confess that it had been a trick. She wanted passionately that he should make some attempt to win back her respect for him.

'Phillip, what was the name of the man in Harley Street to whom you went? The one who gave you the diagnosis and the diet?'

'Lockson,' he said. 'Harwood Lockson. I forget the number.'

'You're sure it was Harwood Lockson?' she asked.

He flared up at once.

'Of course I'm sure. Do you take me for an idiot or what? What's the idea, anyway, of this catechism?'

She looked him steadily in the eyes and then turned her back and walked away, sick at heart.

But the expensive diet ceased abruptly with that chicken, nor did Phillip make any comment, nor Gail offer any explanation.

The rheumatoid arthritis bogey had been laid.

It was soon after that that Gail found herself pregnant.

She had suspected it for some days, but when a visit to the doctor confirmed its likelihood she kept her secret wrapped in her own mind and could not bring herself to tell Phillip.

There had been one discussion on the subject of her having a child, and it had turned into a bitter quarrel which she could never forget.

She had spoken of giving up her work in due course, coming home and making a real married life for them.

'And a baby, Phillip,' she said. 'I shall want one.'

It had never occurred to her that he would wish to deny her that, and his reply stunned her.

'There aren't going to be any more children, Gail,' he said.

'What do you mean by anymore? I haven't got any yet,' she said.

'No, but I have, and two kids are enough for any man in these days.'

'Your children are very dear to me, Phillip,' she said, 'but they're not like my own and never could be. I want at least one child of my own, and I don't want to wait too long for it.'

'Then I'm afraid you're going to be disappointed,' he said, with that air of finality he always gave to an argument, as if when he had spoken no other opinion was possible. 'You're always on at me about what I don't do for the children, about their needing a better education than they're getting, better clothes, new this and new that. Well, how can you suggest burdening me with still another?'

The argument was the more revolting because of the subject on which they argued, and what had been something tender and sweet and holy for Gail became a degrading thing of pounds, shillings and pence, and before they had gone far, Phillip had hurled at her this terrible, unforgettable insult: 'Do you think I want to father the grandson of Jeremy Marlin, swindler and thief, and only not a gaol-bird because he hadn't the spunk to face the music?'

That had crumpled Gail up, and she never forgot it to her dying day, never forgave it to Phillip Westing, though she had to forgive him so many things.

Life had closed over the sore, but it was still there, and so when she found that she was indeed to become a mother to Grumpy's grandson, she kept it to herself for days and weeks, and told Phillip only when she felt it could not much longer be hidden.

Before she told him, she had gone to Jeffrey Templar with her news, sure there of kindness, sympathy, genuine gladness for her. Jeffrey, she felt, would wipe out for her to some extent the stain of Phillip's harsh, unjustifiable words from a mind she longed to make sweet and lovely, holy ground on which the feet of her child might walk.

There had been, too, at the back of her mind the secret fear that Phillip had deceived her over the repayments for the house, since he had deceived her over so much else, and Jeffrey, she knew, would never ask for the money, which he always considered lent to Gail and not to Phillip.

But in this case her fears had been unfounded. The money had been paid faithfully, month by month, whilst she had been keeping him and his children without any contribution from him.

'You should have had the house in your name, you know, Gail,' said Templar. 'Though Westing has been paying his cheque to me every month, it's really been your money, because, without you, his money would have been absorbed in maintaining the home. I pointed that out to him the other day when he seemed inclined to talk a bit big about *his* house. It's your house, Gail, or should be, and I don't mind telling you that if you had done as I wanted and had it put in your own name, I'd have given you the rest of it. But I'm not going to give it to Westing.'

She smiled rather ruefully. She would have been so thankful to know the house was hers and paid for, especially now, when she would have to leave Hannam's and have nothing at all of her own.

'That's just the way Phillip talks,' she said. 'He knows it really is mine, or that it's really my money that is paying for it. Of course he could not pay three pounds a week for a house unless I relieved him of his responsibilities in other directions, so he knows that in actual effect it is I who am paying for the house. Still, that doesn't arise now because—very soon we shall have to make other arrangements, and he won't be able to go on paying the three pounds a week. I'm going to leave Hannam's. I—Jeffrey, I'm going to have a baby.'

She spoke very simply, but he knew what lay beneath those words, the dreams, the hopes, the joy, the fears—all womanhood.

His eyes lost the hint of hostility which was always in them when they spoke of her husband, and a very tender little smile hovered over his lips and the brightness of his blue eyes was faintly dimmed. He had so greatly desired a son!

But to Gail he said: 'My dear, that news makes me very happy for you. You could not tell me anything I would rather hear. When is it, do you think?'

'December, possibly a Christmas present,' she said.

'I'm so glad, Gail. You'll have to take better care of yourself now,' for of late he had thought her thin and peaked, though he did not often see her, and of course marriage always altered a girl.

This, however, would put everything right, and he was genuinely glad for her.

'I haven't told Phillip yet,' she said, 'so when he comes to you, as he'll have to, to ask you to make different arrangements about the mortgage, don't tell him I told you first, will you?'

'Of course I won't,' he agreed, but when she was gone he felt sorry she had admitted that to him.

She should have told her husband first, not just a friend, even so old a friend as he was. There was something wrong, he felt, if Gail had not at once told Westing her glad secret.

When she did eventually tell Phillip his reception of it was not as bad as she had feared.

'Well, I'm not going to pretend that I'm enthralled at the prospect,' he said, 'but I suppose it can't be helped, so I'll just have to put up with it. Dunno how it happened, but mistakes will happen even in the best regulated families.'

'That was all. If Gail were disappointed, if she had retained enough romanticism to hope for something sweet and unforgettable, some little vignette of memory upon which she would look back later with tenderness, she told herself that she could not have expected anything different, and at least Phillip did not show the annoyance and resentment she had almost anticipated.

Tentatively, some days later, she asked him if he would make new arrangements to meet the different position when she left Hannam's, and he frowned but agreed, though she found, when she had come home to take Mrs. Brigg's place and prepare for her baby, that Phillip was not disposed to allow her anything like the sum she had given Mrs. Brigg for housekeeping, though before long there would be another to provide for.

She asked him, rather nervously, for a little money to buy wool and material to make the layette, but he refused curtly.

'I haven't got anything to spare,' he told her. 'You must do as other women do, and save it out of the housekeeping.'

'But, Phillip, it's so small now that it's all I can do to pay the weekly bills, and things mount up. The bill for gas seems bigger every time.'

'Well, you must cut down on it,' he said. 'I don't use the gas.'

'You turn on the gas fire to dress by in the mornings,' she pointed out.

'Well, I'm not going to freeze just so that you can be extravagant over other things,' he said, and stalked away.

She would not have a row with him. That, at least, she owed to the child who with every day grew more real and individual to her, filled her with a gladness such as she never dreamed could be hers, the child who was to make up for everything she had lost, everything she had missed. Many things she would never have, but this one thing, this precious child, would be hers – not even Phillip's, since he did not want it and displayed no interest in it. In fact, when one evening, in her exuberant joy, she had not been able to keep to herself a speculation about the child, some foolish little thing which is one of many in the heart of the expectant, happy mother, he had looked across at her sourly and said, 'Anybody would think no woman had ever had a kid before.'

'Well, they may have, but *I* haven't,' said Gail.

'Well, it's no novelty to me,' said Phillip cruelly, and after that she never mentioned the baby to him again. They went on as if no child were expected, and all her radiant dreams, her imaginings, her hopes for its future, her plans and fancies, were kept to herself.

Yes, truly this was her own child and hers alone! Phillip's part in it had been so insignificant! He had not even known he had given her a child.

She still had some of Kip's hundred pounds in the savings bank, though she had had to break into it to buy some of the furniture for her home, but again she felt reluctant to use it for clothes for Phillip's baby, though felt she would have to do so in the end.

She had not seen Kip in all these months, though when she had been most miserable, and especially during the fortnight she bad been away from Phillip, she had known great temptation to go to the theatre and see him. She had not gone, however, but one day, when she had been into the West End to look at the most exclusive shops for baby clothes and try to remember how they were made so that she could copy them, she had yielded to the temptation of going past the Irving Theatre. She would just look at Kip's photographs, which would be on the outside, advertising his new play, which had followed *The Roundabout.*

She looked at them all, her heart in her eyes because there was no one there to see, and as she gazed at the wide, fine brow, the steady eyes which seemed to look straight at her, the sensitive nostrils, the mouth that was both strong and tender, she knew that nothing would ever pluck from her heart the man whom so deeply she had loved.

Phillip could have ousted that love from her heart, but he had loved himself too much and had sent her back to Kip, unsatisfied, aching, lonely.

With a little sob she turned away – and the next moment was almost in the arms of Kip himself. She had turned so swiftly, walked so unseeingly, that he had had to catch at her to keep from bowling her over as he left the private door of the theatre, and then he had seen who it was.

'Gail!' he said, and again, with a wondering gladness, '*Gail!*'

'Oh, Kip,' she said, and felt the world spin about her and then stand breathlessly still.

He was there. She was with him. The world was narrowed into one square of pavement. There was nothing else beyond it.

'Come and have some tea with me, Gail,' he said. 'We can't stand here.'

His voice was gay, his eyes shone, the hand that slipped in the old familiar way beneath her elbow to turn her about was warm and vital. Its touch thrilled her.

'Not anywhere where—people will notice me, Kip,' she, said nervously, and then Kip's eyes, travelling for one swift moment over her figure in the coat which was not a very successful camouflage for her figure, understood, and she saw him look into her face, and there was a swift stab of pain in his eyes, and she understood so well – so well.

His car was parked in the old spot, and he helped her into it with tender care for her, and her mind went swiftly and unpreventably to Phillip, who never troubled to take care of her, who stalked across the road and waited impatiently at the other side for her to join him, got on a bus in front of her, left her to find a seat as best she could.

Kip took her to a quiet little tearoom where, in an alcove, they could talk without being interrupted or overheard.

But when they were seated there, and their order given, they could find nothing to say.

Meeting Kip had brought colour to Gail's cheeks and relit the soft fires in her eyes, and her coming motherhood had given her a poise and a fine delicacy of feature which she had not possessed before. The bud that had been Gail had flowered, but not for him.

'Dear little Gail,' he said.

'You know, Kip?'

'You're going to have a baby, Gail, aren't you?'

It seemed so natural to be talking to him like that, without reserve or preliminaries, mentioning the most important thing straight away.

'Yes.'

'You're glad, aren't you?'

"Terribly glad, Kip. About Christmas.'

'And this is September. Oh, Gail—'

'I know, dear.'

Yes, she did know what he was feeling, knew too that her joy would be utterly complete if this were Kip's child, not Phillip's.

But she would not think of Phillip now. There was all the rest of life to think of him. This hour, this little hour, was Kip's.

'Tell me about yourself, Kip,' she said.

He smiled and shook off the slight melancholy of his thoughts.

'Oh—I have my children, too, though they're not as exciting as yours, nor as satisfying nor as precious. *The Roundabout* is still on, but I moved it to the 'George', with Palmer in the lead, and have a new one at the 'Irving', *Brittle Glass*, in which I am playing myself.'

'I read the notices of it in the paper. They were good,' said Gail.

'So-so. The critics were pleased with me for giving them the mixture as before, but I still hope to write another *Roundabout*. I shan't get Priscilla back. She tells me she is going wholly maternal now. You women!'

Gail laughed, and they spoke of Priscilla and her baby daughter, of John and Jacko, of the Millers, of almost everything but Gail herself, but at last, when she said she must go, he held her hand very tightly under the table.

'Happy, Gail? *Really* happy?' he asked her, for when the first radiance of their meeting had passed he thought he could see a faintly drooping look about her.

She smiled and nodded her head. Kip must not think there was anything not quite right between her and Phillip.

'Yes, Kip,' she said, and he had to be content with it.

'Alright,' he said, 'but don't forget that I told you that if Phillip did not make you happy, I'd murder him, and that still goes and will always go.'

She laughed.

'You won't have to,' she said, and then it was time for her to leave him, and she laughed again and held her head very high to hide the tears in her heart.

'Don't come with me, Kip,' she whispered, and he let her go, watched her until the swinging door had shut her from his sight, and sat there with his hands clenched, and a deep furrow between his eyes, so sure that everything was not right with her.

She had laughed and talked and told him of the children, had said she was happy – and yet—and yet …

'Oh, Gail, my dear, my dearest,' he thought. 'If it could have been I to whom you are going back, to whom you are going to bear your child. Gail—Gail …'

Chapter Ten

'Coming for a walk, Gail?'

She was very tired. Housework to one who is not accustomed to it is one of the most tiring things in the world, and for months Gail had swept and dusted, scrubbed and polished, washed dishes and clothes, cleaned brass, done all the jobs which even a small house requires when, like 5 Reedsdale Road, it is not a very modem house. She had had no help, not even the weekly blessing of a charwoman, and though throughout her pregnancy her health had been good and she had ailed nothing, she had had that additional burden to carry about with her.

Now, on that Sunday evening, she longed for nothing more than to sit down and put her feet up, but after spending the morning in bed and the afternoon lounging in a chair with the Sunday paper, whilst Gail cooked the family dinner and then washed the dishes with the help of Joyce, Phillip felt the need of exercise, and since he hated his own company and would never go anywhere or do anything alone, Gail must go with him.

'Perhaps the children would like a walk,' she said. 'I'm rather tired.'

'Rubbish,' said Phillip in his peremptory manner. 'I don't want to go on a kids' outing. Besides, a walk will do you good. You need exercise after being in the house all day. Come on.'

Exercise! Ye gods!

She was so tired she could scarcely lift one foot after the other, but Phillip knew no compassion. He wanted to walk. He did not want to walk alone. Gail was his wife. Therefore Gail must walk. To his mind, the logic was unanswerable.

But after a time pains began to shoot through her, and she stopped and clung to the railing of a house, whilst Phillip still strode on ahead and did not become aware of her delay in following him for some time. Taking a walk did not necessarily imply that he wished for conversation with her. Indeed, in these days they had so little in common that he scarcely ever troubled to talk to her at all, spending his hours at home in moody silence alternating with bitter invective against the world in general and his lot in particular.

All the world, in fact, was out of step but Phillip Westing.

When he saw that Gail had stopped he stood waiting for her to catch up with him, and since she did not at once hurry forward to do so, he came back to her grudgingly.

'What's up?' he asked ungraciously.

He was so boorish in his general manner to her now that she often asked herself wearily whether he really did hate her, or whether it was just too much trouble to be polite to her. Kind he had never been.

'I feel ill,' she said.

He granted unsympathetically.

'Eaten too much, probably,' he said, though he never troubled himself to find out whether she ate or not.

She did not refute his statement. It was not worth it.

'I'd like to go back now,' she said, and he turned and began to walk back the way they had come, taking no notice of her but leaving her to drag back, helping herself by the railings. She felt sick and faint, and her chief terror was lest she should fall down in the street. Nobody was about on that dismal October evening, and she felt that if she fell she might lie there for hours before anyone found her. Phillip was evidently disposed to ignore her very existence since she had thwarted him in his desire for a walk.

Somehow she got back to the house, finding that Phillip had left the front door open for her, though he was nowhere to be seen, and she crawled up the stairs, holding the bannisters, and so into the bedroom, where she fell thankfully on the bed dressed as she was, lacking even the strength to take off her coat.

She had no idea how long she had lain there, though dimly she heard the children come up to bed, and downstairs the wireless was chirping away from some foreign station.

At last Phillip came into the bedroom, switched on the light, and looked at her as she lay on the bed, still fully dressed.

'Thought you'd gone to bed,' he said in a surly voice, and she knew he was aggrieved at having been left alone for a few hours, though he had not felt it incumbent on him to go up and see how she was, or if she needed anything.

'I feel so ill,' she said weakly.

His reply was a grunt, and he began to undress without taking any more notice of her, so that presently, realising she could not lie there all night as she was, she dragged herself off the bed and somehow managed to undress and get into bed. She was icy cold, but it never occurred to her to ask him to get her the hot-water bottle for which she longed. Somehow nobody ever did ask Phillip Westing for such small services, his wife least of all.

She slept fitfully, waking now and again to pain and wondering what had caused it, what she had eaten to upset her.

By morning, however, the pain was so acute that she had to rouse Phillip.

'Phillip—I'm so sorry—I feel so ill,' she said.

He sat up reluctantly. He was always difficult to wake, and resented being roused when he had to get up, and now, with a glance at his watch, he saw that it still lacked an hour to his usual time, so with a grunt he turned his back on her and went to sleep again.

Gail waited, and at last crawled out of bed and went in to rouse Joyce.

'Darling, I feel so ill. Would you get the breakfast for me this morning? And put on Dad's shaving-water? I'm going back to bed.'

When Joyce came in to wake her father he looked at Gail in surprise.

'Aren't you going to get up?' he asked her.

'No. I told you when I woke you before. I feel too ill,' said Gail, deathly white against the pillow.

He gave a sound between a grunt and a sniff.

'Well, you know what's the matter with you, don't you?' he said brutally. 'You're in labour.'

Gail swallowed and stared at him. It had never occurred to her. The child was not due for another two months, and she had been so normal all the time.

'But—it's too soon,' she said weakly.

'Well, it's probably a miss,' he said unfeelingly. 'I'll go out to telephone for the doctor when I'm dressed.'

But before he could finish his dressing it was apparent that this could not wait, and Joyce was bundled next door to telephone for the doctor.

Months ago there had been some acrimonious discussion about Phillip expressing the opinion that there was no need for Gail to go into hospital, but that all she needed was a midwife, and she could then go on conducting the affairs of the household from her bed so that neither he nor the children should suffer.

Gail had put her foot down on this, though on no other thing. She insisted on hospital, and that she be relieved of the household cares for at least that period.

The doctor looked grave. She must be got away at once. There were complications.

She clung to his hand.

'Doctor Penning, you won't let me lose my baby?' she asked him piteously.

'No, my dear. That's alright. I'll look after you,' he said, but outside the room he told Phillip privately that he feared greatly for the loss of either mother or child, if not both.

'I'll do everything humanly possible, Mr. Westing,' he said.

'Do what you like,' said Phillip, and when the ambulance came Gail was almost carried into it.

The Sister came to Phillip as he stood uncertainly in the hall.

'Don't worry, Mr. Westing,' she said soothingly. 'Your wife will be alright. She's young and strong. We shall do all we can. Of course there are difficulties, but everything possible will be done. Would you like to wait in here?' opening the door of a small, unoccupied ward.

'How long will it be, do you think?' asked Phillip.

'About an hour, the doctor thinks. If—if there is anything—well, we should let you go to her, of course.'

She left him so that she might go back to Gail.

For almost an hour they worked to save Gail and her baby, but eventually it was obvious that only one life could be saved, and that life the unconscious mother's.

'Better go and tell the husband,' said the doctor to a nurse, when there was nothing more to do for Gail, who lay like a marble woman, ignorant, uncaring. 'He knew it was touch and go, but at least we've saved the mother. He must be frantic by now.'

But when the nurse went to the room in which Phillip had been asked to wait, he had gone. Another nurse who had taken a cup of tea for him said that he had left immediately, had not waited even five minutes after they had taken Gail away for her ordeal.

Phillip had gone home to have a good breakfast, and then had set off for business, calling on the way to see a man about some new files he was needing. It took some hours to locate him by telephone to tell him that his wife still lived, but that the child was dead.

That was another of the things for which Gail never forgave him. His callous indifference to whether she lived or died, whether, if it be her last hour on earth, she would need him. At the time she was too grief-stricken at the loss of her baby to care greatly for anything, but that fresh proof of his real nature and the true position she held in his thoughts sank like iron into her soul forever.

Priscilla came quickly, was her first visitor, for on her way to the hospital Gail had remembered that she was to have seen her friend that afternoon and had asked Phillip, in between the agonising shafts of pain, if he would telephone to her. She had scarcely expected that he would trouble to do so, but in the afternoon Priscilla came, and Gail heard her cool and lovely voice in the reception hall near her room.

She should not have had visitors so soon, but the sister had been so deeply shocked by the indifference of Mrs. Westing's husband that she allowed this visitor a few minutes with the patient. Gail was normal now in body, and this gentle, soft-voiced visitor could do her no harm.

Priscilla brought pink carnations, a great fragrant sheaf of them, and laid them by Gail's bed.

'Thank you, Priscilla,' said the girl weakly, but she closed her eyes and said little else, and soon the older woman, with deep distress and pity, went softly away again. She knew that the vastness of Gail's sorrow for her baby went too far yet for any friend, however loving, to reach her, and she guessed also that Gail was remembering that she, Priscilla, had two children and a devoted husband, whilst Gail had nothing, not even memories, to stay her in this hour.

Phillip came in the evening to stand awkwardly by her bed, and she neither knew nor cared what his thoughts were at that moment.

He glanced at the mass of flowers which the day had produced – Priscilla's carnations, great tawny chrysanthemums which had borne Jeffrey Templar's card, and a bowl of white roses which had come without a card, but which Gail knew Kip had sent. Priscilla must have rung up these two men, and their first thought had been to show their sympathy and affection in the only way they could.

Phillip, who had come empty-handed, looked back at her.

'Sorry I couldn't bring you any flowers, my dear,' he said. 'I tried one or two places, but they were sold out.'

Gail smiled a little without looking at him. She knew that right opposite his office was a very large flower shop on which such a charge could never, in any circumstances, be laid, but she said nothing. She was glad he had not brought flowers. They would have seemed an insult just then.

There was nothing for them to say to each other, these two joined in the closest human relationship but poles apart in spirit, but when, after a few minutes, Phillip said he thought he had better go, Gail let a little of her heart's bitterness well from her.

'You're glad my baby is dead, aren't you, Phillip?' she asked in a hard, small voice.

'Well, dear, perhaps it's for the best,' he said, brightening a little at her method of approach. After all, she could not be feeling it so badly if she could speak like that. 'You'll soon get over it, you know.'

'I shall not want another baby,' she said. 'I could not go through it all again.'

He thought she meant the anguish of her labour, which had been so futile, but she would have endured that many times, and in greater degree, for women are made that way, fortunately for the survival of the race. What she meant was those months of his neglect, his indifference and worse. Children should have happiness in their conception and the months of their creation, and Gail could not give such happiness to Phillip's child.

She saw the relief and the complacence. How kind Fate always was to Phillip! In everything he got his own way. He had only to desire things to take a certain course for him, and they took it.

'I'm glad you have come to the conclusion that it isn't worth it,' he said with his first touch of heartiness. 'After all, we've got the other two children, and two are enough for anyone in these days, heaven knows. Be quick and get well and come home again,' but Gail, lying on her pillows with that small, secret smile hovering about her lips, knew that he was thinking of his comfort when he looked forward to her being at home again.

A day or two later Jeffrey Templar came.

Gail, very low in body and mind, as she was bound to be when the first exhaustion had passed, felt her eyes fill for the first time when she saw his kind, friendly face and the compassion in the shrewd blue eyes.

She took his hand, and on an impulse drew it down against her cheek.

'M'dear,' he said gently. 'I'm so very sorry. You know that.'

She let the tears fall weakly on that hand, strong and kind, that had never refused her help, never turned her away. Could she feel she had nothing, when these two friends remained to her, Jeffrey and Priscilla?

True to his practical nature, he assured himself that she needed for nothing material.

'You won't have to be worried about money or anything?' he asked her.

'No, Jeffrey. It's—wonderful of you—but you've always been wonderful to me.'

'Nonsense, m'dear,' he said. 'I believe you see me through rose-coloured spectacles and wearing a halo.'

'Slightly on one side,' added Gail with a smile, alluding to his habit of giving his hat a slightly rakish tilt, revealing the boy behind the middle-aged, successful man of the world. It is that everlasting boy in men which is so endearing to the women who love them, for a woman's love is so largely maternal.

She recovered her physical health quickly, almost too quickly, for in three weeks she was back at the little house which was again her prison, and she could realise now how the sweet hope of her child had stayed her, given point to her existence and made everything else insignificant.

Phillip, after the first brief pseudo-kindness, quickly relapsed into the old moods of surliness. Nothing was right for Phillip Westing, though, to an impartial observer, very many things might have seemed right for him.

One of the most irksome parts of his petty tyranny, Gail now found, was his curtailing of the housekeeping money in every possible way. He bought her a book, analysed in detail, and made her enter into it every penny she spent, going through it at the end of the week and marking threepence here, sixpence there, even odd pennies, which he considered need not have been spent, and the next week he would give her that much less until housekeeping became a nightmare to her and she was afraid to buy even absolute necessities, and certainly had nothing at all to spend on herself.

Phillip had never asked her how she had contrived to pay for the nursing home.

Eventually she went to see Mr. Hannam again.

He was apologetic.

'I'm sorry, Miss Marlin.' (She had always remained that to him, though, of course, he knew of her marriage.) 'If I could ask you to come back to us in your former capacity I should be only too glad, but business is not good. People don't care for antiques in the same way, and frankly I could not afford an extra salary. If, however, you would be prepared to work on commission, I might be able to give you jobs now and again, finding things I want, pieces to complete a set, special period pieces and so on.'

'I'd be glad of anything,' said Gail gratefully, and she found that the little money she could earn in this way from time to time kept her and the children in clothes, and helped her out with the housekeeping in difficult weeks.

But of course he did discover that she was earning money.

The discovery came from an outside source, a man whom he met in business casually and who also had contacts with Hannam's.

'I know you—or, rather, your wife, Westing,' this individual had said with bland unconsciousness of the wasps' nest he was stirring up. 'Doesn't she do work for Hannam's? I believe the old boy told me you were with Bradey's. He thinks the world of her, you know. It seems that last week she ran some old prints to earth which he'd been wanting for years, and bought them for him at a price which left him almost in tears of gratitude to her.'

Phillip said nothing, but when he came home that evening Gail saw the signs of the gathering storm and sent the children off to bed early, in spite of their protests.

When the storm broke he accused her of everything he could think of – deception, theft, undermining the characters of his children, an illicit association with Hannam (who was sixty-eight and a grandfather), neglect of his home – a long series of accusations which reduced her to a state of impotent fury.

In vain she explained, tried to justify herself, denied this, admitted that, he refused to listen, shouting her down until she realised that he had no intention of allowing her a voice in her own defence.

'I wonder if you know how I hate you, Phillip,' she said at last in a tone of concentrated bitterness and fury.

'I know you do. You make that apparent. You only stay with me so that I shall have to keep you. You'd rather be my widow than my wife, wouldn't you, you cold-blooded, sexless woman. Well, why not get rid of me? There's the carving-knife. Stick it into me. Go on! Stick it into me!' he taunted her, and pushed the knife, still lying on the table, towards her until the handle touched her fingers. 'Ha! Haven't got the pluck, have you? Rather do your miserable little cheating behind my back, wouldn't you?'

For an hour he had taunted her, accused her, goaded her, knowing her quick temper and delighting in rousing her to fury, and Gail knew for an awful moment that she was capable of doing what he tempted her to do with that evil-looking knife, and so she turned and fled, out of the room, out of the house, anywhere out of reach of his jibing tongue, out of sight of his cruel face with its mocking smile.

It was a bitterly cold night, but she walked about with neither hat nor coat and in her thin house shoes, hour after hour across the bleak, deserted common, careless of the drizzling rain, until at last, exhausted and beaten, she crawled back to the house, expecting that she would find Phillip waiting up for her and possibly ready to begin the quarrel again.

But he had not even waited up. Careless of where she was, or in what physical and mental condition, he had gone to bed, and when she staggered up the stairs, wet and chilled through, he was in bed and peacefully asleep!

In the morning she was hot and shivering, but rose as usual to see to the breakfast and get the children off to school, and to give Phillip breakfast half an hour afterwards, because he always refused to get up until the very last minute, though she had more than once pointed out to him the waste of gas and food in making two breakfasts when one would have done.

He did not speak to her, but gave her a sly, triumphant look as he went out, a look which showed her plainly that he felt he had had the best of last night's quarrel, and Gail struggled through her day knowing that she was in a fever and ought to be tucked up in bed and kept warm and free from worry.

The next day she had to give in, to Phillip's unconcealed irritation, seeing that he had had to have the breakfast left for him by Joyce or take the unthinkable alternative of cooking fresh food for himself. The child had brought Gail a cup of tea, but Phillip did not ask her if she wanted anything else done.

When he came home that evening he was displaying a loud, raucous, obviously artificial cough, which was especially loud and raucous whenever he came near the bedroom where Gail still lay. She sighed. She knew the signs, and next morning, when Joyce called him, he told her in a hoarse whisper, accompanied by the cough, that he was not well enough to get up. He thought he had the flu.

They could not both lie there with no one to do anything in the house, and though Joyce had offered to stay at home, Gail knew she was working hard for a scholarship and could not afford the loss of a day, so she struggled out of bed, dressed herself, and did what was necessary in the house.

When Phillip was about again he made capital out of what he called 'my bad illness' in order to glean from anyone who came his way that pity without which he seemed unable to exist. The fact that he did not get it from Gail turned him further against her, but she would not prostitute her intelligence to pander to his vanity, though she had to prostitute her body for the lusts of his.

The net result of his discovery that she was earning money, however, was added comfort for her, for she need not now hesitate to take commissions from Hannam's and from other houses which previously she had felt bound to refuse, and her income grew to larger, if still very modest, proportions. She was given some sketches to make for various purposes, and one of the museums employed her in the compiling of a new illustrated guide to the collection, which work not only brought her good remuneration, but also brought her into touch with cultured and pleasant people who liked her personality and her work and were glad to put in her way anything which might help her.

She ignored Phillip's cheese-paring ways, ceased to care whether he cut her housekeeping money down or not, and merely permitted herself to despise him in secret when she saw how pleased he was to have the last of his responsibilities taken from him. He still paid a pittance into the house, calling it grandly 'your housekeeping allowance', but he knew, and Gail felt sure he knew, that the bulk of the responsibility was left on her whilst he presumably saved his money, for except for his clothes and his cigarettes, he spent nothing. She was told once that he had the reputation amongst men of leaving a bar before it was his turn to pay for the round, and she believed it.

They moved into a better house, largely because for a long time Phillip had grumbled about the one which, at the time of their marriage, had seemed almost luxurious to him. He had soon forgotten the discomforts and sordid ugliness from which he had come, and found 5 Reedsdale Road too small, too crowded, inconvenient, difficult of access – a hundred things which Gail had accepted and would have continued to accept.

However, he harped on the one string until she agreed that they might move. For one thing, she could now afford help in the house, and a little maid would give her more time for the increasing needs of her work.

In the negotiations for the new house Phillip completely Justified Jeffrey Templar's original estimate of him, for he refused to agree that any part of the money paid for the present house was either Gail's or due to her efforts, asserting that all the payments made had been out of his pocket, as the cashed cheques could prove; that accordingly there was no justification in Gail's claim to be part owner of this house, and therefore of the new house whose initial payment was to be met out of the net proceeds of the sale of 5 Reedsdale Road.

She ceased to argue the point, and again Phillip got his way, but he had dropped even lower in her respect for him. It was found necessary, after all, to put more money down on the house in order to get a building society mortgage, and Phillip took Gail up to town to dinner one night, to her vast surprise and greatly to her pleasure and appreciation, only to reveal to her later that he wanted to borrow two hundred pounds from her.

It was all the money she had, and it had been laboriously saved for some purpose which she would not admit even to herself as yet, and she knew that he could only have known of her possession of that sum by prying about amongst her papers.

'I've felt for a long time that this little house is not good enough for you, my dear,' he said to her, and she wondered if he really thought she believed him, and said nothing.

'There's another thing, Gail. I can get rid of the mortgage Templar holds over our heads. I've never liked the man. I don't like his attitude to me, and I don't like his interest in you.'

Gail was roused to a defence of Jeffrey.

'Don't be idiotic, Phillip,' she said. 'Mr. Templar has no interest in me except a more or less fatherly one.'

Phillip did not really believe in many of the things of which he frequently accused her. It was simply that it seemed necessary to him to find things for which to condemn her. He hated her efficiency and feared her success.

'Well, anyway, I'd rather owe money to a building society than to Jeffrey Templar,' he said, and Gail dropped the subject.

They moved into the new house, and at first her belief that it would make a lasting change for the better in their lives seemed justified. Phillip liked the larger rooms, the added importance it gave him to have a better address, and though he still neither brought visitors to the house nor encouraged Gail to do so, he took a pride in the place and expressed himself satisfied with it.

He became more expansive in his talk, and his periods of moody silence were fewer and shorter, and Gail listened with what interest she could to his political distributes, his condemnation of the Government whatever they did, and his tales of his own prowess in the office, where, if he were to be believed, Gail felt he must be heartily disliked by both colleagues and employers.

Once she offered a faint protest.

'If I'd ever been as rude as that to my employer, I should have expected and deserved the sack,' she said, when he had boasted about some reply he had made to Mr. Bradey, of whom actually he stood in wholesome fear so that she doubted if he had ever used the words he claimed.

He sneered.

'You always were a boot-licker,' he said. 'Look at the hours you used to work for that blighter Delaney without a penny overtime.'

She would not argue with him, especially about Kip.

She often wondered in after years that she had remained with him so long, put up with so much, allowed him to dominate so many valuable years of her swiftly passing youth. She found her answer in his children, in their love for her, their dependence on her for happiness, their development along the lines she herself had chosen for them.

Joyce seemed to be shooting towards womanhood like a rocket, growing tall and willowy, a delicate loveliness succeeding the prettiness of childhood. She always seemed to Gail a strange flower for Phillip Westing to have produced, and could only conclude that Joyce was like her mother, for neither in appearance nor in character did she appear to have inherited anything from her father. She was intelligent but not brilliant, and she quite unaffectedly preferred home life to a career, and hoped she would marry young and have babies. She consciously modelled herself on Gail, who felt herself to be hopelessly inadequate as a model, but who in consequence found herself living up to the best in her and keeping down the worst in order that Joyce might not someday look her in the eyes and accuse her.

Hugh was a different proposition, tough, wiry, aggressive.

But there were happy times, even gay times, nearly all of them of Gail's making. There were occasional, if very rare, jaunts to town, to a pantomime or a variety show, Phillip deciding the price of the seats and knowing that Gail would wish to have something better, so that they compromised on going into the better seats, and Phillip paying for his own whilst she paid for the other three. He called this 'going fifty-fifty.'

Chapter Eleven

'Goodbye, Gail. Goodbye, darling, and—thank you—thank you for everything.'

There was almost a sob in the happy voice, and Gail held her step-daughter, today's bride, closely for a moment.

'Goodbye, sweet. All happiness. Don't keep your husband waiting, my darling.'

Joyce laughed, the joyous laughter of pure happiness.

'How lovely she's looked all day!' said Gail to the man who stood sulkily with, and yet not a part of, the gay crowd.

Phillip Westing did not reply save by a non-committal grunt, but Gail took no notice. He had too long ago ceased to exist as a force in her life, and she would not allow anything to dim the happiness of Joyce's wedding day.

Gail, at thirty-one, looked scarcely more than a girl herself today, in her perfectly cut dress of rust-coloured crepe, banded with soft summer fur, a string of clear, golden amber her only adornment. She wore the colourings of autumn, but there was no suggestion of autumn in her smooth face with its delicate unobtrusive make-up and her slender figure.

The years that had brought her experience had added to, rather than lessened, the attraction of her youth. Looking at her, one realised that this was a woman who could give much to life, but knew now what she had to give and that she would ask much in return.

Hugh came back to her. He had not shot up like Joyce, but had remained no more than medium height, and had probably, at twenty, stopped growing. He was dark, thin, wiry, impish, with a little of the cynicism which now and again aped his father's and would later on spoil his present boyishness, though Gail had fought against it and made him able to laugh at himself, which Phillip Westing would never be able to do.

Hugh slipped a hand within her arm.

'Good show,' he said.

'Joyce looked lovely, didn't she? And I think she's going to be happy with Ray,' said Gail on a note of happiness tinged with that sadness inescapable when a beloved bride has gone joyously to fulfil her destiny.

They paced the garden. The guests would be leaving soon, and Gail on duty again, but for just these few minutes she could take her leisure.

'Tired?' Hugh asked her.

'No, but—since you ask me that, I may as well tell you that I'm planning to take a little holiday,' she said, and there was a certain note in her voice which made him glance swiftly at her.

'Dad going?' he asked.

'No,' said Gail, and there was one of those brief silences more pregnant than words.

It was Gail who broke it.

'Hugh, you're alright at Dickenson's, aren't you?'

'Yes. Fine. Old Dickenson was about yesterday, and he talked to me and I showed him my new model, you know, the eighty-eight, and he was quite keen about it, and I shouldn't be surprised if he asks me to make it on a larger scale, with more detail.'

'That's good. I thought you were getting somewhere with that,' she said. 'I'm so glad for you, Hugh, I shall enjoy my holiday better.'

'Where will you go?' he asked her.

'Oh—I don't know—anywhere, everywhere. I have no plans. I shall pack my nicest clothes and my roughest, so as to be ready for anything, and I shall start from Folkestone, which seems to me such a nice, clean place to start from, and I shall go to—oh, Switzerland, Germany, Italy, anywhere my fancy guides me.'

'You sound as if it were going to be a long holiday, Gail,' said Hugh, looking at her closely.

'Maybe,' she said. 'I've been wanting this holiday for a long time, but I also wanted to wait until—oh, until you were settled and Joyce was married. Your father has never liked Ray.'

'Does he ever like anybody?' asked Hugh with a little laugh.

He knew what she meant. If she had gone away, leaving Joyce with her father and still unmarried, Phillip might somehow have contrived to spoil that romance, even to ruin it irretrievably. Gail had made up her mind that it should not be ruined. Also, Phillip had not wanted Hugh to go into Dickenson's, and the two had been more or less at loggerheads over it during the whole two years. If Hugh had gone into Bradey's, to occupy the stool Phillip had found for him, he would have been earning more than he had been all this time at Dickenson's and able to pay his own way at home. As it was, he had little more than pocket-money whilst he learned his job, and Gail had had to keep him. If she had been away for some time, with Hugh still struggling for notice and advancement, Phillip might have forced him to give up his chosen work from the sheer need to earn his keep.

Gail did not comment on Hugh's unfilial criticism. The time had gone by when she felt the need to protect Phillip from his children's eyes. If they now saw him as he was, it was his own fault, not hers.

'You think Dickenson will give you a lift-up, Hugh?'

He nodded.

'Jukes says so,' he said, and Gail heard the little note of pride behind the laconic reply, and shared that feeling of accomplishment.

They walked again for a few moments without speaking, and then he said, apparently apropos of nothing: 'Bob Hastings and his wife are moving from their flat into a little house. They asked if I'd like to go in with them, nearer the works, and all that. I said perhaps, presently.'

She held his arm more closely. She knew what he was trying to say to her. He wanted her to know that he would be alright, that he was on his feet.

'I like Bob,' she said, 'and Janet's a dear.'

He knew she had understood.

'You've been pretty swell to us, Gail,' he said.

'You've been pretty swell to me,' she said with a smile.

'Gail—'

She waited. Hugh had never found it easy to express himself.

'Gail? I often wonder why you did it—married Dad, you know.'

'Oh—I was young, romantic, couldn't get the man I wanted, was too impatient to wait, took the man who seemed to want me,' she said, her tone light, casual, matching her smile.

'And there were us, Joyce and me,' he said.

'Mmps.'

'You're still young, Gail.'

She laughed a little.

'You still think that thirty-one is young?' she asked, teasing him a little.

'It's young enough,' he said, and then she saw that some of the guests were looking for her, wanting to leave, and she pressed his arm again and left him, going across the grass to them, serene, charming, sure of herself, a woman who knew herself to be liked and who liked in return.

Later, when they had all gone, when Hugh had wandered off on some business of his own, and the little maid was able to sit down and rest after Gail and the daily woman had helped with the clearing up and the washing of dishes and glasses, the mistress of this pleasant house was free to attend to her own concerns.

They had left their second house some two or three years ago, Phillip having quickly discovered that it no more suited his ever-increasing sense of his own importance than had 5 Reedsdale Road, and since then they had been living in a more distant suburb, in a delightful modern house with a garden and a view. Gail had found most of the money for it, but she had by that time reached a stage when it was not difficult for her to find a few hundreds, nor greatly to miss them if, as seemed probable, they went beyond recall, as did everything else of hers which Phillip could handle.

Phillip was lounging in an easy chair by the open window, the warm July sunshine reluctant to leave the garden though the evening had set in.

It was a good place, a pleasant place, but to Gail it had never been more than that. She had cared for it and worked in it and for it because her nature demanded that she do her best for anything in her environment and left to her care, but it had never been a home, though she had lived in it for several years.

Phillip did not look up from his book. It was only Gail.

But she spoke to him, rather surprisingly. He did not like to be spoken to when he was reading, and had always made it clear.

'Phillip, can you spare a few minutes?' she asked quietly.

He lowered his book without putting it down.

'I suppose so,' he said ungraciously.

'I am going away,' she said.

He frowned.

'What, just now? Just when Joyce has gone, and Hugh is always out?' he asked. 'You know how I hate to be left on my own.'

'I'm afraid you will have to get over that,' she said in a very clear, level tone. 'I am leaving you, Phillip.'

This time he put the book down and did not even remember to mark the place. He stared at her, his jaw dropping a little, and then he closed his lips like a trap.

'What's the idea?' he said, shooting the words at her from that tight mouth.

'Simply that my job here is done, and my life is my own again,' she said.

'What do you mean by that? You're still my wife, aren't you?' he snarled.

'Legally perhaps, but neither physically nor mentally,' said Gail calmly. 'I have not been your wife for some years, as you know.'

'That's not been my fault,' he rapped out at her.

'I know. I'm quite willing to admit that I have been the one to end that side of our marriage. It was an indignity to both of us to retain the physical relationship when our minds were utterly dissociated. I won't say our souls, because you don't believe in souls. You believe only in bodies.'

'You can't leave me. I shall not allow you to do so,' said Phillip pompously. 'You are my wife in the eyes of the world, and my wife you will remain.'

She smiled.

'Oh no, Phillip, you can't keep me here like that, you know,' she said, amused. 'The days have gone by, however much you may regret them, when you could tie me to the bed-post or look me up or starve me into submission. I don't belong to you. I belong to myself, and now that my job here is done, Joyce happily married, Hugh safely settled in the work he really wants to do and will do well, I can begin to pay the debt I owe to myself. I don't suppose it has ever occurred to you, Phillip, that I am entitled to any happiness or pleasure just for myself, has it?'

'You're talking a lot of rubbish,' he said. 'Pleasure? Your life's nothing but pleasure, with servants to do your work for you so that you can go gadding about—'

'I work,' put in Gail mildly.

'Work? What you call work,' he said contemptuously. 'Besides, there's no need for you to work. I provided a home for you, and you chose to find your work outside it, and now you try to put the blame on me.'

'I think you're a bit confused, Phillip, but the only thing I have to say, in passing, is that your refusal to accept your responsibilities and your essential meanness both of mind and money forced me to find a means of earning a living, and my own hard work made it a success. However, I am not going to enter into the old futile arguments, nor am I going to quarrel with you, however much you want to quarrel. I need not have told you I was going. I could have walked out of the house and left you to find out. I am telling you, however, and I am quite definitely leaving you.'

'Who's the man?' he demanded wrathfully, assuming a menacing attitude over her.

She drew back.

'Don't get yourself into a state, Phillip,' she said. 'We're not alone in the house, and I'm not afraid of you—nowadays. As for your question, it is typical of your mentality and needs no answer.'

'You can't deny that there's another man then?' he asked sneeringly. 'Well, who is he? Out with it!'

'You fool,' said Gail contemptuously. 'You can't believe, because it hurts your pride too much, that a woman would prefer to live alone than to live with you. There is no other man.'

'I don't believe you,' he said furiously. 'I tell you this much, though. I'll never divorce you. I'll never set you free to give to another man what you won't give me. Understand? No matter when you ask it, nor how, nor why, I'll never give you a divorce. Understand?'

Her lip curled and she turned away.

'You really are a fool, Phillip,' she said. 'But then, if you weren't, you'd have had the sense to see on which side your bread was buttered and been at least civil enough to me to make it possible for me to tolerate you. You have everything to lose and little to gain by my going, and you know it. It's too late. My mind is quite made up. I am going away tomorrow and I shall not come back,' and she walked out of the room and upstairs to her own bedroom, where she went on with the packing not yet finished.

Her heart was beating quickly. Though she had betrayed nothing of the things she had felt in that interview, it had not been easy for her to keep her self-control in face of his gibes and anger, but she was glad that she had been able to say just what she had meant to say and no more.

At this house they had had separate rooms. Gail had arranged it without reference to him, and he had, to her surprise and relief, accepted the arrangement without comment, though many times he had tried her door handle and found the door locked against him, nor had she at any time admitted him. That chapter of their life was closed, and if he had been unfaithful to her, as she felt was very probable, she neither raised the question nor wished to know. Her continuance of their life together had nothing to do with him.

In the morning, everything was ready, the big case with her best dresses and light shoes, her hat-box, the smaller case with strong shoes, mackintosh and an old tweed suit, a little dressing-case and necessities for a night or two.

She looked at herself in the glass and smiled.

She saw a slender, graceful woman in grey travelling kit, sturdy little shoes of lizard skin to match her fitted bag, good grey gloves, little pull-on hat of grey-blue felt with a jaunty quill through its crown. There was a light in her eyes, and the touch of colour in her cheeks and the red of her lips had not come out of boxes, though she did not despise these in times of need.

She dusted her nose with powder again, stood upright and drew a deep breath.

She was free.

At last, after all these years of bondage, she was free!

A tap at the door brought her to it.

'Please, madam, the master says will you go and have a word with him?' asked the maid, a frightened look on her face.

'Where is he, Florence?' she asked.

'In his room, madam. I think something's wrong,' she said, and Gail, with a little exclamation of annoyance, went along the corridor and opened the door of her husband's room.

Phillip lay half on the floor, half on the bed, groaning, his head in his hands.

She stood looking at him for a moment, her eyes narrowing, her mind going back to those other times when, as a last resort, he had pretended severe illness. Was this just another of those things? Or was she really to have the cup of freedom dashed from her lips before she had had time to taste it?

'What's the matter?' she asked him in a cold, unfeeling voice.

'Shut the door,' he gasped, and she shut it.

'Gail, I—oh Gail—I couldn't bear you to go and—I've taken poison. I—wanted you to be free of me. It—it was all—I could do for you.'

He had overdone it. With those last sentences he had destroyed the effect he had striven to create.

She went across to the dressing-table where a tumbler lay on its side, artistically disposed, a little white substance at the bottom of it.

She wetted her finger, dipped it into the substance, and tasted it. Then she went to the medicine cupboard over the wash-basin, looked for what she wanted, and found it – a small white box. There was a still damp finger mark on it, as if Phillip had had the idea whilst washing or shaving, and had hastily put it into operation.

With the box in her hand, she went across to where Phillip lay groaning, though furtively watching her, wondering if he had underestimated her power of penetration.

'Get up, Phillip,' she said, and he struggled to his feet, swayed violently, caught at the bed for support and finally sat on the edge of it, holding his throat between his two hands.

'Burns,' he said weakly. 'Burns.'

'You're overdoing it, Phillip,' said Gail, her voice crisp, faintly amused and yet contemptuous. 'Soda mint tablets don't burn, you know.'

He rolled his eyes at her.

'What do you mean? Who's taken soda mints?' he asked, not quite sure if that really was the box she had in her hand.

But it was. She was looking at it more fixedly, as if memory were waking, and a frown replaced the smile.

'You know, Phillip, I'm just thinking – trying to remember – you did have soda mints in this box, but the other day I thought they were not quite good any longer, and I *believe* – I can't be sure, but I *believe* that this was the box into which I put those tablets the vet left for poor Tombo's ears. You remember he said we must be careful not to let Tombo lick them because they're poison—good heavens, Phillip, I think I must have put them in this soda mint box. Why, what's the matter?' as he got up from the bed, covered the distance between them in a stride and snatched the box from her hand, staring at it in incredible horror.

'My God, Gail! You didn't—you couldn't—you've poisoned me! You've killed me! Send for a doctor! Tell him he must come at once! Say it's life and death! You've poisoned me!'

But Gail was laughing, very gently, very indulgently laughing.

'Poor Phillip, so you did take soda mints, did you? Don't worry. I put the rest of poor Tombo's tablets in the fire. You haven't eaten any. I should get dressed now if I were you. The soda mints won't do you any harm, though it's usual to take them after a meal and not before.'

He had seen that she was ready, even to her hat, and he caught at her hand.

'Don't leave me, Gail. I know I didn't take poison, but I wanted to. I can't go on living if you leave me. I'm a sick man. I shan't trouble you long. I've never told you, but it's my heart. The doctor—'

She drew her hand away and now she was not laughing. There was a sick feeling inside her. If only he could have retained the semblance of a man she might have stayed with him, but this weakling, this snivelling little bully of a man – what had she to do with him any longer?

'Phillip, don't,' she said. 'Don't demean yourself and me. We've had so much of that – rheumatoid arthritis wasn't it the first time? And then cancer, consumption, pneumonia – and now heart disease. It doesn't work, Phillip. It will never work anymore. Face up to life. Be a man. Stand on your own feet. You're not old. Forty-five is nothing in these days for a man. There's time for much in your life yet, but only if you are a man and meet whatever comes like a man.'

'Don't go, Gail,' he said, and tried to clutch her again, but she eluded him, walked past him and out of the room, closing the door behind her.

Outside, she drew a deep breath of relief. So much she had endured, so much. Not at this last moment was she to be cajoled into surrender.

Florence was bobbing about anxiously.

'It's alright, Florence,' said Gail. 'Your master will be down very soon. Give him a nice breakfast and see that his coffee's hot and that there's plenty of hot milk. Is the taxi here?'

'Yes, ma'am,' said Florence. 'I hope you have a nice holiday, ma'am. Oh, thank you, ma'am,' fervently, as Gail put a pound note into her hand before picking up her dressing-case. The other luggage had gone down to the cab.

Five minutes later Gail had gone, without one backward glance, and in an hour's time she was in the train for Folkestone.

Chapter Twelve

'Nothing else, madame?'

'Nothing else, thank you, André.'

'*Paris Soir*, madame?' said the little waiter, handing her the paper.

She smiled and took it.

'Thank you, Andre,' she said, but sat for a little while on the hotel terrace with the newspaper in her hand, not caring to read it, wondering what to do, whether she should not, after all, go home.

She had had a wonderful time, seen beauty and wrapped her soul in it until she felt that nothing sordid and unlovely could ever hurt her again whilst that memory lasted; she had met people, had fun, spent a lot of money – but perhaps she ought to now go home.

Home.

Where exactly would home be?

She had no definite plans, except that she would like a garden, so that ruled out her other liking for a London flat. Perhaps she would live in the flat, but have a tiny cottage somewhere and go there at the weekends, have some kindly woman there to look after it for her and welcome her so that she would have a feeling of home-coming.

She could afford that, if she were careful, and she had no desire for extravagant or luxurious living.

During the years when she had been waiting for Joyce and Hugh to grow up she had been consolidating her own position, and eventually the unbelievable had happened and old Erasmus Hannam, dying, had left her the complete stock of a business which had been moribund for years, and which, in his will, he had almost apologised to her for bequeathing to her.

That had been three years ago, and Gail had worked like a slave to revive a business which had once been able to keep dead and gone Hannams in something more than just comfort.

The turning out of the old storerooms had revealed treasures which the old man had not known he possessed, amongst them half a dozen plates which Gail knew had been sought the world over by a wealthy American collector, who had at length come to the conclusion that they were non-existent.

Gail had been able to name her own price, an exorbitant one which had made her quake whilst she waited for his reply, but he paid up like a lamb, and with the proceeds of the sale Gail had been able to take a lease on new and more suitable premises, where she could display to advantage her china and exquisite old glass, some brasses which also had been hidden for a generation or more, and the famous Ellendale miniatures which had been the choice morsels of Hannam's known collection.

She had put in charge of the shop a man whose honesty and knowledge were beyond praise, and she herself had used her energies outside, attending sales, hunting bargains, always improving her acquaintances with the business, and always ready to seize every opportunity of outside work for museums, collections and private individuals to whom her skill with pencil and colour could be useful.

So she could afford to live in reasonable comfort, even modest luxury, especially now that she had only herself to keep, neither Joyce nor Hugh, nor need she be responsible for the partial dependence and constant demands of Phillip.

Sitting on the terrace of her Paris hotel, where she had come in her journeyings, possibly her last stopping place *en route* for home, she found herself strangely, rather disappointingly, reluctant to take up the new life. Once its loneliness would not have worried her, but for ten years she had not lived alone, and she would miss the comings and goings of the children, miss even the difficult, depressing presence of Phillip himself.

She turned to the newspaper, idly glancing through it, and came to the English column, which gave news of the doings and whereabouts of her countrymen in the French capital.

And a name arrested her eyes, the name of the man of whom she had tried not to think for years.

Strange that she should see this name now, just new.

Mr. Kipling Delaney, the celebrated English actor-playwright, has arrived at the "Hotel Guillaume", where he expects to spend a few days.

Kip in Paris! She glanced out across the boulevard over which the terrace looked. Some distance away, through a narrow opening in the buildings, she could just see the tall block with its name in shining lights, HOTEL GUILLAUME.

Somewhere behind those lights was Kip!

She scarcely knew she had had the impulse, but she was moving towards the telephone when she realised it, and stopped short.

No, better not. Better let things remain where they were. She had come to a place of comparative peace. The old aching was no longer intolerable. It was as if she thought of someone dead, some lovely thing she once had had but no longer grieved over losing. Better leave things like that.

It was nine years since they had met, and for the last four of them she had not even been able to see him because he had given up acting in order to write and produce his successful plays.

Two years ago Gilda had died. Gail saw the announcement in the papers but she did not write to him. She had made her life, such as it was, and to meet him again would only complicate it and she did not know whether he would even want her to contact him, though that thought sent a shaft of pain through her.

She had not allowed herself to look too far ahead. She had more or less come to terms with Phillip, her terms rather than his. She no longer quarrelled with him or even argued. If he asked her anything about her business, she told him, though she knew such questions had been prompted by his bitter jealousy. Apart from the business which kept her fully and pleasurably occupied, her only interest lay in Phillip's children who had become more and more attached to her as the years went by. Now, her self-imposed burden which she had never regarded as a burden, could be laid down and she was free.

She put aside the newspaper and went to dress for the evening.

She was going to see *Samson and Delilah*, to hear a famous pair whom she might never hear together again. It was one of the things for which she had come to Paris. She was not truly a music-lover, but some things she loved to hear, and this was one of them.

She amused herself by dressing *en grande toilette*, the position of her seat in the opera-house justifying it, and she wore a gown she had bought in Brussels, heavy charmeuse in a deep, dull gold, with a necklace of rough turquoise which she had picked up at a sale, had had cleaned and re-set and retained for herself. She wore the same blue stones in her ears, whilst her hands were bare save for the narrow gold band of her wedding ring.

She had a cape of very nearly Russian sable, and wore it with an air so that only a connoisseur in furs, seeing it on her gracious, almost regal figure, would have dared to question its integrity.

Gail knew, and hated its insincerity, but she could not have afforded the real thing. Besides, she had so few occasions when she could wear a fur cape at all.

She had a seat in one of the boxes, an end seat of the tier, and was arranging herself comfortably and hoping that the second seat would not be occupied, when suddenly she saw Kip.

He was alone, in evening dress, standing in the gangway a little below where she sat, and at first she thought he was waiting for someone. Then a girl attendant asked him a question, and his reply came audibly to her in that voice trained to make its faintest whisper carry.

'*Merci. Je suis seul*,' and the girl, giving him a coquettish glance, looked at his ticket and began to lead him up, nearer to Gail.

When he was on a level with her, so near that she could have touched him, the girl paused and pointed along the row on the other side.

Gail did not pause to think. She did not consciously think at all, save that in a moment he would be gone, swallowed up amongst that sea of expectant faces.

She leaned forward.

'Kip!'

For a split second he stood quite still, and she thought he had not heard her. Then he turned round slowly, and was looking into her eyes, unbelieving, dazed with surprise.

'Gail!'

The attendant, believing him satisfied, had gone to help someone else, and they remained there, these two, lost in the contemplation of each other and this thing that had happened to them.

Then Kip glanced at the empty seat beside her.

'Are you alone?' he asked.

'Quite,' said Gail, a thrill in her voice at the wonderful truth of that.

'Wait. I'll see if anyone is coming into that seat. If so, I'll find others,' and he was gone.

Soon he would be back, everything arranged. Everything always did arrange itself marvellously for Kip. After the years of Phillip's bungling ineptitude, his fear of doing anything unconventional which always made them miss the best of everything, it was lovely to hear Kip's calm 'I'll find others'. He came back and opened the door of the box.

'Come along, Gail.'

'Is the other seat taken?' she asked.

'I don't know. I didn't ask. There was a private box,' and he slid a hand beneath her elbow and took her to where an attendant waited to show them to their box, a little velvet-hung sanctuary where she was alone with Kip.

They smiled into each other's eyes and needed no words, even if they could have found them, but presently, when he had taken her cloak and bought her a programme and a big box of extravagantly beribboned chocolates, he spoke softly.

'How wonderful you look, Gail.'

'And how wonderful you look, Kip.'

They laughed. Oh, but it was good—good—to be together again, and when the lights went down, his hand slipped through her arm and found her fingers, which curled about his own, and so they sat, entranced by the music, entranced by each other, poised between heaven and earth, in that special place which is the prerogative of lovers.

Now and then they spoke a little.

'Are you in Paris alone, Kip?'

'Yes. And you?'

'*Moi aussi.*'

It was enough. What else did they need to know? The night was young, and no one in the whole wide world could lay claim to them unless or until they chose.

'Where are you staying, Gail?'

'At the Ambassadors. You're at the Guillaume.'

'How did you know?'

'*It was in Paris Soir.*'

'And you didn't let me know?'

'I didn't know if you would want to know.'

'*Oh, Gail!*'

They sat hushed by the exquisite beauty of the voice which sang Samson to his destruction.

'Mon cœur s'œuvre à ta voix.'

Kip slid an arm about Gail's shoulders, and held her so.

'As my heart opens at your voice, beloved,' he whispered, and then she knew that nothing had changed for them, that everything was the same – and yet everything gloriously different.

They sat on for a little while after the last note of music had slipped away into memory, the last round of applause ceased, but in their hearts was no consciousness of ending, but rather of beginning.

Finally they turned to each other with questioning eyes.

'We'll go somewhere and talk,' said Kip. 'Evening in Paris, and you, my sweet! Was there ever such blessed juxtaposition? And see what you have done to me already, to give me a word like that!' and he laughed for pure joy of this moment, and Gail tucked a hand within his arm and laughed with him.

To be with him again! To hear his laughter! To be able to laugh at small, silly jokes again! It was to be re-born.

'I know just the place,' said Kip, and he took her to a roof garden high over Paris, a place of palms in pots, and straggling shrubs and great jars of flowers, of little nooks and discreetly shaded lights which made no attempt to vie with the lights of Paris, the sort of place which one would find in no other city in the world.

Kip ordered a gala supper with champagne, and over it they talked, and Gail told him of her business, its successes and failures, of Joyce and Ray honeymooning somewhere in Scotland, of Hugh and his aeroplanes, whilst Kip spoke of his plays, and so, always going round and round the circle of things, they came gradually to its centre.

'And—Phillip, Gail?' asked Kip at last, when she had told him of her holidaying through Europe alone.

She met his eyes steadily.

'I've left Phillip, Kip,' she said in a quiet voice.

He drew a deep breath.

'What may I say to that, Gail? That I'm sorry? You know it isn't true. I am glad. But I'm sorry that things had to go that way for you. I've grieved for you all these years. I've known, of course, that you were not happy in your marriage.'

'Priscilla?' asked Gail.

'Yes, and Cora, though she has been more reticent. It's been a nightmare to me to think of you being unhappy, of all women in the world, *you*. And to be so helpless. What could I have done for you at any time? Priscilla always told me I could do nothing, but it was a ghastly business to stand by and not even try to help you.'

'You couldn't have helped me, Kip. Nobody could. I just had to dree my own weird,' she said with a little smile.

Oh, she could afford to smile now! Kip was there, and Phillip already growing like the memory of an unpleasant dream on waking.

'Anyway, you're not going back to him again?' he asked, and there was authority in his voice. He was making a statement.

'No, I'm never going to do that,' said Gail quietly. 'That is finished.'

He squared his shoulders.

'So—it's forward for us, Gail?'

She nodded her head, that bright head, that well-remembered gesture!

'You know about Gilda?'

'Yes, Kip. It was in the papers.'

'But you didn't write?'

'No. It was difficult. There were the children. They depended on me so much. I couldn't let them down, and—I didn't know how you still felt about things. I wanted you to be—free.'

'I was in chains from the moment I met you. I never wanted to be freed from them but I couldn't have come to you. I had to wait for you to come to me. Have you come, beloved?'

'If you want me, Kip,' she said very simply, and he pushed aside the flimsy little table and took her in his arms.

'If I want you? If I *want* you? Oh Gail, my dear, my dearest, the years I've longed to do just this,' he said, and in his beautiful voice was the note that only she had heard, would ever hear.

'Phillip—'

'Need we talk about him? Does he matter to us anymore?'

'He'll never divorce me, Kip. He told me so.'

'I imagine that's typical of the man. Having done his best to wreck your life and make it a burden, he'd keep you from having happiness now. Does he know about me?'

'No. That's the odd thing. Eaten up with jealousy as he was, accusing me of affairs with all sorts of men including poor old Mr. Hannam, he never even thought of the one man it could have been, the only man I love or have ever loved. I didn't even tell him when I left him. You see—I didn't know we should ever find each other again.'

His arm tightened about her and he kissed her. The little waiter, hovering near, decided that they would not want anything else. Of all the people in the world who love a lover, there is none to equal a Frenchman.

'Ah, l'amour, l'amour!' he sighed as he went away.

'And now that we have met—what, beloved?'

'I'm in your hands, Kip,' she told him, softly and sweetly.

'I love you so utterly, Gail. With all the best in me because the best has been you and for you. I won't say "and with the worst", because there has been nothing bad in my love for you. Always you have kept me to the best, so that whatever I have done has been worthwhile, even if only I myself have known how I've laboured to cut out the cheap, the insincere, the catchpenny of the crowd who have got themselves into the habit of liking anything I offered them. Even now, with you in my arms, you have the best of me, Gail, because, if I had to, or if you wanted it so, I would ask no more of you than this. My love for you is a giving, not just a seeking, Gail.'

She looked into his eyes with a shining glory in her own, and he saw the woman she had become and knew a deep, abiding thankfulness. Phillip Westing had not been able to hurt her, not the brave, bright spirit of her, not the deep woman's soul.

'It can be a seeking, Kip,' she said. 'I belong to you. I have always belonged. I did violence to the best in me in marrying Phillip, though I think that he could have made our marriage a success when I was young. Kiss me, my love, my dear. I am yours, yours only and forever.'

Almost as if that kiss were to them a sacrament rather than an earthly consummation, their lips met and clung, and for a moment time and place were no more, past and future alike forgotten.

When they came back to a world which still would have none of their dreams, Kip spoke to her very gently.

'Darling, when will you come to me? I am not going to think of our future together as a furtive thing.'

'I will come to you anytime, anywhere,' she said very simply.

'Bless you for that, my sweet. Then—not here and now, Gail, not in Paris, and as if we were snatching at a chance meeting. I have to go back in a few days, to clear up one or two things, and then I can be free for several weeks. I will go tomorrow, and if you will let me know where and how I can keep in touch with you, I will telegraph to you where to meet me. Will you do that? Come to me somewhere?'

'To the ends of the earth, beloved,' said Gail.

'I could not wait so long,' he said with a little smile. 'I'll think of something, make a plan, and we'll meet—when? In a week's time?'

She nodded, misty-eyed with happiness, all her world radiant, filled with light.

'I shall be waiting for you, Kip.'

'You'll stay here in Paris?'

'Yes, at the Ambassadors.'

'Alright. Then I'll wire to you time and place. If it's the other side of Europe, can you manage it? Get there alone?'

She laughed.

'I could find you anywhere,' she said. 'Besides, I've had to find my way for ten years, you know.'

He laughed, but there was anger in the back of his mind, anger against Phillip to whom those ten years had been given.

A pair of young lovers had been near them, heedless of them as they themselves had been heedless, but now they moved, the boy's arm round the girl's waist, her eyes looking up into his, smiling.

Gail gave a little sigh, the mere breath of a sound.

'We have been young,' she said with a wistful thought of the years gone beyond recall, the wastage of them, and a phrase came into her mind, 'the years that the locusts have eaten'. But Kip gathered her closely and would have none of it. 'We're still young, beloved,' he said. 'Our hearts are young because life beats in them so strongly, and all the future is ours, and all the happiness we've never had. "Grow old along with me; the best is yet to be".'

She clung to him.

'Oh, Kip, it may be quite wrong. So many people would condemn us, will condemn us if they ever know. But inside me, I'm alright with myself. I am giving you nothing that is not mine to give. You are hurting no one in the world by loving me. Oh, Kip, I'm glad to be alive! Glad that you and I managed to get into the world together!'

They kissed in a farewell which, for the first time, held no sadness. There had been so many goodbyes. This was a greeting.

He left her at her hotel. They were not to see each other again until that meeting he would arrange.

The next morning, Gail, with laughter in her eyes, sent off a telegram to Jeffrey Templar.

Please send me a hundred pounds 'Ambassadors' Paris. Gail.

She had the money, but did not want to ask Hurst at the shop for it, nor even to give her address to her bank manager. She was afraid, as she always had been, lest Phillip should follow and find her. She could not conceive of his thinking her worth the fare to Paris, but with Phillip one could never be sure, and it was better to be on the safe side.

Jeffrey Templar, getting her telegram, sat with it in his hand and smiled. What was the monkey up to now? He had seen Westing in the street only the day before, so knew that Gail was alone in Paris, at least so far as her husband was concerned.

He rang for Miss White.

'I want a hundred pounds in ten-pound notes,' he told her, and disregarded her suspicious look, nor did his manner admit of any of the arguments which her long service sometimes justified.

He put the money into an envelope with a note.

If this is for hats, come and show them to me when you get home. J.

Then he sealed the envelope and went himself to register it to Gail in Paris.

She smiled when she read what he had written. Dear Jeffrey. He would never ask her what the money was for, she knew, and if she never paid it back, it would make no difference to him, though of course she would (and did) insist on paying it. She began, gaily, delightfully, to spend it.

Nothing that she had ever had before would do for her new life, or that part of it which would be Kip's.

She did not buy wildly, nor in vast quantities, but she knew her Paris, and she went about her shopping with method, and kept rigidly to the list she had made out, refusing to be tempted by gay little hats, frilly frocks she might never wear and which would crush, however carefully they were packed, and which she would not be able to wear more than once without pressing or possibly cleaning.

Only in her lingerie did she let herself go, and there is no place in the world where lingerie is more enthralling, more seductive, than in the Paris shops.

She bought one or two tailored suits, knowing them to be her style, two evening dresses which would survive innumerable packings, and a colourful, embroidered jacket, tight-fitting and essentially

Parisian, which would turn any of her dresses into a gala affair. She bought filmy lace blouses, and good shoes and stockings, but with all her care was appalled to find how little remained of Jeffrey's hundred pounds – little, but enough to take her anywhere in Europe in response to Kip's summons.

It came after five days of waiting, days when every known emotion had possessed her.

Meet me at Innsbruck Station four-thirty fifteenth, it said, and there was no signature. How should she need one?

Innsbruck. The name had always sounded magical to her though she had never been there.

Innsbruck.

She went to Cook's office in the Place de la Madeleine, talked to a pleasant young man who did not know he was booking her to paradise, and went back to her hotel in a dream.

Innsbruck! For the rest of her life that name was to hold the wonder and the glory of the heavens for her.

On a breathless day of shimmering heat, she left the Tyrol Hotel, where she had stayed for the night, and walked across to the station, over the wide, cobbled square.

It was all so strange. In Paris, Brussels, Cologne, Berlin, Rome, one might as well be in London, so much had all great cities in common, so cosmopolitan their populace, but here in the quaint old Austrian town, fabled into antiquity, she could not but be in a foreign land. In the morning she had wandered about the town, its broad main street ending abruptly in little more than an alley, cloistered on either side with tiny shops of embroidery, leather goods, shoes – always and inevitably shoes! She saw the golden gate, shining in the sun, and the great statue in the middle of the Maria Theresienstrasse which would effectually prevent that gracious thoroughfare from ever becoming a great highway. She found the triumphal arch, the Triumphpforte, rather sad reminder of Austria's lost greatness.

And she looked up and out beyond the city at the mountains which ringed it, hemmed it in with their majesty of eternal snow.

She felt that no other place on earth could be more fitting to her meeting with Kip. Had he known how she would feel when he sent her that telegram?

It seemed incredible that he should be coming to her here, where she felt so utterly a stranger, so isolated, but here she was, waiting for him in the booking-hall, in a powder-blue dress and a big white hat, looking no more than the girl she felt, eager, palpitating, dewy-eyed, coming to meet her lover.

She saw him suddenly, and her heart stood still.

All she saw was Kip, his tall form conspicuous for its height and distinction of bearing even to other eyes than hers, for porters migrated to him by instinct whilst other people vainly tried to summon them, and he was giving directions about his baggage, having seen Gail and flashed her one moment's recognition so that she stood quite still and waited for him.

Life was to hold many exquisite, breathless moments for her, but never a more perfect one than that in which she had first seen Kip on Innsbruck Station, knowing that he had come there to her and for her, alone out of all the millions of human beings in the world.

Having disposed of the question of his baggage, he came to her, purposefully, his eyes seeking hers, eager, glowing.

Their hands met.

'Gail.'

'My dearest.'

He put a hand under her elbow.

'I'm filthy and untidy, and what I need most in the world is a bath,' he said, though to her he looked as immaculate as ever, and not in the least as if he had just finished a twenty-four hour journey. 'Let's go across to the Tyrol and I'll have one there, and after that—well, we'll see. Are you packed?'

'Yes,' said Gail happily. 'I was at the Tyrol last night, so my things are there.'

He nodded approval.

'Sweet you look,' he said. 'I love you in blue.'

'I bought it for you,' said Gail, and wondered if he knew that every thought had been his in all that week, sleeping or waking.

The porter with the baggage was at the hotel already, and the smiling, English-speaking manager himself at the door to welcome the visitor, to place the whole vast hotel at the service of an English gentleman who wanted to use it to have a bath.

'The suite is ready, my sir,' he said, bowing and rubbing his hands, but not in such a fashion as to express subservience. It was rather the action of a man who anticipates a great treat.

'Suite? It's a bath I want,' said Kip in his smiling, good-humoured fashion. 'Is the water hot?'

'But assuredly, assuredly, beyond all doubt in the world,' said the manager, and Kip laughed and turned aside to speak to Gail before following him.

'I know these suites,' he said. 'Probably a place as big as royal apartments in a palace. Come up and wait for me to get clean enough to kiss you?'

She nodded and laughed, and they went to rooms on the first floor which almost bore out Kip's anticipation of them, a huge drawing-room complete with palms and grand piano, a bedroom with two enormous canopied beds and wardrobes as large as rooms, and a vast, cold bathroom with, to Gail's infinite amusement, two baths in it.

The manager said he would send a chambermaid, and bustled off, and Kip looked at the baths and laughed.

'Complete with *every* modern convenience,' he said. 'Could hospitality go further? Oh Gail—beloved—' as the realisation of her presence there in Austria with him broke in on his nonsense and shook the laughter from his face and left it grave with the love he bore her, the love which had waited so long for fulfilment.

Gail came to him.

'Have you to be so very clean?' she asked him, and he swept her into his arms and held her there, and heaven was their own again.

The chambermaid, her arms full of warm towels, had to cough to attract their attention, and they separated and laughed, and she laughed with them, sharing their happiness, for such is the delightful way of the true Austrian.

'You wouldn't like to stay on here a bit, Gail?' Kip asked when he came back from his bath to find her in the sitting-room waiting for him.

'What was your plan?' she asked him.

He put an arm about her shoulders and led her to the window, where they could look out along the valley of the Inn, and at the vista of the mountains with their snowy crests going up into the clouds.

'Up there, along that ridge,' he said, pointing it out to her, 'is a small hotel I found once, a place to which I thought (quite futilely then) I would like to bring the woman I loved. That was why I told you to meet me in Innsbruck, it is a few hours' ride from here. We can get a car. We could see the moon rise behind the mountains, and we should, I think, be quite alone there. They have rooms waiting for us, but if you would like to stay here a little while—just tonight perhaps?'

Gail looked towards the mountains, and back at the ornate room.

'Let's go to the mountains, Kip,' she said, and he sighed in relief and held her closely.

'I hoped you'd say that,' he said. 'I thought you would. It's what I want too. We'll have dinner here, whilst we are still in civilisation, and then afterwards we'll go to Rigourden together."

'I shall have to change if we're having dinner here,' said Gail.

He looked at the blue dress with regret. She looked so charming in it.

'Yes, I suppose you will,' he said. 'We could dine up there, but somehow I'd like to have our first dinner *en prince*. Besides, I want the pleasure of seeing other men admire you and envy me for a man of superb good fortune,' with a little laugh which she knew hid a deep feeling of pride in her.

Lovely to have a man proud of her again! After having been taken for granted for so long by Phillip, pushed into the background as something of no account, or merely a part of the furniture for his comfort and convenience, lovely to be thought of as a unique and desirable woman who bestowed a favour on a man by her company!

She dressed for his delight and her own, and wore a dinner gown of deep cream lace, its little coat hemmed and collared with soft dark fur, a lovely, feminine gown which revealed, by subtly hiding, the gracious lines of her figure, its alluring curves which still were adorably slender. She wore no jewels, but Kip, meeting her in the sitting-room of the suite which for the time being he had used as his own, took from his pocket a long flat case, opened it and put over her head a string of pearls, lustrous, perfectly matched, a thing of such sheer beauty that she exclaimed almost in awe.

'Oh—Kip!' she breathed.

'Dearest, I'm not going to give you a lot of jewels. I think you know why. Jewels are not associated in my mind with happiness or with love. But I wanted you to have these. I have been collecting them for you, telling myself that they were not really for you at all, though I knew in my heart that no other woman would ever wear them whilst I lived. They are ten years of thought of you, Gail, ten years of love and aching desire and sorrow, ten years of grief for your griefs, ten years which, thank God, can never come again.'

She could not speak. She stood fingering the pearls with loving hands that trembled.

'A rosary,' she said at last in a whisper, and then, against his lips: 'Thank you, Kip, for every thought of those years, and thank you for having made tonight possible.'

They held each other for a long moment, and then he set her free, hearing the break of her breath, knowing how highly strung were her nerves at this moment.

'Come. Let's go down, my queen,' he said. 'I am a king tonight.'

They dined gaily, sumptuously, their hearts laid bare in their eyes and in their laughter and in their sudden silences for all to see, though they did not even remember that they were not alone, and afterwards they went away to change into simpler clothes, and Kip made arrangements about the car, and when they slipped away out of Innsbruck, the moon was already risen.

It took them an hour and a half on the steep, winding mountain roads to reach Rigourden, but when Gail stood on the wide balcony of their room in the tiny hotel which seemed to cling precariously to the side of the mountain, the valley below with its silver river running through it, the high peaks and the white snow above them, she knew that they had chosen wisely in preferring this to the opulent comfort of the Tyrol.

Kip, who had been paying the driver and talking to him of other days and other drives ahead, came to her through the open doors of the bedroom, put his arms about her and drew her back against him so that her head lay against his shoulder.

'Thoughts, beloved?' he asked her softly.

'I don't think I had any,' she said. 'Can one think when one is feeling so intensely?'

He let his cheek rest against her soft hair, a deep thankfulness for her in his heart, a vow that nothing he would do should ever hurt her, ever make her regret this supreme gift of herself.

'Gail, I want you to know that there has never been anyone else. Gilda, of course, when we were very young, but that was so soon finished. In all the years, ever since I've known you, there has never been anyone else. I'm glad to know that now, glad to be able to tell you so. I have waited for you, my sweet, my very own.'

The thought of Phillip came like a cloud between herself and the sunshine of her happiness. If only Phillip had never been!

'Kip, I'm sorry there was Phillip,' she said, for she must share her every thought with him, take him into the innermost places of her mind.

'Don't be sorry for anything, my dear heart,' he said. 'Tonight, and ail our future, is made up of the things the past has given to us and taken from us and made us suffer. We are so much more sure of our happiness, and it is so much safer in our hands than would have been possible had we had it when we were ten years younger in years and experience and knowledge. We have learned the value of happiness, to count each little bit of it as something won, something precious. Youth is so ready to squander its happiness, believing that the cup is inexhaustible. We know that it is a gift of the gods, dealt out to us sparingly, so that we catch each drop as it comes, hold it, guard it, never risk spilling it. We might have lost some of our happiness had I been able to take you all those years ago.'

She turned in his arms, love and desire and all the needs of her woman's body and soul seeking the ultimate fulfilment of his.

'Oh, Kip, do you wonder that I love you?' she whispered, and he saw the look in her eyes, felt the drooping sweetness of her body against his own, and lifted her in his arms and carried her back into the room.

Oh, the wonder of those weeks together! The radiant, incredible happiness that was to be found in each other!

They stayed at Rigourden for the first week, chained there by their love, living to the full every moment of every enchanted hour, and then, almost without a plan but each somehow knowing exactly what would please the other, they wandered through Austria, finding its quiet by-ways unknown to the tourists, coming now and then on some town of sufficient importance for them to have a suite in an hotel, where Gail wore her loveliest clothes, and Kip, unable to find enough expression for his love, showered gifts upon her so that laughingly she protested that he would have to buy a pantechnicon to get her home.

But mostly they found the quiet places, tiny inns perched on a mountainside where they found gentians, or chalets nestling in the lush valleys of the Tyrol, where their room had a bare, scrubbed floor and an enormous wooden bed piled high with feather quilts, and downstairs, in a little wine parlour, they ate the peasant dishes, unfamiliar, marvellously cooked, delectable.

'I shall grow a tummy,' said Gail, unable to resist the good things, the Wiener *schnitzel* cooked with wine, the *apfelstrudel*, the sweet drinks in tall mugs which were so disconcertingly potent.

'I shall love you just the same when you are thirteen stone,' Kip told her. 'There will be so much more to love!'

But she guarded for him the beauty of her body, which he loved.

The thing she had dreaded most had not come to pass. Marriage with Phillip had shown her how revolting physical love could be, and she had feared lest, because of that revulsion, which had been so horrible a feature of her married life, she find herself unresponsive to Kip, drained of vitality.

But Kip's love was a thing as remote as the stars from Phillip's self-appeasing lust, which had held no reverence for her, no appreciation of her own feelings, nothing but the desire of his own flesh to which Gail, as a wife, must submit herself at all times.

Kip's love was deeply reverent but no whit less passionate because of it. Rather could he take her to undreamed-of delights because he loved her mind in equal measure with her lovely, surrendered body.

'I can never understand how a man can have any desire to make love, even just physical love alone, to an unintelligent woman,' he said to her, lying by her side in one of those monstrous, downy beds which seemed to rise up all round them as if they were embedded in warm clouds suspended above the earth. 'Loving is so much a mental and spiritual rapture that without the mind to appreciate it, the body must lack this last ecstasy that I find in you, Gail. It's because our minds are so deeply in tune, so exquisitely in love with each other's mind, that we can enjoy this lovely intimacy of our bodies.'

His spirit and his body explored her own and found nothing but sweetness there, and his worship of her was a healing balm to the wounds of Phillip, who had prated to her recoiling mind of his 'rights' and ravaged a body she had learned to loathe.

Kip's tender care of her was a thing to marvel at after her husband's casual disregard of her as anything but a vehicle for his pleasure. Kip laid a carpet at her feet so that they might know no rough places nor be touched by the mud and the mire of life.

Once she spoke of the financial side of their relationship.

They had been dining in a famous restaurant (they had reached Vienna) and Gail had been revolted by the sight of a lovely young girl with an old, palpably rich man who was fawning on her.

'Horrible,' said Gail with a little shiver. 'What is it? Free love or matrimony?'

Kip grinned. He loved the touch of the prude that would always remain in Gail.

'Matter o' money, whichever it is,' he said.

'Money's horrible,' said Gail, and then laughed because all day long, in the entrancing Viennese shops, Kip had been showering money on her without listening to her protests.

She leaned across the table to him.

'Darling, I'm letting you spend all this money on me because I know you love doing it and because it's such a novelty to me, but I'm glad I've got my job and am actually independent of you. I want to say just this to you, my darling. Your money makes it possible for us to do wonderful things together, like this, for instance, but everything would be just the same in my heart if you were poor and could give me nothing. I'd work for you, Kip, scrub and wash and polish for you, and every moment of living would still be unutterable joy if you could give me nothing but your love. You know that, don't you?'

'Yes, my sweet, thank God I do. But I've never been more glad that I can give you almost anything a woman can want—almost, my dearest. Oh Gail, if only I could marry you!'

She knew how that longing permeated all his love for her, not because he was afraid of the insecurity of the tie between them, but because he wanted to make her honoured amongst women, lived always in fear lest this divine linking of their lives should ever bring her a moment's dishonour or pain or regret.

'Darling, we couldn't be any happier,' she told him, her eyes like misty stars, like deep pools. 'Sometimes I feel almost glad we can't be married. It makes us know our love as such a strong thing. We don't need all the majesty of Church and State to make sure that we don't run away from each other. No one has had to say to us "You're tied up good and strong. You can't get free. You, Kip Delaney, can pop into Gail's bed whenever you like. And you, Gail, have got to let him and like it! All the might of the great British constitution is behind him, so move over and make room!" Darling, I might not love having you in my bed nearly so much if the State and the Church were with you!'

There was tenderness in her laughter, that music of their happy love, which was pure joy.

For her, the one possible regret in their unmarried state was that she could not bear his child.

They had discussed it frankly, as they could discuss anything. Sometimes they held widely divergent opinions and had respect for each other's point of view, never insisting on their own, but in this thing they had no divergence.

'It can't be, Gail, my dear, my most dear,' Kip had said. 'Let's not harbour vain regrets. The gods have given us so much. We must let them hold back one gift without demur.'

'I know, my beloved. I'll be content. I *am* content,' Gail said.

After much thought, Kip maintaining that no possible harm would be done him by being cited in a divorce action, Gail had decided to ask Phillip for a divorce, but first she had invited herself to the flat in which Joyce and Ray had nested like a couple of love-birds. The flat had been found for them and the key-money, disguised under the term 'fixtures and fittings', paid by Gail, who could not bear the thought of their starting their married life in 'rooms' as so many young couples have to do.

She had asked Hugh to meet her there. He was living in a boarding-house close to them, having promptly left his father when he realised that Gail was not coming back and refused to live with Joyce and Ray.

They were all there when she arrived, and though Ray would have left them on some flimsy excuse, she would not hear of it.

'No, you're one of the family,' she said. 'Joyce would tell you anyway, so you may as well stay and hear it first hand,' smiling at Joyce's husband, of whom she was very fond.

'Have a glass of your own sherry first?' for she had sent them a case of wines for Christmas. 'To fortify you?' he asked, getting the glasses.

'She doesn't look as if she needs to be fortified,' laughed Joyce. 'You look beautiful and you get younger every day.'

'Thank you, darling,' said Gail.

Hugh, who had seen what it was to have no courtesy, none of the social graces, had taken her mink coat, her Christmas present from Kip, and she was wearing a dress of leaf-green wool and her pearls. She looked what she was, a poised and successful woman, a happy woman, above all a loved and loving woman, and there is no greater beautifier than that. Gone were the little lines of worry, of always having to be on the watch against giving imaginary offence or the smallest reason for the one-sided quarrel in which she had kept herself silent when all her instincts had been to lash out with her tongue.

'Come on, 'fess up,' said Joyce. 'What have you been up to?'

Gail looked from one to another and saw only love in their eyes.

'Well, darlings, I'm not really nice to know because—I'm a scarlet woman. I've got a lover and—'

The look on the three faces and their burst of laughter stopped her.

'Is that all?' asked Joyce. 'My sweet, as if we didn't know! We've known it for ages.'

'But—but—how could you know? We thought we'd been so careful,' she said ruefully.

'Not careful enough for the lynx eyes of your children,' chuckled Ray.

'He's such a heavenly man, darling,' put in Joyce. 'I always tell Ray that if I'd seen him first, he wouldn't have had a chance.'

'You wouldn't in any case,' her husband told her drily. 'A rag and a bone and a hank of hair!'

Hugh said nothing, but his face too showed her that he knew and did not mind, even approved!

She looked from one to another.

'You know then? Who he is, too?'

'Mm. Kipling Delaney. We saw you with him on the first night of his play, the one with the waterfall in it, and you didn't need to shout it any louder, not to us anyway. We've been so glad for you, darling, so very glad,' and Joyce came to sit on the arm of her chair, to hug and kiss her.

'Well!' said Gail, a little misty-eyed at this proof of their never-failing love. 'What can I say? Who else knows? Your father? That is really what I came to tell you. I want to marry Kip. I'm going to ask your father again for a divorce. He refused it when I left him, said he never would.'

'How like him, the skunk,' said Hugh, speaking for almost the first time. 'Can't you make him?'

Gail gave a wry smile.

'Could one ever make him do anything he didn't want to do?'

'But he must know by now that you'll never go back to him. Fancy going back to him after Kipling Delaney!' said Joyce with a sigh of rapture. 'Fancy going back to him in any case! He made our lives sheer hell, and it must have been worse for you than for us. Why did you stay with him so long?'

'You know why,' said Hugh before Gail could speak. 'It was for us, wasn't it?'

She nodded but could not speak. She would not have expected Hugh to be so perceptive. Joyce perhaps, but not Hugh.

She stretched out a hand to him and he took it, came round to her other side and put an arm about her shoulders, and she knew that it had been worth it, worth all the tears and the unhappiness and the frustration. They had grown up loved and cared for, guided to the best of her ability and now they were happy human beings, good citizens, honest, truthful, able to take their place in the world.

She did not take all the credit of that to herself, for she had had good material to work on, but left to their father, sharing his grudge against life, his bitterness and distrust of all men, would that good material have stood the test?

They talked a little while longer and then she rose to go. Her car stood outside and Ray offered to drive her home, but she refused.

'No, dear, thank you. I—I'm meeting Kip,' she said, and oh, the relief of being able to speak of him like this, naturally and without fear!

The past six months had been made up of spells of intense happiness and of the waiting time for the next to begin.

She had taken a little house just outside London where he could come to her easily and quickly, carrying on with her work though he had not wanted her to do so.

'Let me, Kip. I must be occupied. I can't just sit and wait for you, wondering if you'll come, eating my heart out for you when you can't.'

In spite of his repeated assurances that it could not hurt him, she would not live with him openly unless they could marry.

'I don't mind for myself. I should glory in it, in having everybody know that I belong to you, your chosen woman, but people have built up a sort of legend about you, have never been able to say or to think anything—sordid about you. They know of the long years when you had Gilda, looked after her with such care and were utterly faithful to her. I don't want to spoil what they think of you. Someday Phillip will set me free. He must. He can't hold me forever.'

So they had made a private heaven of their own, and did not stay in England when they were together. He came to the little house to visit her but never stayed the night. He would send her a telegram instead, telling her where to meet him and when and she would go gladly, eagerly, a woman so much in love.

Meet me at Basle eighteenth three o'clock
Meet me Milan twelfth three-fifteen
Meet me Florence twenty-third noon
Paris fifth four-thirty

Those telegrams! She kept them in a locked box and felt that when she was a very old woman they would still give her a thrill, revive for her memories sweet as lavender and roses, though nothing could ever rival for her the sweetness or the magic of that first one:

Meet me Innsbruck fifteenth four

But they knew this spasmodic happiness was not contenting them. They wanted a home they could share openly and they wanted a family.

Phillip was still living in the house which her money had bought, his stubborn pride keeping him there, but Joyce had told her that he had no servants, not even a daily woman, to clean and cook for him. He had dismissed the mother and daughter who had been with Gail for some years and the daily woman, finding out how much she was expected to do for lower wages, had promptly dismissed herself, and as her husband was the gardener, he had done the same.

Once or twice, for very pity and shocked at the uncared-for state of the house which had been immaculate in Gail's time, Joyce had spent a day there cleaning the few rooms he used and cooking something for him, but it had had to be a Saturday because she had gone on with her job after she married, and Phillip had been there too, whining and morose. When he did one of his well-known acts, pretending to be at death's door and in a faint voice demanding that Gail be sent for, Joyce told him brusquely to 'get up and stop putting on an act' and she had not been since.

• The letter which he received was from Jeffrey Templar. He and Kip had persuaded her to let him handle it rather than let Phillip know where she was living and go there and create a scene. Apparently he had never tried to find her, as he could have done by following her from Hannam's, and her whole being shrank from seeing him again. In fact, the fear of him in which she lived was a contributory factor to her decision to ask him to divorce her.

Jeffrey's letter was short and business-like, merely telling him that she wanted him to divorce her, citing Kipling Delaney.

Phillip's reply was typical of him.

Dear Templar – he *wrote, getting a spiteful satisfaction out of that form of address* – *I have no intention of divorcing my wife. I am waiting for her to return to my home and expecting her to do so. Yours,*

P. *Westing.*

'Well, it's rather what we anticipated,' said Jeffrey, showing it to her.

'Isn't there anything we can do, Jeffrey?' Gail asked unhappily.

'There's one thing, but you wouldn't like it. You could run up bills all over the place in his name, and you could leave him to pay your income tax, though the latter would take time as you've always paid it yourself.'

'He could put one of those notices in the paper saying that he was not responsible for my debts,' hazarded Gail, who disliked the idea intensely.

'Not worth the cost of the advertisement in law, m'dear. He'd still be held responsible.'

'I couldn't do it, Jeffrey. For one thing my pride wouldn't let me, and for another it would look so bad for Kip if people knew about us. Isn't there *any* other way?'

'Not in law, no. I've been sailing very near the wind, as it is, asking him to divorce you. Divorce in this country is supposed to be a punishment of the guilty, not a reward! You might just possibly have gone to the courts yourself with a plea of mental cruelty, but it's very difficult to establish, depending almost entirely on the views of the judge, and you couldn't do that now. I'm afraid there's nothing you can do, Gail, though I'm more sorry than I can say. I'm not advising you as a lawyer, mind, but suggesting merely as a friend that if you and Delaney are quite resolved that you want to spend the rest of your lives together, you should do it openly, changing your name to his. That's quite easily done.'

'We don't want that, Jeffrey. We want to marry and have a family, live a normal, decent life.'

He put a hand on her shoulder.

'Sorry, m'dear,' he said gently.

He had told her quite truthfully that there was nothing he could do for her but a day or two later he made an opportunity of seeing Kip, and whilst there was nothing anyone could have seized on in what he said, and it would have been grossly illegal if there had been, he had none the less been able to sow in Kip's mind a seed which was quick to germinate.

He might be able to buy Gail if the price he offered were high enough! He was a rich man, probably far richer than anyone knew, and he would count no cost too high, though his lip curled at the thought of it and he hoped she would never know.

It was difficult and dangerous and it had to be carefully planned but it was made easier by the instantaneous gleam in Phillip's eyes when, meeting him by the chance that was part of the careful planning, Kip put his scheme quite casually to Phillip.

'I hadn't realised that it was you whom I was going to meet, Mr. Westing,' he said, pretending surprise and some discomfort, an easy thing for Kipling Delaney to do. 'Still, I take it we can both look on this purely as a matter of business? When I considered buying the business of Bradey & Sons and they arranged for me to go over the books with their accountant, I naturally had not anticipated that it would be you.'

Phillip Westing was no fool and he very much doubted that, but he did not let it appear.

He had known for some time that the firm was in low water and might have to go out of business, and it had worried him a lot, for though he had achieved a reasonably good position there, he was not a qualified accountant and would find it difficult to find another job to match it.

Kipling Delaney had been in touch with Bradey's for some years, his interest in them having started with the engravings they had made at the time of Mr. Chives' death, but Phillip had been surprised when he made the tentative offer to buy the business which was the cause of the present interview. It was taking place after office hours on the premises of Bradey and Sons.

After a cursory examination of the books, Kip said that he might be prepared to pay something in the neighbourhood of five thousand for the business, and this was where the gleam of understanding had come into Phillip's eyes, for he knew that the business was not worth even half that sum and that he himself could buy it for a few hundreds.

'You are willing to offer that for the business, Mr. Delaney?'

'For the business, yes,' said Kip, eyeing the other man steadily. 'I rather think, though, that you yourself have made an offer for it, Mr. Westing?' though both men knew that Phillip Westing could not think in hundreds, let alone thousands.

'Er—yes. I have been considering it, Mr. Delaney.'

The business was old-fashioned and needed a considerable sum spent on new machinery and equipment if it were to survive, but Phillip knew that Kip had no intention of buying it at anything like five thousand pounds, if at all. On the other hand, if he himself offered, say a thousand pounds for it, Kip would buy it from him for five thousand and let it cease to exist.

'I might even step up my offer to, say, ten thousand,' said Kip smoothly. 'That would depend, of course, in whose hands it was at the time of sale, Bradey's or yours. You are an intelligent man, Mr. Westing, and if I bought it, it would be on the understanding, on a gentleman's agreement of course, that I paid, say, a thousand pounds when it passed into your hands and the balance—later.'

The proposal was understood perfectly. Ten thousand pounds, which was more than the business was worth, would enable Phillip to buy it forthwith, and the balance would be paid to him when he had got his divorce from Gail. He knew implicitly the 'gentleman's agreement' which could not be put into writing.

Ten thousand pounds! And costs as well as damages for the loss of his wife!

Phillip lowered his eyes from Kip's. Even he felt slightly ashamed of the transaction and knew that there was contempt in the other man's eyes.

But if he wanted Gail, why should he not pay for her? Phillip knew that she would never come back to him, and now he did not particularly want her. He would be well rid of her and might even marry again himself, but it would be to some simple, homely woman this time, not that bitch with her grand ways and her ability to make far more money than he himself could earn!

So, very shortly afterwards, in righteous indignation at her conduct, Phillip Westing instructed a firm of solicitors to sue on his behalf for divorce against his wife, citing Kipling Delaney, and though no defence was offered, the case caused a slight stir, the co-respondent being who he was.

Gail was indignant at the amount claimed and granted as damages; for, said the judge severely, Phillip Westing had lost only a wife but one who had been able to contribute largely to their joint home, thereby involving him in considerably more expense than his own position justified, and had left him for a rich and well-known man who could give her a better position. The skill of Phillip's lawyers had brought this into the supposed picture and since the suit was undefended, there was nothing to say to refute it.

'Never mind, my sweet,' Kip told her, but was glad that she did not know how much he had really paid for her. She would have been so angry, bless her! 'You were cheap at the price! Come on. I'm going to buy you a diamond as big as St. Paul's!'

Give Back Yesterday

Helena Clurey has it all – a devoted husband, money and family. She is happy and secure, but her apparent contentment is about to be shattered by a voice from the past. Mistress she may have been, but that is not the way it is put to her: 'you were not my mistress - you were, and are, my wife.'

The Weir House

Philip wants to marry Eve. It is her way out - he is rich, not too old, and has been in love for years – but not a man she can accept. He has even secretly funded her lifestyle, such that it is. Eve feels trapped. Unlike her friend Marcia, who cheerfully accepts an 'ordinary' life without complaint, Eve has known better and wants better. A chance encounter then changesthings – Lewis Belamie pays her to act as his fiancée for a week. Adventure, ambition, and disappointment all follow after she journeys to Cornwall with him, where she eventually nearly dies after what appears to be a suicide attempt because of a marriage that has seemingly failed. However, the mysterious and mocking Felix really does love her. Just who is he; how does Eve end up with him; and what part does 'The Weir House' play in her life? Has Eve's restlessness and relentless search for stability ended?

Through Many Waters

Jeff has got himself into a mess. It is, on the face of it, a classic scenario. He has a settled relationship with one woman, but loves another. What is he to do? It is now necessary to face reality, rather than continually making excuses to himself, but can he face the unpalatable truth? Then something beyond his influence intervenes and once again decisions have to be made. But in the end it is not Jeff that decides.

Misadventure

Olive Heriot and Hugh Manning had been in love for years, but marriage had been out of the question because of the intervention of Olive's mother. Now, at last, she was of age and due to gain her inheritance and be free to choose. A dinner party had been arranged at the Heriot's home, 'The Hermitage' and Hugh expects to be able to announce their engagement. Things start to change after a gruesomely realistic game entitled 'murder', which relies on someone drawing the Knave of Spades after cards are dealt. Tragedy strikes and other relationships are tested and consummated – but is this all real, or imagined?

Printed in Great Britain
by Amazon